DEATH AT BREAKFAST

John Rhode was a pseudonym for the author Cecil Street
(188   64), who also wrote as Miles Burton and Cecil
W   aving served in the British Army as an artillery officer
        he First World War, rising to the rank of Major, he
        riting non-fiction before turning to detective fiction,
        uced four novels a year for thirty-seven years.

        list of detective stories grew, so did the public's
        for his particular blending of humdrum everyday
        the startling appearance of the most curious kind
        . It was the *Sunday Times* who said of John Rhode
        must hold the record for the invention of ingenious
        f murder', and the *Times Literary Supplement*
        d him as 'standing in the front rank of those who
write   tective fiction'.

   Rh   e's first detective novel, *The Paddington Mystery*
(1925   introduced Dr Lancelot Priestley, who went on to
appea   in 72 novels, many of them for Collins Crime Club.
The F   estley books are classics of scientific detection, with
the e   lerly Dr Priestley demonstrating how apparently
impo   ible crimes have been carried out, and they are now
highl   sought after by collectors.

JOHN RHODE

Death at Breakfast

COLLINS
CRIME
CLUB

COLLINS CRIME CLUB
An imprint of HarperCollins*Publishers*
1 London Bridge Street
London SE1 9GF
www.harpercollins.co.uk

This paperback edition 2017

First published in Great Britain by Collins Crime Club 1936

A catalogue record for this book is available from the British Library

ISBN 978-0-00-826875-6

Typeset in Sabon by Palimpsest Book Production Ltd, Falkirk, Stirlingshire

Printed and bound in Great Britain
by CPI Group (UK) Ltd, Croydon CR0 4YY

MIX
Paper from
responsible sources
FSC
www.fsc.org FSC™ C007454

This book is produced from independently certified FSC™ paper
to ensure responsible forest management.

For more information visit: www.harpercollins.co.uk/green

Contents

Contents

Prologue

Victor Harleston stirred uneasily. He grunted, then opened his eyes. Was he awake? Yes, he thought so. He stretched himself, to make quite sure of the fact.

It was still dark behind the closed curtains, on this January morning. Too dark for Harleston to see the time by his watch, which lay upon the table beside his bed. He was too lazy to stretch out his hand and switch on the light. Instead of this, he lay still and listened.

Very little noise came to him from without the house. Matfield Street was a backwater, lying not far south of the Fulham Road, and comparatively little traffic passed along it. One or two early risers were evidently about. Harleston could hear the hurried tap of a woman's heels upon the pavement. This passed and gave place to a popular tune, whistled discordantly. A boy on a bicycle, probably. Considering that the window of his bedroom looked out at the back of the house, it was surprising how distinctly one could hear the noises from the street, Harleston thought idly.

But these were not what he was listening for. His ears were

tuned to catch a familiar sound from within the house. Ah, there it was! A rattling of crockery. Janet would be along soon with his early tea. Harleston pulled up the eiderdown a few inches, and composed himself for a few minutes doze.

Then, suddenly, his memory returned, and in an instant he was wide awake. It was the morning of January the 21st, the day which was to make him rich! No more dozing for him now. Rather an indulgence in luxurious anticipation. Before the day was out, he could be his own master, if he chose. He hadn't decided yet what he should do. Better not throw up his job at once. People might wonder. On the whole, it would be best to wait until the Spring, then take a long holiday and consider the future. There was no earthly need for a hurried decision.

He heard a door slam, somewhere downstairs, and then steps approaching his room. Janet, with the tea. It must be half-past seven.

Then the expected knock on the door, and a girl's voice, 'Are you awake, Victor?'

'Yes, come in,' he replied.

The door opened, and the girl placed her hand on the switch, flooding the room with light. She wore a gaily coloured apron, and was carrying a tray. Seen even this early in the morning, she was not unattractive. Full, graceful and unhurried in her movements. A slim figure, with her head well set upon her shoulders. Her face was certainly not pretty, but, on the other hand, it could not be described as ugly. Plain Jane, she had been called at school. And the nickname aptly described her. Janet Harleston was plain, without anything special about her face to capture the attention.

If you looked at her twice, you did so the second time because your curiosity was aroused. You wondered if her expression was natural to her, or whether something had occurred that moment to cause it. You noticed the sullen droop of her lips, the hard, unsympathetic look in her grey eyes. A sulky girl, you would have thought.

Her behaviour on this particular morning would have strengthened that impression. She put the tray down upon the table by Victor Harleston's bed, and left the room without a word.

He made no effort to detain her. His mind was too full of plans for the future to find room for trifles. He raised himself to a sitting position, blinking in the sudden light. Seen thus, his face appearing above his brightly striped pyjamas, he was definitely unlovely.

Victor Harleston was a man of forty-two, and at this moment he looked ten years older. His coarse, heavy face was wrinkled with sleep, and his sparse, mouse-coloured hair, already beginning to turn grey, had gathered into thin wisps. These lay at fantastic angles on his head, disclosing unhealthy looking patches of skin. What could be seen of his body was flabby and shapeless. His eyes were intelligent, almost penetrating. But there was something malefic, non-human about them.

He yawned, disclosing a set of discoloured teeth, in which were many gaps, and looked about him. Janet was still upset, then. She hadn't troubled to draw the curtains or light the gas-fire. Well, he couldn't help her troubles. She'd get over them in time. She'd have to.

This last reflection brought a grin to his face. He loved to feel that people *had* to do what he wanted. At present, the number of such people was disappointingly small. Janet, and a few juniors at the office. It galled him to think that, up till now, he had himself had to do what his employer wanted.

Up till now! Money was a precious thing, to be carefully hoarded. There was only one way in which a rational man was justified in spending it. The purchase of freedom for himself, and of servitude for others.

Still, he would have to make up his mind about Janet. He might make her an allowance, and tell her to go to the devil. But the prospect of parting with any of the fortune now within his grasp was repugnant to him. Why should he make Janet an allowance? Why part with one who was, after all, an efficient and inexpensive servant? He would only have to replace her, and the money spent on the allowance would be utterly thrown away, bringing him no benefit. Yes, that was the plan. He would stay here, in this house which was his own and suited him. But he wouldn't spend the rest of his life earning money for other people. He would enjoy himself, and Janet should continue to look after him. But she must never be allowed to guess at his sudden access of fortune. That was a secret to be hugged to his own breast.

As for her temper, that had never troubled him yet, and it was not likely to now. She was too dependent upon him to let her ill-nature go to extremes. Dependent upon him for every mouthful she ate, every shred she wore. It was a delicious thought. He could dispose of her as he pleased. And it pleased him that she should remain and keep house for him. Victor Harleston poured himself out a cup of tea, added milk and sugar, and left it to cool.

He resumed his interrupted train of thought. No need to take seriously her threat of the previous evening. She would leave him, and go and stay with Philip until she found a job for herself! Not she! She knew too well which side her bread was buttered to do a silly thing like that. Jobs that would suit her couldn't be had just for the picking up. There was only one job she was fitted for, that of a domestic servant. And what would Philip, with his high-flown ideas, say to that? It was all very well for the young puppy to encourage her. He wasn't earning enough to keep her, that was quite certain. And he had a perfect right to forbid Philip the house, if he wanted to.

Victor Harleston drank his tea, and got out of bed. His first action was to draw the curtains. A sinful waste to use electric light if he could see to dress without it. Yes, it was a bright morning, clear and frosty. He switched off the light. Then he took a cigarette from a box which stood on his chest of drawers, and put the end of it in his mouth. He found the box of matches which he always kept hidden in a drawer, underneath his handkerchiefs. He struck a match, turned on the gas-fire, and lighted it. With the same match he lit his cigarette. No sense in using two matches when one would serve. Then he put the box back in its accustomed place.

As he did so, a sheet of paper which he had placed on the dressing table the previous evening caught his eye. It was a business letter. He read it over again, and smiled. All right. He had not the slightest objection to receiving something for nothing. He would try the experiment, right away.

Standing in front of the gas-fire, warming himself, his thoughts reverted to his impending fortune. He picked up a pencil from the mantelpiece, and with it made a few calculations on the back of the letter. The resulting figures seemed to please him, for he nodded contentedly. Quite a lot of money, if carefully husbanded.

He folded the letter in half, and tore it across. Then put the two halves together, folded them as before, and once more tore them across. With each of the four scraps of paper thus produced he made a spill. These he added to a bundle of similar spills which stood in a vase. No sense in wasting matches, when with one of these one could light a cigarette from the gas-fire.

He took his dressing-gown from a hook behind the door, put it on, and went along to the bathroom.

I

A Mishap While Shaving

1

Doctor Mortimer Oldland, though no longer young, was still full of energy. He would tell his patients, sometimes rather acidly, that hard work had never killed anybody yet. It certainly showed no signs of killing him. His extensive practice in Kensington left him very little leisure. But he always seemed ready at any moment to tackle a fresh case or to persevere with an old one.

He believed in early rising, summer or winter. By half-past eight on the morning of January 21st he had finished his breakfast, and was sitting over the fire consulting his case-book. As the clock struck the half hour, the door opened, and the parlourmaid appeared. 'There's a lady called to see you. sir. She says it's urgent.'

'It's always urgent when ladies call at this hour,' replied Oldland calmly. 'I suppose she has brought the usual small boy, suspected of swallowing a sixpence?'

'No, sir. She's alone, and seems in a terrible state. She was too upset to tell me her name. And I don't think I've ever seen her here before, sir.'

'All right. I'll see what I can do for her.' Oldland put down his case-book, and walked into his surgery.

He was confronted by a distraught woman, a perfect stranger to him. 'Oh, Doctor!' she exclaimed, as soon as he appeared. 'Can you come round at once? My brother has been taken very ill, and I don't know what to do for him.'

Oldland's experience had made him a pretty fair judge of character. She did not seem to him the sort of woman who would fly into a panic over nothing. 'I'll come,' he replied shortly. 'Where is your brother?'

'At home, 8 Matfield Street. It's quite close . . .'

'So close that it will be quicker to walk there than ring up for a taxi. And you can tell me the details as you go.'

He picked up his emergency bag, and they set off, Oldland walking at his usual smart pace, the girl, for it was evident that she was quite young, half running to keep up with him. In broken words she described the symptoms. Her brother had come down to breakfast as usual, but complaining of not feeling very well. He had drunk a cup of coffee, but had been almost immediately sick. He had complained of being terribly giddy, and had seemed unable to walk. On leaving the dining-room, he had collapsed on the floor of the hall, where he lay, unable to speak or move.

'I see,' said Oldland. 'We'll see what we can do for him. By the way, I don't think I caught the name?'

'Harleston. I'm Janet Harleston, and my brother's name is Victor. He's only my half-brother, and he's a good deal older than I am. I keep house for him. I've never known him like this before. He's always perfectly well.'

Oldland asked no more questions, and they covered the remainder of the distance in silence. The front door of number eight Matfield Street was standing ajar. Janet Harleston ran up the half-dozen steps which led to it, and pushed it open.

Oldland followed her into a narrow, linoleum-laid hall. He had no need to inquire the whereabouts of his patient. Victor Harleston lay huddled on the floor. At a first glance Oldland saw that he was completely unconscious. He examined the patient rapidly, then took a syringe from his bag and administered an injection. 'Is there a sofa handy?' he asked sharply.

Janet was standing by, watching him anxiously. 'Yes, in the sitting room,' she replied. 'Just through this door.'

'Is there a maid in the house?'

'No, my brother and I live alone. We have a charwoman, but she doesn't come until the afternoon.'

'That'll be too late. He's a heavy man, and I hardly think we could manage him between us. Will you run out, please Miss Harleston, and fetch a policeman. There's one at the corner of the Fulham Road, I noticed him as we passed. Tell him I sent you. He's sure to know my name.'

She ran out obediently, and Oldland resumed his examination of the patient. Victor Harleston, his toilet completed, was more presentable than he had appeared in bed. His hair was brushed and neatly parted, and his clothes, if not smart, were clean and nearly new. But he had apparently cut himself while shaving, and the patch of sticking-plaster adhering to his cheek was scarcely an ornament. Oldland, holding his pulse, shook his head ominously.

Within a couple of minutes Janet returned with a policeman. He and Oldland exchanged nods of mutual recognition. 'This young lady asked me to come along, sir . . .' he began.

'Yes, that's right, Carling.' Oldland cut in curtly. 'Poor

fellow. Taken ill. I want to get him on to the sofa next door. You take his shoulders, and I'll take his legs. That's right.'

The two men carried Victor Harleston into the sitting-room, Janet following them. The unconscious man having been deposited on the sofa, the policeman turned to go. But Oldland detained him. 'Don't run away for a moment' he said. 'I may want you to help me move him again presently. Miss Harleston, I want you to run over to my house again. When the parlourmaid opens the door, ask her to give you the small black case which is lying on the mantelpiece in the surgery. The black one, mind, not the red. And bring it back here as soon as you can.'

For the second time she ran off, and Oldland listened to her footsteps as they descended the front steps. As though to satisfy himself of her departure, he went to the front door and watched her till she disappeared round the corner of Matfield Street. Then he came back to the policeman. 'Your turn to run errands, now, Carling,' he said. 'There's no telephone in this house, that I can see. Slip round to the nearest box, and ring up Scotland Yard. Ask for Superintendent Hanslet. He knows me well enough. And tell him that there's a job waiting for him here. I'll stop in the house until he comes, or sends somebody else. Got that?'

'Yes, sir,' replied Carling. 'Will you want me again?'

Oldland shook his head. 'Neither you nor I can do any more for this poor chap. He'll be dead within the next few minutes.'

Left alone with his patient, Oldland's expression changed. His usual rather cynical smile gave place to a look of sternness such as few of his friends had seen. He picked up the inert wrist once more, and remained holding it until the irregular pulse had fluttered into lifelessness. Then, with a sharp sigh, he composed the body in a natural attitude, and stood for a moment looking at it as though he half expected the departing soul to reveal its secret. At last he shrugged his shoulders, and abruptly left the room.

He had already taken in the arrangement of the house. Two doors opened off the hall. The one nearest the front was that of the sitting-room, into which Victor Harleston had been carried. The second door was ajar, revealing a table laid for breakfast. Evidently the dining-room. At the end of the hall was a flight of steps leading downwards to the basement, and another flight leading upwards to the first floor. Oldland hesitated for a moment, then walked into the dining-room.

It was adequately furnished with objects of a peculiarly ugly type. A heavy, clumsy looking table stood in the middle of the floor, which was covered with a rather worn carpet. On the table was spread a white cloth, apparently fresh from the wash. The room contained a set of dining-room chairs, two of which had been drawn up to the table. One of these had been overturned, and lay on its side. The other, on the opposite side of the table, seemed to have been pushed back hurriedly.

Oldland inspected the preparations for breakfast, being careful, however, to touch nothing. In front of the overturned chair was a respectable meal. A couple of fried eggs and two rashers of bacon on a plate. These had not been touched, and were now cold and greasy. The knife and fork lying beside the plate were not soiled. A second plate, on which was a piece of toast, broken in half, but otherwise untouched, and a pat of butter. A cup, which had evidently been drunk from, empty but for some dregs of coffee at the bottom.

The meal laid at the other side of the table was more modest. No eggs and bacon, merely a plate with toast and butter, some of which seemed to have been eaten. A cup of coffee, full and untouched. At this end of the table stood a coffee-pot. Oldland, anxious to disturb nothing, did not lift the lid. Beside it stood a jug, about a third full of milk which had once been hot. In the centre of the table was a toast-rack, with four pieces of toast still in it. There was also a butter dish, with a few pats of butter, and a cruet with salt, pepper, and mustard.

At one end of the room was a recess, with a window looking out at the back of the house, over an unkempt patch of garden. In this recess was a roll-top desk, with the top closed. Oldland noticed that the key was in the lock. This key was on a ring with three others of various kinds. Two of these were Yale keys.

Oldland, who had quick ears, heard the sound of hurried footsteps on the pavement. He returned to the hall, in time to confront Janet Harleston as she entered the house. 'I'm sorry, Doctor,' she said breathlessly. 'But the parlourmaid said she couldn't find the black case anywhere.'

'No, I'm afraid you had your trouble for nothing. Miss Harleston,' Oldland replied. 'It was in my bag all the time. I found it just after you had gone.'

'Oh, I'm so glad!' she exclaimed. 'How's poor Victor? Is he any better?'

'I'm sorry to say that your brother is dead, Miss Harleston,' replied Oldland, with what seemed cruel curtness.

But amazement, rather than grief, appeared to be the effect caused by this bold statement. 'Dead!' she exclaimed incredulously. 'But he was perfectly well when I took him his tea at half-past seven.'

'That may be, Miss Harleston. You understand that, under the circumstances, I cannot give a death certificate, and that I shall have to communicate with the coroner?'

12

She shook her head helplessly. 'I don't know anything about these things, Doctor. Does that mean there'll be an inquest?'

'I'm afraid so. In any case, arrangements will have to be made to take the body to the mortuary. Have you any other relations alive, Miss Harleston?'

'My mother and father are dead. But I have another brother. Philip, who lives in Kent. He's my real brother, a year older than I am. He was here to supper yesterday evening. I'd better send him a wire to come up at once, hadn't I?'

'Plenty of time, plenty of time' replied Oldland absently. He glanced at his watch. Past nine o'clock! His car and chauffeur would be waiting for him. He had a long round of visits to pay that morning. But he couldn't leave this sinister house, yet. It was a damnable nuisance. 'What was your brother's occupation?' he asked abruptly, more for the sake of continuing the conversation, than because he felt any interest in the matter.

'He was a clerk in an accountant's office. Slater & Knott is the name of the firm. Their offices are in Chancery Lane. Victor had been with them for years.'

'Had he many friends in London?'

She shook her head. 'No, Victor wasn't the sort to make friends. He . . . Oh!'

Janet Harleston broke off with a sudden exclamation. She seemed suddenly to have remembered something, and Oldland glanced at her with a faint renewal of interest. 'You were going to say?' he suggested.

'I was going to say that as far as I know, he hadn't any friends, and then I remembered the man at the door, when I went to fetch you. I've been so upset, that I never thought of him again until this moment.'

Oldland might have pursued the subject, but at that

moment the door bell rang insistently. 'I'll answer it,' he said. 'I expect it's somebody for me.' He walked swiftly to the door and opened it. On the threshold stood Superintendent Hanslet himself. 'Morning, Doctor!' he exclaimed cheerfully. 'What's the matter here?'

Oldland made no reply, but drew him inside and propelled him into the sitting-room. Janet, motionless in the hall, watched them with wide-open, frightened eyes, but said nothing. It was not until he and Hanslet were standing together in front of the sofa that Oldland spoke. 'That's what's the matter,' he said curtly.

Hanslet took a step forward, and bent over the body. 'Dead?' he asked.

'Dead,' replied Oldland grimly. 'I was called in, and reached here at five-and-twenty minutes to nine. The man was then alive, but his condition was hopeless, and he died a few minutes later.'

'What did he die of?' asked Hanslet suspiciously.

'Acute poisoning of some kind. And it appears that he lived alone with his half-sister, the girl you saw in the hall just now. The rest is up to you. I've got my work to attend to. You know where to find me if you want me.'

And before Hanslet could protest, he had slipped out of the house.

2

The superintendent shrugged his shoulders. He had always considered Oldland a bit eccentric, though he fully recognised his abilities. The two men had been acquainted for some few years.

Though Hanslet continued to stare at the body for some few moments, he did so more out of curiosity than in the hope of learning anything from it. He was fully prepared to accept Oldland's statement. The problem before him would be simply expressed. The task of the police was to find out how the poison had been administered, and by whom.

Hanslet turned swiftly on his heel, and left the sitting-room, to find Janet still rooted to the spot where he had last seen her. 'Allow me to introduce myself,' he said. 'I am Superintendent Hanslet of the Criminal Investigation Department. Acting upon information received, I have come here to make inquiries. To begin with, may I ask you your name?

She started, as though his words had awakened her from a deep reverie. 'My name?' she replied. 'Janet Harleston.'

'And the dead man was your brother?'

'My half-brother, Victor Harleston. My father married twice. Both he and my mother have been dead for some years.'

'You and your half-brother lived here alone?'

'Yes. My father left the house to Victor. I stayed with him to look after him, since he was not married.'

'I see. Now, will you tell me what you can of your brother's illness? Everything that you can remember, please. But we need not stand here. I expect you would like to sit down?'

She led the way into the dining-room, and sat down stiffly upon one of the chairs which stood against the wall. Hanslet seated himself beside her. Before them were displayed the remains of the interrupted breakfast.

Janet began to speak without emotion, as though she were describing some remote event, entirely unconnected with herself. 'I took him up his cup of tea at half-past seven, as I always do. He was all right then. I'm sure he was, for he looked just the same as he always did. I put his tray down by his bed . . .'

Hanslet interrupted her. 'One moment, Miss Harleston. Did you speak to your brother when you took him his tea?'

'I asked him if he was awake, before I opened his door, and he answered me.'

'You didn't ask him how he was, or any similar question?'

'No,' she replied sharply. 'I didn't speak to him while I was in his room.'

The tone of her voice did not escape Hanslet. It was clear to him that brother and sister had not been on the best of terms. But he did not comment on this. 'What happened next?' he asked.

'I don't know. I went down to the kitchen to get breakfast. It was a little after eight when I brought it in here. Victor came down a few minutes later. I saw that he looked rather pale, and I noticed that he had a piece of sticking-plaster on his face. I asked him if he had cut himself shaving, and he said something about any fool being able to tell that, since he wasn't in the habit of putting plaster on his face to improve his appearance. I saw that he was as grumpy as usual, and didn't say any more.'

Hanslet made a mental note of that phrase, 'as grumpy as usual.' 'You had no reason to think that your brother was seriously ill?' he asked.

'Not for a few minutes. I poured out his coffee and passed it to him. Usually he eats his breakfast and then drinks his coffee. This morning he took a piece of toast and a pat of butter, but though he broke the toast in half he didn't eat any of it. And he didn't eat any of the eggs and bacon I had done for him, either. He seemed impatient for his coffee to get cool, and, as soon as he could, he drank it all off at once.'

'Had he previously drunk the cup of tea which you had brought him?'

'I don't know. I haven't been up to his room since. I saw that his hand shook as he held the coffee-cup, and I wondered what was the matter. After he had drunk his coffee, he sat for a minute or two in his chair, twitching all over. Then he got up, as though he was so stiff that he could hardly move. He was so clumsy that he upset his chair. Then he staggered to the door, waving his arms and trying to speak. He was very sick as soon as he got into the hall, and then he swayed for a moment, and fell down flat. I ran out to him, and saw that he was very ill. He didn't seem able to move, and he couldn't speak. I thought he had a stroke, or something. So I ran out at once to fetch the doctor.'

'Is Doctor Oldland your usual medical attendant?'

'Oh, no. We had no regular doctor. Nobody has been ill in the house since my father died, and the doctor who attended him has gone away now. But I had often noticed Doctor Oldland's plate when I was out shopping, and as he lives quite close, I went to him.'

'Since there was nobody else in the house, you had to leave your brother alone while you went for the doctor?'

A puzzled look came into her face. 'That's the funny part about it,' she said, using the adjective in its commonly perverted sense. 'I opened the front door and ran out, almost colliding with a man who was coming up the steps. He said, "Excuse me, are you Miss Harleston? I'm a friend of your brother's." I told him that my brother had been suddenly taken ill, and that I was just going for the doctor. He replied that he would stay with him while I was gone. I ran on towards Doctor Oldland's, and I was so upset about Victor that I never gave the man another thought.'

17

'But you and Doctor Oldland found him when you came back, I suppose?'

'No, that's the funny thing about it. We didn't, there was nobody here.'

'Are you sure that this man actually entered the house?'

She hesitated. 'I'm almost sure. You see, I was in a desperate hurry, and only stopped on the steps for a moment when he spoke to me. I feel pretty certain that he walked through the front door as I ran away, but I didn't look back to see what had become of him. I'm sure I didn't shut the door, and Doctor Oldland and I found it ajar when we got back here.'

'I gather that this man was a stranger to you, Miss Harleston?'

'I had never seen him before. He said he was a friend of my brother's, which would have surprised me if I had had time to think, for I didn't know that Victor had any friends. Oh! I've just thought! Perhaps he meant that he was a friend of Philip's.'

'Philip?' Hanslet repeated inquiringly.

'Yes, my real brother. He was here to supper last night, and perhaps this man thought that he had stayed for the night.'

'Can you give any description of this man?'

'I'm afraid I can't. I shouldn't know him again if I saw him. You understand how it was. I was thinking only of getting the doctor as soon as I could, and I didn't take any notice of him.'

'How long were you away from the house?'

'Oh, not long. Not more than ten minutes, I should think. Doctor Oldland was very good, and came back with me at once.'

Hanslet nodded absently. He was rather puzzled as to his

next move. He wanted this girl out of the house, and yet it was imperative that she should be kept under close observation. 'Have you any friends in London?' he asked.

'No, I hardly know anybody. Victor didn't like people coming to the house.'

'I don't like the idea of you staying here alone, after the shock you've had. You mentioned your brother Philip. Where does he live?'

'At Lassingford, near Maidstone. He manages a fruit farm there. I could go to him. He asked me, yesterday evening, if I couldn't go and stay with him for a few days. That's what all the row was about.'

So there had been a row. Hanslet had already suspected as much. And then he had a bright idea. 'Look here, Miss Harleston!' he said. 'I'm going to put you under the care of a friend of mine. He'll send a message for you to your brother, and do anything else you want him to. Now, run upstairs and put on your hat, and we'll go out and get a taxi.'

He watched her go upstairs and into a bedroom, the door of which she shut behind her. It might have been her brother's room, but he had to take that risk. However, she appeared again a few minutes later, dressed to go out and carrying her bag. Hanslet met her at the foot of the stairs. 'Perhaps you had better give me your keys,' he suggested.

Without protest she handed over a bunch, which Hanslet put in his pocket. 'Now, I'll just write a note to this friend of mine,' he said. 'Then we'll be ready to start.'

He took out his notebook, and scribbled a few lines on a blank leaf. 'Dear Jimmy. This is Miss Janet Harleston. Keep your eye on her till further orders. Let her send any messages she likes, but secure a copy of them. She is not, at present, to be detained.'

They went out of the house together, and walked as far as the Fulham Road. Here Carling was still on duty. Hanslet beckoned to him, and drew him aside. 'Get a taxi, and take this lady to the Yard,' he said. 'She's not under arrest, so treat her as politely as you can. When you get there, ask for Inspector Waghorn and give him this note.'

Carling saluted. A purring taxi was stopped, and he helped Janet into it, clambering in beside her. Hanslet watched them drive off. He went to a nearby telephone box, and put through two calls, one to the divisional police surgeon, the other to the police ambulance station. Then he returned to number eight, Matfield Street, where he went into the sitting-room and sat down in the most comfortable chair. He was in no hurry. Plenty of time to get things straight in his mind before he started looking about.

The case was a very simple one. The dead man and his sister had been the sole occupants of the house. That cleared a bit of complications out of the way, at the very start. There was no uncertainty as to the cause of death. Oldland had said that it had been due to acute poisoning. Oldland was a cautious chap. He would not have committed himself so definitely, if he had not been certain.

In such a case, there were three possibilities to be considered. In the first place, accident. For instance, Harleston might have put poison in his early tea, in mistake for his usual daily dose of Kruschen. In the second place, suicide. He might deliberately have poisoned himself, though this, on the face of it, seemed unlikely. And in the third and last place, murder. The poison might have been administered by somebody with intent to kill.

If the evidence pointed to murder, there was only one person upon whom suspicion could fall. His half-sister. Nobody else had had access to him, by her own admission.

The visionary figure standing on the doorstep, even had he really existed, could have had no connection with the crime, since Harleston had obviously taken the poison before he appeared on the scene.

Hanslet had not been very favourably impressed by Janet Harleston. She had told her story readily enough. Almost too readily, perhaps. But she had displayed very little sign of grief at her brother's death. She had almost given Hanslet the impression that the event was a relief to her. She showed a lack of half-sisterly feeling, to say the least of it. And, by her own confession, she had quarrelled with her brother, as recently as the previous day.

The superintendent rose from his chair, passed into the hall, and went upstairs. He opened the door of the room into which he had seen Janet go. Her bedroom, quite obviously, from the articles which it contained. This room had a window looking out over Matfield Street. Next to it was a smaller room, used as a box-room. On the other side of the landing were two doors, one leading into a bathroom and lavatory, the other into a second bedroom. Both these rooms had windows looking out at the back of the house, over the tiny plot of untended garden.

This second bedroom was certainly the one occupied by Victor Harleston. The bed was unmade, and his striped pyjamas had been carelessly thrown upon it. Hanslet's eye was immediately caught by the tray which stood on the table beside the bed. This was obviously the tray upon which Janet Harleston had brought her brother's early tea. Hanslet examined the objects which stood upon it. A tea-pot, about one-third full of tea, now cold. A cup and saucer, the former containing dregs. A sugar-basin, with a few lumps of sugar in it, and a milk-jug, about half-full.

Hanslet examined the room with considerable care. But he could find nothing unusual about it, nothing for instance, which might suggest poison. There was no bottle or other receptacle which seemed in any way suspicious. He passed into the bathroom. This was in a state of considerable disorder, but again it appeared to contain nothing suspicious. He went downstairs again. The ground floor of the house he had already explored, and he continued his way to the basement. Here he found a kitchen, pantry, scullery and larder. There was nothing in any of them beyond the usual food and appliances to be expected in such places.

He was still poking about when he was summoned by a loud knocking on the front door. His visitor proved to be the police surgeon, Doctor Bishop.

'Well, Superintendent, what have you got here?' the latter asked in a business-like tone.

'Come inside,' Hanslet replied, 'and I'll show you.'

The two went into the sitting-room where the body still lay. Doctor Bishop listened attentively to the superintendent's account of what had happened.

'Oldland,' he said. 'Yes, I know him. Very sound chap. If he said the man died of acute poisoning, you may take it that he did. Your trouble is I suppose, to find out where the poison came from.'

'I've a pretty good idea of that already,' Hanslet replied. 'Look here, doctor. The man had a cup of tea soon after seven. He had nothing else until he drank a cup of coffee about half an hour later. Immediately after taking the coffee he was violently ill. No amount of poison in the coffee would act so quickly as that, would it?'

'I shouldn't think so,' said Doctor Bishop thoughtfully. 'It would seem more reasonable to suspect the tea.'

'That's just what I thought. Now then, doctor, if you'll be good enough to come upstairs I'll show you the whole outfit still untouched.'

They went up to Harleston's bedroom. Dr Bishop removed the lid of the teapot and sniffed its contents.

'Ah!' he exclaimed, 'I shouldn't care to drink that tea. Here, smell it for yourself.'

Hanslet followed his example.

'It smells to me more like rank tobacco than tea,' he said.

'Yes,' replied Dr Bishop. 'And that's the characteristic odour of nicotine, a most virulent poison of which two or three drops would probably be fatal. I don't think you need look much further for the cause of this man's death. But what I can't understand is how he came to drink the decoction which smells like this. And it probably tastes even filthier than it smells, but I shouldn't advise you to try. I'll take the contents of the teapot and the dregs in the cup and send them to the Home Office for analysis.'

'We'd better look round and see if there's any more nicotine about the place, I suppose,' he said. 'Just to make sure.'

They searched the house, but without any further results. The coffee on the dining-room table had no suspicious smell, but Dr Bishop decided to send this for analysis just as a matter of precaution. The food in the kitchen and larder appeared to be equally free from nicotine. And then it occurred to Hanslet that if Janet Harleston had administered the poison, the most likely place to look for it was in her room. They went upstairs again. Conspicuous in the centre of Janet's dressing table was a bottle labelled 'eau-de-Cologne' and containing a liquid of a dark brown colour. Dr Bishop looked at this suspiciously.

'I've never seen eau-de-Cologne that colour before,' he said.

He took the stopper from the bottle and applied his nose to it. 'There you are,' he said, 'a most remarkable odour which seems to be a blend of eau-de-Cologne and nicotine. This liquid is a strong solution of the latter in the former, I'll be bound. This bottle must go with the rest for analysis.'

There seemed to be little more to be done for the present. The case was clear as daylight. Harleston had been poisoned by nicotine administered in his early tea, and his sister was the only person who could have administered it. Well, Hanslet thought, she was in safe keeping till she was wanted, anyhow.

Dr Bishop went off with the material for analysis. A few minutes after his departure the ambulance men arrived and the body was taken away to the mortuary. Hanslet remained alone in possession of the house.

It seemed, on the face of it, as though there was nothing more to be done in Matfield Street. And yet Hanslet could not tear himself away. He had an uncomfortable feeling that the house possessed some secret which he had not yet succeeded in penetrating. Everything hitherto had been too simple, too obvious. Why should the girl have left that most compromising bottle on her dressing-table when she had had every opportunity of removing it? Why had she not cleared away the tea-tray before summoning Dr Oldland? And yet, unless Harleston had himself put the nicotine in his tea, her guilt was manifest.

Once more Hanslet began to prowl restlessly about the house. His wanderings took him into the bathroom. Here there were abundant signs of Harleston's toilet. The bath had recently been used and had been cleaned. On a ledge beside the wash basin was an array of shaving materials. A safety razor, rinsed and not dried. A stick of shaving soap, and a shaving brush. Rather to Hanslet's surprise he found that the brush was already dry. Yet Harleston had undoubtedly shaved himself that morning. The smoothness of his cheeks was sufficient evidence of that. And he had cut himself while doing it.

He had certainly cut himself. There were two or three drops of blood on the edge of the basin. A roll of sticking plaster and a pair of scissors lay beside the shaving brush. The only towel in the room was a rough bath towel, and curiously enough, there were no traces of blood on this.

However, there was nothing here to throw any light upon Harleston's death. Hanslet, remembering the bureau which he had seen in the dining-room, went downstairs once more. The bureau stood as Oldland had noticed it, with the key in the lock. Hanslet opened it. Immediately inside were a few sheets of headed notepaper. He removed these and made a further search. Harleston appeared to have used the desk to contain his private papers and accounts. There was nothing else of interest in it.

Hanslet glanced at the sheets of headed paper. They bore the inscription of Novoshave Ltd. with an address in Oxford Street. He wondered idly how they came to be in Harleston's possession. He put them back where he had found them, locked up the desk and put the bunch of keys in his pocket.

There was a second bureau in the sitting-room, and Hanslet thought that it might be as well to examine this. He found it locked, but the lock was a very flimsy affair, and he had no difficulty in breaking it open. Inside was an untidy mass of letters and household bills. It was easy to guess that Janet was the user of this bureau. Hanslet picked up the letters and glanced through them. One, signed Philip, caught his eye. It bore the address, Hart's Farm, Lassingford, and was dated on the previous Friday. Its contents were brief and to the point.

'DEAR JANET. I will come up on Sunday afternoon and put forward the proposition I mentioned to you before. Victor, I suppose, will make himself unpleasant about it, as usual. If only you could get him out of the way there would be no difficulty.

Cheerio, Yours, PHILIP.'

Hanslet smiled grimly as he read this last sentence. Get him out of the way! He was pretty effectually out of the way now, at all events. And what was this proposition that brother and sister had between them?

Hanslet tore himself away from the house at last, still not quite satisfied in his mind. His immediate problem was, how to deal with Janet Harleston. Should he arrest her on the evidence he had already obtained? On the whole he thought better not. Let her remain at large for the present until the case was complete. It would, for instance, be necessary to ascertain the source of the nicotine.

3

Junior Station-Inspector James Waghorn, familiarly known to his associates at Scotland Yard as 'Jimmy' had made considerable progress in his career. Since he had so nearly lost his life in the course of his investigations in the Threlfall Murder, he had become considerably more circumspect. He had found favour with his superiors and now occupied a room of his own at the Yard. Although not yet entrusted with cases of the first importance, he had more than once made himself useful as an assistant to men of greater experience. Hanslet in particular found him a very useful collaborator.

Jimmy was the finished product of Cambridge and the Metropolitan Police College. To his relatively high standard of education, he added an intense enthusiasm for the profession which he had adopted. He thoroughly enjoyed police work, especially that part of it which dealt with the detection of crime. Already he had learnt to combine the experience of the older members of the Force with a certain natural ability for differentiating between the false and the true.

The arrival of Janet Harleston, escorted by the imperturbable Carling, afforded him no surprise. Hanslet was given to issuing instructions without adding any explanation. His duty was to entertain this girl, without the slightest knowledge of the why or wherefore. She was obviously under the influence of some strong emotion, but what it was Jimmy found himself unable to discover. She seemed to think that Jimmy knew what had happened and their conversation was, at first, not very explicit.

But it soon transpired that her most pressing desire was to communicate with her brother Philip. Jimmy offered her every assistance and assisted her to compile a telegram. In its final form this read as follows:

'Harleston, Hart's Farm, Lassingford. Victor dead very sudden come at once to Scotland Yard.

JANET.'

This telegram was despatched at once and while awaiting the reply Jimmy set himself to study his unexpected visitor.

He soon made up his mind that whatever emotion it was that gripped her it was not profound grief. She neither wept, nor showed that frozen look so often produced by a sudden bereavement. The death of Victor had not touched her heart, of that Jimmy felt pretty certain. Was she suffering from remorse? Possibly, but Jimmy thought not. It seemed to him rather that she was puzzled—profoundly puzzled. And perhaps, as the occasional flick of her eyelids seemed to suggest, she was relieved.

She displayed no desire to talk about what had happened at Matfield Street. Indeed, after her first nervousness due to her unfamiliar surroundings had left her, she showed no disposition to talk at all. Jimmy tried her on two or three subjects but obtained no response. In the end they relapsed into a rather uncomfortable silence.

All at once she spoke abruptly, as though her thoughts had taken a practical turn.

'Oh, I ought to let Mr Mowbray know at once,' she exclaimed.

'Mr Mowbray?' inquired Jimmy politely.

'Yes, he's our lawyer. He'll have to see to things, won't he?'

It struck Jimmy that Mr Mowbray might have more to see to than the girl realised.

'Where does he live?' he asked.

'In Lincoln's Inn. Perhaps you could telephone to him for me.'

Jimmy hesitated. If he were to telephone the lawyer, he would almost certainly come round to the Yard at once and insist upon interviewing his client. This might not conform to Hanslet's wishes. Jimmy had already learnt that under certain circumstances, detectives do not welcome lawyers. The latter had a way of seeing further than their clients. They would suggest a refusal to answer certain questions, or even object that those questions should not be put. Hanslet would probably turn up sooner or later to interview this girl, and he might not be best pleased if he found her under the protection of her lawyer. So, on the whole, Jimmy thought it best to temporise.

'I think it would be better not to telephone,' he said. 'Telephone messages are so apt to be misunderstood. Besides, Mr Mowbray might not be in his office. Suppose you write him a note and I'll have it sent round at once?'

She wrote a note, Jimmy contriving to overlook her as she did so. It was very brief, stating merely that Victor had died suddenly that morning and that she was going down to stay with Philip. It did not seem to occur to her to mention that the police were already in charge of the matter.

She gave the envelope to Jimmy, who left the room with it. He found a messenger and handed over the note to him with instructions that it was not to be delivered until three o'clock that afternoon. Then he returned to Janet, who had once more relapsed into silence.

He was greatly relieved when, shortly before eleven o'clock, he was summoned to Hanslet's room. The superintendent welcomed him with a grin.

'Well Jimmy, how are you getting on with that charming young woman I sent you?' he asked.

'Oh, pretty well, so far,' replied Jimmy cheerfully. 'She's not exactly communicative, and I haven't got any information out of her. Here are the copies of the only two messages she has sent so far.'

Hanslet looked at these and nodded. 'Yes,' he said, 'I know something about Philip, but who's this fellow Mowbray in Lincoln's Inn?'

'Her lawyer. But I've taken steps to see that he doesn't get that message till this afternoon.'

Hanslet laughed. 'You're a bright lad, Jimmy,' he said approvingly. 'I think I'll go and see this Mr Mowbray before he gets the message. Now, sit down and I'll tell you what it's all about.'

Jimmy listened with interest to his superior's story. At its conclusion he said nothing for a few moments, then:

'This girl doesn't look to me like a murderess.' he exclaimed.

Hanslet fixed him with a critical eye. 'If you can tell by inspection whether a woman is a murderess or not, you'll be a valuable acquisition to the Force,' he said. 'There doesn't seem to be a shadow of doubt about it. They were alone in the house, the poison was found in her room. And yet, Jimmy, my lad, in spite of everything that stares me in the face, I don't believe she did it.'

This was a remarkable admission for Hanslet. He seemed to realise this, for he added hastily, 'Don't let that go any further, Jimmy. It's merely the expression of my private opinion. A man would never have left all that damning evidence lying about. But in the case of a woman, you never can tell. She may have lost her head when she saw the effect of the poison upon her brother. Poison is all very well in theory, but it's a nasty, sticky business in practice. I dare say she didn't realise the unpleasantness involved. Her first instinct was to run for the doctor, and as soon as he appeared on the scene it was too late for her to do anything to cover her tracks.'

'I wasn't thinking so much of the evidence as of her state of mind,' said Jimmy.

'State of mind! What do you know of her state of mind? She's probably been thinking a hell of a lot since it happened.

I feel almost sorry for her, though. It's a clear case of either murder or suicide. There's no possibility of death having been accidental. And, if it was murder, she is the only possible culprit.'

Their conversation was interrupted by the ringing of Hanslet's telephone bell. The expected Philip Harleston had arrived, and was asking for his sister Janet. Hanslet winked knowingly towards Jimmy.

'Here's the third party,' he said. Then turning towards the telephone, 'All right, bring him in here.'

It was not long before Philip Harleston appeared. He was a fresh-faced, rather simple looking young man, with a decided likeness to his sister. He seemed rather disconcerted at finding himself at Scotland Yard and shifted nervously from one foot to the other. Hanslet motioned him to a chair.

'Well, Mr Harleston, you know what has happened,' he said curtly.

'My sister sent me a wire,' replied Philip in a puzzled voice. 'I don't understand it at all. Victor was perfectly well when I last saw him. And that was only yesterday evening.'

'You were on very friendly terms with your half-brother, I expect,' said Hanslet innocently.

Philip scratched his head with a peculiar gesture of uncertainty. 'I don't know that we were particularly friendly,' he replied. 'I didn't like the way he treated Janet. Of course, he had to provide a home for her, but that was no reason for making her slave for him as he did.'

'Your sister was dependent upon her half-brother?'

'Completely. She had nothing whatever of her own. Now, of course, she'll be independent.'

Hanslet glanced triumphantly in Jimmy's direction. Here was the first hint of motive coming as a gift from Heaven.

Victor Harleston had made his sister slave for him. His death made her independent. The reason for the murder became immediately apparent. However, Hanslet did not pursue the subject. He preferred to learn the relations between these three people from an independent source. He seemed at the moment more interested in Philip's visit to Matfield Street.

'You had supper at your half-brother's house yesterday evening, did you not?' he asked.

'Yes, I went there to see Janet and she asked me to stop,' Philip replied. 'I had a suggestion to make to her which I knew that Victor would not like. I knew she was a bit run-down and wanted a change. So I suggested to her that she should come and stay with me in the country for a bit.'

'And this suggestion did not meet with your half-brother's approval?' Hanslet asked.

'Most decidedly not. In fact, he put his foot on it at once. He said that his bargain with Janet was this. He provided for her and in return she kept house for him. Who was going to do her work while she was away? Was he expected to pay somebody to come in? In fact, Janet's place was at Matfield Street and she could only leave there with his permission.'

Hanslet nodded. 'And you accepted your half-brother's decision without protest?' he asked.

Once more Philip scratched his head. It was evidently a characteristic gesture. 'Well, I don't know,' he replied slowly. 'I told Victor just what I thought of his behaviour and we had a few words. In the end he told me to get outside the house and stop there. If I liked to take Janet with me, I might. But if she went it would have to be for good. He would wash his hands of her as he would be entitled to.'

'What time was it when you left the house?' Hanslet asked.

'About nine o'clock. I caught the nine forty-five from Charing Cross.'

'What is your occupation, Mr Harleston?'

'I am the manager of a fruit farm. I have a small cottage and I could easily put Janet up. The trouble is that what I earn would not be enough to keep both of us.'

'I think you said that your half-brother's death will make your sister independent?' Hanslet suggested.

'Yes, that's right,' Philip replied cheerfully. 'There's nothing to prevent Janet coming and living with me now.'

Hanslet made no reply. He pressed a button upon his desk and a few seconds later a messenger appeared. 'Will you take Mr Harleston to Inspector Waghorn's room, please,' he said. And then, turning to Philip, 'You'll find your sister waiting for you there,' he added.

Philip left the room in charge of the messenger.

'Well, that's that,' said Hanslet. 'Victor Harleston's death seems to have come as a godsend to those two young people. I don't want them hanging about Matfield Street. Run along and talk to them, Jimmy. Persuade Philip Harleston to take his sister away with him. Only, keep your eye on them. And if they show any signs of making a bolt for it, have them detained.'

It was by now lunch-time, a meal which Hanslet never missed if he could help it. He went out and had his favourite chop and a pint of beer. He then decided to pay a visit to Mr Mowbray. He thought it probable that he would secure some useful information from this quarter.

Mr Mowbray occupied a dark and musty office in Lincoln's Inn. Hanslet was received by an elderly clerk, who immediately told him that on no account could he see Mr Mowbray without an appointment. Hanslet, however, produced his card, and this had the usual effect. The clerk shuffled off with it into an inner office. He reappeared a few minutes later with the information that Mr Mowbray would make an exception to his invariable rule and see the superintendent at once.

Hanslet passed into the inner room and found himself confronted by a wizened old man with a peevish and distinctly unwelcoming expression. From his appearance Hanslet guessed that he had been interrupted in his quiet after-lunch doze. The lawyer glared at him.

'Well, Superintendent,' he wheezed, 'what is your business?'

'Not a particularly pleasant one, I'm afraid,' Hanslet replied. 'Mr Victor Harleston, of eight Matfield Street, was one of your clients, I believe?'

'Was!' exclaimed the lawyer. 'Was? Is, you mean. What about him?'

'He died under extremely suspicious circumstances about nine o'clock this morning,' Hanslet replied equably.

'Eh! What's this?' exclaimed the lawyer. 'Why wasn't I told about it before?'

'The information has been conveyed to you at the earliest possible moment, Mr Mowbray. Perhaps you will be good enough to give me certain information respecting your late client.'

The lawyer looked at him obliquely. 'I must first demand an explanation of the words you used just now,' he replied. 'Suspicious circumstances, I think you said. In what way were the circumstances of my client's death suspicious?'

'It is believed that Victor Harleston died as the result of acute poisoning,' said Hanslet deliberately.

'Then an inquest will be held?' Mr Mowbray snapped.

'That is so. It is in view of this inquest that I am asking for information.'

'Well, what do you want to know?'

'First of all I should like information as to Victor Harleston's age, occupation, and so forth.'

'Victor Harleston was forty-two. He has for many years been employed as a clerk by Messrs. Slater & Knott, Accountants, Chancery Lane. I have every reason to believe that his work has given his employers the fullest satisfaction.'

'Did he possess means beyond his salary?' Hanslet asked.

The lawyer glanced at him suspiciously. 'He enjoys the proceeds of a trust established by his father,' he replied.

'Were there any conditions attaching to this?'

This question seemed to rouse the lawyer from his apathy. 'A most ridiculous affair altogether,' he exclaimed. 'Victor's father, Peter, was always doing the most unaccountable things. He made this foolish will without consulting me and I always told him that trouble would come of it.'

'May I ask for an outline of the provisions of the will, Mr Mowbray?'

'Well, I suppose you've a right to know,' the lawyer replied ungraciously. 'Peter Harleston began life as a van boy. After that he became an assistant in a greengrocer's shop. He managed to save money and when his employer died he bought the business. He made a very good thing of it and at the time of his death he was the owner of the house in Matfield Street, and had other investments amounting to between ten and fifteen thousand pounds in all.

'Peter Harleston married twice. By his first wife he had Victor and a girl who died young. By his second wife, he had a boy Philip and a year later a girl, Janet. Peter and his second wife died within a few months of one another, about three years ago.

'Peter was one of those people who imagine that after they are gone their children will squander the money which they have so laboriously amassed. He imagined that he had found a way of preventing this. Victor was already in a good position in an accountant's office. Philip he provided for by buying him a small share in a fruit farm which carried with it the position of manager. Victor as the eldest son and the one who took most after his father secured the lion's share. Peter, in that ridiculous will of his, left him the house in Matfield Street, with reversion to Philip if Victor died without issue. The remainder of Peter's estate was to be formed into a Trust so long as he provided a home for his half-sister Janet. Those were the testator's actual words. There was no explanation of this exceedingly vague term. There was no provision made for Janet getting married or for her wishing to leave her half-brother's roof of her own accord. Of course, had I been consulted I should never have allowed such lamentable looseness of expression.'

'And in the event of Victor's death?' Hanslet suggested.

'I'm coming to that, I'm coming to that,' replied the lawyer testily. 'In that case, the proceeds of the Trust were to be divided. If Victor had married, his widow, or, failing her, his children, were to receive one-third share. The remaining two-thirds were to be enjoyed by Philip and Janet in equal proportion. If Victor had not married, the proceeds of the Trust were to be divided equally between Philip and Janet.'

'The three children were, of course, aware of the contents of their father's will?'

'Naturally. It was my business to inform them. In fact, Philip came to see me not long ago. He wished to know whether it would be possible for the Trustees to provide for his sister independently. He inquired as to Janet's condition should she decline to continue to live with her half-brother.'

'I should be interested to know what you told him.' said Hanslet.

'Told him! My dear sir, I could only refer him to the conditions of the will. Victor was to enjoy the proceeds of the Trust so long as he provided a home for Janet. Whether she availed herself of that home did not affect the issue. If she left it, Victor was under no obligation to support her. He would, however, be bound to re-admit her should she at any time decide to return.'

This Hanslet thought was sufficient for the moment. He took his leave of the lawyer, and, since he found himself in that neighbourhood, he decided to call upon Victor Harleston's employers in Chancery Lane. He ascertained that the offices of Slater & Knott were situated in Cobalt Buildings, and proceeded thither. He was received by Mr Knott, a keen, alert looking man of between thirty and forty, who seemed very much surprised to hear of the sudden death of his employee.

'Why, I've never known Harleston have a day's illness,' he exclaimed. 'I couldn't understand it when he didn't turn up this morning. I don't think he's missed a day for years. In fact, if I didn't hear in the course of the day, I intended to go round and see him after office hours and find out what was the matter.'

'Has Victor Harleston seemed in his usual health and spirits lately?' Hanslet asked.

Mr Knott smiled. 'Health, yes,' he replied. 'As for spirit, well, he never displayed any exuberance in that respect. He was always a quiet, rather morose sort of chap who seemed to avoid his fellow-men. I have an idea that he disliked friendship because of the expense attached to it. So far as I know he never drank, and smoked only the cheapest cigarettes he could buy. He was the last person in the world to spend a penny when a halfpenny would do as well.'

'He carried out his duties efficiently?' Hanslet asked.

'Perfectly. Like a machine without any imagination. In our profession that's not a bad thing in its way. I suppose you've got the idea of suicide in your mind. I can only tell you straight out that I know of no reason why Harleston should have committed suicide. No financial or business reasons, I mean. But fellows like that who have no resources beyond themselves often do these unaccountable things.'

'Can you tell me if Harleston has any connection with a firm of Novoshave in Oxford Street?'

Mr Knott looked at the superintendent, sharply. 'May I ask what makes you ask that question?'

'Only this. I found some of their headed notepaper in his desk at Matfield Street.'

Mr Knott seemed relieved. 'Oh, is that all!' he exclaimed. 'Naturally, we don't like discussing our client's business with anybody. I think I can account for the presence of that headed notepaper. We are the auditors to Novoshave Ltd. Harleston was employed upon the job most of last week at their offices and no doubt he took some of their paper home to work upon. He had no connection with Novoshave except as our employee.'

Hanslet rather perfunctorily asked one last question. 'There was no suggestion that Harleston might lose his job, I suppose?'

Mr Knott shook his head. 'Good heavens, no!' he replied. 'There was no reason why Harleston should not have stayed with us till the day of his death. We always found him a very useful man, so useful that we paid him a special bonus of a hundred pounds at the beginning of this year.'

From Chancery Lane Hanslet returned to Scotland Yard. On his desk he found a message awaiting him. It was as follows.

'Dr Priestley would be glad if you could find it convenient to dine with him this evening. Oldland, who would like to see you, will be present.

H. MEREFIELD.'

Hanslet smiled. 'So the Professor's on the job already, is he?' he muttered. 'You bet I'll go. But I'm afraid there isn't enough meat in this case to suit the old boy's appetite.'

4

Dr Priestley, who lived in a spacious if rather gloomy house in Westbourne Terrace, was, in his own line, a distinguished scientist. His name was hardly familiar to the general public, but to his fellow-savants he was very well known indeed. He was a man of considerable means and since his retirement from a professorship, he had devoted himself to scientific criticism. His articles and monographs, though usually couched in somewhat acrid terms, were treated with profound respect in the learned world.

But in addition to his scientific employment, he had a hobby. This hobby, which he liked to pursue in secret, was criminology. He maintained that criminology, properly treated, presented problems of absorbing interest to the scientist. Many years ago he had made Hanslet's acquaintance. They had become fast friends and Hanslet got into the habit of laying his more difficult cases before the acute brain of the professor.

It happened that Dr Oldland was one of Dr Priestley's oldest acquaintances. It was natural therefore that he and Hanslet should meet frequently at the professor's house. The reason for the present invitation was fairly obvious. Oldland had told the professor about his experience of that morning, and some feature of his account had interested the latter. In any case dinner at the house in Westbourne Terrace was an event to be remembered. Hanslet was always ready to enjoy an excellent meal in such distinguished company.

So that evening at eight o'clock he sat down at the professor's table. He found himself one of a party of four, the other two being Oldland and Dr Priestley's secretary, Harold Merefield. The professor never encouraged the discussion of problems during dinner, holding that such a procedure might divert his guests' attention from their food. It was not until the company was assembled in the study afterwards that he made any reference to the Harleston case.

'Oldland tells me, Superintendent, that you and he met under rather peculiar circumstances this morning,' he remarked.

'We met because Oldland sent for me,' Hanslet replied. 'He had been called in to attend a suspiciously sudden case of poisoning and he seemed to think that I ought to know about it.'

'It was a devilish awkward,' said Oldland reminiscently, helping himself to a whisky and soda. 'There was I, alone in the house with that girl and a remarkably suspicious looking corpse. I didn't know what the dickens to do. If I went out to call the police I should have had to leave her alone. For all I knew, there might be evidence in the house that she would take the opportunity to destroy. So I hit upon the idea of sending her back to my place for a wholly imaginary black case, and employed her absence in telephoning to you. How did you get on after I left?'

Hanslet laughed. 'So that was the dodge, was it? I was faced with the same difficulty. I got out of it by sending the girl to the Yard and putting her in charge of young Waghorn. You remember him, I expect, Professor?'

Dr Priestley nodded solemnly. 'Yes, I remember him in connection with the Threlfall case.'

'Well, having got rid of her, I started to have a look round,' said Hanslet. 'I sent for Dr Bishop, the police surgeon, to lend me a hand. We didn't have far to look. Harleston's early tea had been liberally doctored with nicotine.'

'Nicotine!' exclaimed Dr Priestley. 'Why, the presence of the most minute quantity of nicotine would surely be detected by anybody with normal powers of taste and smell?'

'I should have thought so,' Hanslet replied. 'The tea in the pot stank like a rank pipe. But there was the nicotine and there was the man dead of acute poisoning. I shall hear tomorrow what the post-mortem has revealed.'

'I can tell you that now,' said Oldland quietly. 'The coroner asked Bishop to carry it out, and he, knowing that I had been called in, invited me to attend. At my suggestion we called in Grantham, the pathologist from the Home Office. The three of us set to work and, if you're interested, I can tell you what we found.'

'Not unnaturally, I'm profoundly interested,' said Hanslet.

Oldland grinned. 'Well, we found the nicotine all right,' he said slowly. 'There's not a shadow of doubt that nicotine

41

poisoning was the cause of Harleston's death. But curiously enough, we didn't find it where you might have expected. In his tummy, that is.'

'Well, where did you find it?' Hanslet asked impatiently.

'Absorbed into his system. You may have noticed that the chap had a piece of sticking plaster on his face, suggesting that he had cut himself while shaving. Well, we removed that and found a nice clean cut underneath it. From the appearance of the edges of the cut we had no doubt that it was through this that the nicotine had been absorbed.

'Now nicotine is one of the most virulent poisons known. Cases of fatal poisoning have been due to nicotine being absorbed through the unbroken skin. A very small quantity taken internally produces rapid death. Priestley will bear me out in that.'

'Nicotine is known to be extremely rapid in its action,' Dr Priestley remarked. 'In the celebrated case of Count Bocarmé, who poisoned his wife's brother with nicotine which he prepared for the purpose, death took place in five minutes.'

'Since in this case the poisoning was by absorption, death was rather less rapid than that,' said Oldland. 'How the nicotine came in contact with the cut, I can't say.'

Hanslet looked in bewilderment from one to the other. 'There was nicotine in the teapot,' he said stubbornly. 'Somebody drank a cup of tea from that pot and there seems no doubt that it was Harleston.'

Oldland shrugged his shoulders. 'I can't help it,' he replied. 'There was practically no trace of nicotine in the man's stomach. Grantham carried off the contents for analysis, of course, but I'm willing to bet anything you like that he won't find more than a trace. Whereas the tissues in the neighbourhood of the cut were literally impregnated with nicotine.'

'You mean that he can't have drunk the tea?' Hanslet asked.

'Not if it was so saturated with nicotine as you suggest. I may as well say that Bishop told me about the tea, and the absence of nicotine in the stomach troubled him as much as it does you. The only theory he could suggest was this. Harleston had not drunk the tea owing to its offensive taste and smell. On the other hand, after he had cut himself, he applied some of the leaves to his face in an attempt to stop the bleeding. I believe that people do employ tea-leaves for that purpose.'

'Well,' Hanslet exclaimed, 'somebody must have put it there,' Oldland agreed readily enough. 'But where did she get it from? That's the question.'

'What is nicotine used for?' Hanslet asked.

Dr Priestley glanced towards his secretary. 'Will you get down the Chemical Encyclopaedia, please, Harold?' he said. 'Thank you. Now will you turn to the article on nicotine, and extract from it the answer to the Superintendent's question?'

Harold turned over the pages of the volume until he found what he wanted. After a moment or two he began to read. 'Nicotine is soluble in water, alcohol and ether, and preparations of it are extensively used for horticultural purposes as an insecticide, also as a dip for the destruction of ticks and other pests on the wool of sheep.'

Oldland nodded. 'That's right,' he said. 'Almost every gardener uses nicotine in some form or another. Fruit growers especially. They make a wash from it with which they spray their trees.'

Hanslet suddenly stiffened in his chair. 'Fruit growers!' he exclaimed. 'Do they, by jove! I learnt this morning that young Philip Harleston is the manager of a fruit farm.'

43

'That certainly suggests the possible source of the nicotine,' Oldland remarked. 'You found some more of the stuff mixed with the girl's eau-de-Cologne, Bishop tells me.'

'Yes, on her dressing table. I've been wondering whether the mixture was made in the hope that the eau-de-Cologne would drown the smell of the nicotine.'

'It's possible,' said Oldland shortly. 'By the way, did the girl say anything to you about a man at the door?'

Hanslet appeared rather astonished at this question. 'Oh, she mentioned him to you, did she?' he said. 'I was inclined to think that rather nebulous individual was an afterthought.'

'She didn't mention him to me until we had had some conversation together. And then she mentioned him quite suddenly, and I think genuinely.'

'You'd have thought it would have been the first thing she would have talked about,' Hanslet objected. 'Dash it all, a stranger on the doorstep just at the critical moment when she was going out to fetch the doctor! According to her account, this stranger volunteered to come in and look after her brother while she was away. Yet, when she returned, he wasn't there and she showed no astonishment.'

'Oh, I don't know,' Oldland replied. 'You must remember her mind was fully occupied with her brother. The momentary incident of the stranger might well have slipped her memory.'

'Well, the stranger, even though he may have been a confederate, cannot have been the actual poisoner,' said Hanslet. 'Unless he was in the house earlier in the morning unknown to its occupants, and I don't see how that can have happened. No, I'm afraid the matter's plain enough. Janet Harleston poisoned her half-brother, possibly at the instigation of Philip.'

Dr Priestley had been listening attentively to this conversation. 'Do you not think, Superintendent, that you are accepting things at their face value without adequate investigation?'

'Well, Professor, I was inclined to think at first that things were too easy,' Hanslet replied. 'But then, I made some inquiries into the question of motive. I went to see the family solicitor. From him I obtained the information that there are only two people who could possibly benefit by Victor Harleston's death. And those two people are his half-sister and brother.'

Dr Priestley frowned. 'Benefit financially, I suppose you mean,' he said. 'Surely you are not yet sufficiently acquainted with Harleston's history to state that nobody else might have found his death desirable?'

'Well no, I suppose I'm not,' Hanslet replied. 'But from what I can hear of Harleston, he was a man without any particular history. He seems to have been mean and uncompaniohable, but otherwise inoffensive.'

Dr Priestley put the tips of his fingers together, a favourite gesture with him, and stared at the ceiling. 'It seems to me,' he said oracularly, 'that the chief interest of this case lies in the manner by which the poison was administered. It appears to be proved fairly conclusively that the poison was not swallowed, but absorbed through a cut sustained while Harleston was shaving. It appears to me hardly probable that Harleston applied the whole of a cup of tea to his cut. He might have dipped a towel in the tea and dabbed this on his face. But that would account for hardly more than a spoonful of the tea. Yet, I understand, the tea-cup found in his room was nearly empty.'

Hanslet laughed. 'Perhaps you will remember a case in which you helped me not long ago, Professor,' he replied.

'Then you asked me if I had looked for lip marks on a wine glass. I remembered that this morning and I particularly looked for lip marks on the cup. I found them, all right. There's not a shadow of doubt that the cup had been drunk from. And yet, here is Dr Oldland, assuring us that the poison had not been swallowed.'

'I do not see that that need present any difficulty,' said Dr Priestley quietly. 'If the poison were already in the tea when Harleston poured out his cupful he certainly did not drink it. The post-mortem evidence is conclusive proof of that. On the other hand, if Harleston drank the cup of tea, the poison was not then in it. We should then be driven to explore the possibility of the poison having been added at some later time.'

'Added later!' Hanslet exclaimed. 'When? Why? And by whom?'

Dr Priestley seemed indisposed to reply. It was Oldland who stepped into the breach. 'I'd hazard a guess to all three parts of your question, Superintendent,' he said. 'When, during the period that Janet Harleston was absent from the house on her errand to fetch me. Why, to produce a false impression. The poisoner may not have known that post-mortem examination would enable us to say positively that the poison had not been swallowed but absorbed through the skin. Finally, by whom, suggests a very interesting speculation. What about the man whom Janet met on the doorstep?'

Dr Priestley protested. 'This is carrying conjecture to an unwarrantable length,' he said severely.

'Sorry, Priestley,' said Oldland contritely. 'That was a wild bit of guesswork, I'll admit. But the facts are there and they've got to be explained somehow.'

'They are more likely to be explained by careful investigation than by conjecture,' Dr Priestley replied. 'The central point, I still insist, is this. How did the nicotine come in contact with the wound? You have, no doubt, made a careful examination of the house, Superintendent. In the course of that, did you find a bloodstained towel?'

'No, it's rather a queer thing, but I didn't,' Hanslet replied. 'I looked for one in the bathroom, but couldn't find it. However, it must be about the place somewhere. I'll have another look.'

'I should very strongly advise you to do so,' said Dr Priestley. 'This morning, you were under the impression that the poison had been swallowed. The cut on the dead man's face had therefore but slight significance for you. Now, however, you know that cut to have been vital. How and when the cut was sustained should be the basis of your future inquiries.'

5

Next morning, upon his arrival at the Yard, Hanslet found the official report of the post-mortem awaiting him. It was a voluminous and highly technical document, but it told him no more than he had already learnt from Oldland.

He put it aside and turned to greet Inspector Waghorn, who entered his room at that moment.

'Well, Jimmy, and what about our two young friends?' he asked.

'I saw them down to this place, Lassingford, yesterday afternoon,' Jimmy replied. 'It's only a village, and, of course, everybody there knows Philip Harleston. He lives in a cottage on Hart's Farm. Nice little place, wouldn't mind living there myself. They didn't know I was behind them all the way, of course. When I had seen them safely installed, I went and had a chat with the local constable. He'll let us know if they attempt to make any move.'

'Janet will have had a summons to attend the inquest by now,' said Hanslet. 'It's fixed for this afternoon at half-past two. We shan't produce any evidence at this stage, and there's bound to be an adjournment. That will give us time to look round. And, since you're here, Jimmy, you may as well come along with me and we'll have another look over that house in Matfield Street.'

On the way Hanslet explained to his subordinate the disconcerting paradox revealed by the post-mortem. 'You see how it is,' he said. 'The experts say that Harleston could not have been poisoned by the tea. They are confident that his death was due to absorbing the poison through the cut on his face. How did the poison reach that cut? That's the question we've got to answer.'

'The only thing I can think of, is that he must have used his early morning tea as shaving water,' suggested Jimmy flippantly.

'You'll have to think of something a bit more sensible than that,' Hanslet replied. 'Here we are, I've got the key in my pocket, and the local people have had instructions to keep an eye on the place.'

The superintendent unlocked the door and they entered. A rapid survey was sufficient to assure Hanslet that nothing had been touched since his last visit. In the dining-room Harleston's untouched breakfast looked more unappetising than ever. The imprint made by the body on the sofa in the sitting-room was still visible. A woman's crumpled handkerchief lay in the hall. It had evidently been dropped by Janet in the course of her hurried departure. Hanslet picked it up and sniffed at it. It smelt faintly of eau-de-Cologne.

Remembering Dr Priestley's hint, Hanslet led the way to the bathroom. He and Jimmy stood just inside the doorway whence they could survey the whole room. On the ledge by the wash-basin they saw the safety razor, the stick of shaving soap and the brush. Thrown carelessly over a towel rail was a bath towel, but this seemed to bear no trace of blood. Only those two or three drops of blood on the edge of the basin showed that the cut must have bled fairly freely.

'We know that Victor Harleston has a recent cut on the right side of his face,' said Hanslet. 'We can't say for certain, of course, that he made this cut while he was shaving himself. The cut may have been caused in some other way. Yet, if we accept Janet's statement, we have confirmation of the shaving theory. She asked him whether he had cut himself shaving and he admitted it rather surlily.

'On the other hand, Janet may have had some reason for her statement. She may have wished to create the impression that her half-brother had cut himself while shaving. Again, where is the towel he must have used? He may have thrown it into a dirty clothes basket somewhere. No, from what one may judge of his habits he was not a very tidy man. Let's have a look round and see if we can't unearth it somewhere.'

They scoured the house without success. In the little boxroom was a clothes basket containing a few items of dirty linen. But the towel they were seeking was not among these. There were no coal fires in the house, so the theory that it might have been burnt was untenable. After an exhaustive search of every corner, they were bound to confess themselves nonplussed.

'I can't make it out,' said Hanslet petulantly. 'What do you do, when you cut yourself shaving, Jimmy?'

'Grab hold of the towel and dab my face with it,' Jimmy replied promptly.

'Exactly. So I imagine does everybody else. In this case, the cut began to bleed at once. These drops on the basin show that. Harleston must have dabbed his face with something, but what? Not the bath towel—there's no blood on that. His handkerchief, as I happened to notice yesterday morning, has no blood upon it. In any case, blood or no blood, the man must have used a towel to dry his face after shaving. Where is it? And there's another queer thing, Jimmy. This shaving brush was bone dry when I looked at it yesterday morning. That seems to me pretty queer, for in my experience a shaving brush remains wet for a long time after use.'

'That is rather queer,' said Jimmy thoughtfully. 'I wonder whether Harleston was right or left-handed?'

'What the devil has that got to do with it?' Hanslet demanded.

'I was just thinking of the technique of shaving. Most people lather their face all over and then begin to use the razor. If they are right-handed, they almost invariably start on the right side of their faces on a level with the ear. If, then, Harleston was right-handed, he probably cut himself as soon as he started shaving.'

'That's rather a neat point, Jimmy,' said Hanslet approvingly. 'But I don't see that it is of any particular use to us.'

'Only this. Apparently he finished shaving after he had cut himself. In which case he must continually have dabbed his face with something, and that something must have absorbed a considerable quantity of blood.'

'Well, since we can't find it, that's hardly helpful.'

'What is he likely to have done with it?' Jimmy insisted. 'His face probably continued bleeding after he had finished shaving. He might have taken this towel, or whatever it was, into his bedroom to use while he was dressing. If you don't mind I'll have one last search in there.'

Hanslet raised no objection to this. Jimmy went into Harleston's bedroom and proceeded to examine everything which the room contained. In the course of his search he came upon the vase containing the spills. He turned these out and looked inside the vase. There was no towel or fragment of rag within it. As he replaced the spills, he noticed the fragment of an embossed word upon one of them. He unfolded the spill, thus revealing the word Novoshave.

Hanslet was still pursuing his search in the bathroom. Jimmy took in the spills.

'Did not you tell me that you found some headed paper belonging to Novoshave Ltd?' he asked.

'Yes, in the desk in the dining-room,' Hanslet replied. 'Why?'

'Because here's a bit of another sheet of the same paper. And this sheet has had a letter typed upon it.'

Hanslet seemed unimpressed. 'Well, that's not a very sensational discovery,' he said. 'You'd much better keep your mind fixed on the towel.'

But Jimmy's imagination had been set to work. Novoshave Ltd. He had seen their advertisement. They were, he knew, a firm who specialised in the manufacture of safety razors and other shaving requisites.

The tiresome and recurrent business of shaving seemed to be the background of this case. It might be worth while ascertaining the nature of the communication from Novoshave Ltd. to Victor Harleston.

51

It was an easy matter to unfold the four spills and so to piece together the letter from which they had been made. It was typewritten and ran as follows:

'DEAR MR. HARLESTON. As you are no doubt aware we are about to place upon the market our new model K. safety razor. This model has certain features which render it the most efficient safety razor yet produced. We are confident that it will meet with a ready welcome from the general public.

'We are anxious, however, to have a few opinions other than our own. For this purpose we have decided to distribute specimens of this model among certain of our friends. We have the greatest pleasure in including you among the number. Enclosed you will find one of our model K. razors in leather case. We have also included a tube of our famous Novoshave cream. This is applied direct to the face and no brush or water are necessary.

'We shall be greatly indebted to you if you will be good enough to make an early trial of the razor and cream, and at your convenience to report to us the results obtained by you.'

The letter was dated January 18th, three days' prior to Harleston's death. He had been in no hurry to make the trial, Jimmy thought. The safety razor found in the bathroom was an ordinary Gillette, not a Novoshave. Nor had the tube of shaving cream come to light. Harleston had apparently been in the habit of using Pears shaving soap. Perhaps he had put away the gift so generously made him by Novoshave Ltd., intending to use it upon some future occasion.

52

Jimmy idly turned over the strips of paper forming the letter. On the back he observed some figures in pencil. These were as follows:

$$20000 - 100 = 19900$$
$$\text{£}100 \quad \text{at} \quad \text{£}5 \ 2 \ 1 \quad = \quad \text{£}5.104$$
$$\text{£}20000 \ \text{at} \ 5.104 \times 200 = \text{£}1020.8$$
$$5.104$$
$$\overline{\text{£}1015.696}$$

Jimmy put the letter aside and proceeded to unfold the remaining spills. These, having been made of fragments of newspaper, contained no information of significance. He resumed his search for the towel, even going so far as to lift the carpet in case it should have been hidden underneath it. At last he was compelled to admit to complete failure.

Hanslet had had no better luck in the bathroom. He seemed put out by his lack of success.

'It's no good wasting any more of our time here,' he exclaimed crossly. 'We'd better get back to the Yard. 'There's plenty to do there. And then after lunch we shall have to put in an appearance at this confounded inquest.'

That afternoon, Jimmy reached the coroner's court before his superior. Not long after his arrival, Janet Harleston appeared, escorted by her brother Philip. Jimmy greeted her and drew her aside. 'There are one or two questions I should like to ask you, Miss Harleston,' he said. 'To begin with, where did your brother shave yesterday morning?'

'In the bathroom, I suppose, as he always did,' she replied. 'I put a jug of hot water in there for him, just after I had brought him his early tea.'

'Did you visit the bathroom again before you left the house yesterday?'

'No, I always tidied upstairs after Victor had gone to the office, but yesterday I hadn't the chance.'

'How many towels were there in the bathroom yesterday morning?'

Janet smiled at the apparent absurdity of the question. 'Well, there was Victor's bath towel on the rail,' she replied. 'And a clean face towel, which I had put over the jug of hot water to keep it warm.'

Jimmy pursued this subject no further. It was very remarkable that this face towel should so mysteriously have vanished. He went on to his next point.

'Did your brother receive a package of any kind on Saturday?' he inquired.

Janet thought for a minute. 'Yes,' she replied. 'A small parcel came for him in the morning after he had left the house. I gave it to him when he came back in the middle of the day and I don't remember seeing it since.'

'Have you any idea who sent him the parcel?'

She shook her head. 'Not the slightest. I didn't take any particular notice. It was just an ordinary parcel, quite small, with a typewritten label on it.'

'What did your brother do with the parcel when you gave it him?'

'I went out of the room directly afterwards. He had picked up a knife and was cutting the string then.'

'In which room was this?'

'In the dining-room. Victor always came home to lunch on Saturdays. The table was laid before he came home and I went down to the kitchen to bring up the food.'

All this sounded reasonable enough. 'If your brother had

opened the parcel what would he have done with the brown paper and string?' Jimmy asked.

'He would probably have put them in the wastepaper basket beside his desk. Now I come to think of it, I believe I remember seeing some crumpled brown paper and string in it when I emptied the basket on Sunday evening.'

'What did you empty the waste-paper basket into, Miss Harleston?'

'Why, into the dustbin, of course. Where else?'

Jimmy smiled ingratiatingly. 'I'm sorry to be so persistent, Miss Harleston, but what became of the dustbin?' he asked.

'Why, I put it outside first thing on Monday morning for the dustman to empty. He's always round between seven and eight, and when he has emptied it, I take the dustbin in again. And of course, he emptied it yesterday morning as usual. I took the dustbin in while I was getting breakfast.'

The court was now about to open and Jimmy had no further opportunity for conversation. The inquest lasted no more than a few minutes. Merely formal evidence was taken and the coroner adjourned the proceedings for a fortnight. Jimmy returned to the Yard, deeply perplexed by the problem of the missing towel.

He sat down to consider the mystery. Towels do not vanish of themselves. This particular towel must have been removed from the bathroom by human agency. Harleston might have removed it himself, certainly. But in that case what could he have done with it? He had not left the house between the time of his shaving and the time of his death. He could not have destroyed the towel without leaving some traces. The search had been so thorough that Jimmy felt convinced the towel must have been removed from the house. By whom? Perhaps by Janet when she went to fetch Dr Oldland. Perhaps by the mysterious man on the doorstep. But why should anyone have removed the towel? For the first time Jimmy saw clearly the answer to this question. Harleston had been poisoned by nicotine absorbed through the cut. He had probably dabbed the cut with the towel. Therefore the towel would show traces of the poison.

This suggested to Jimmy a possible theory. Suppose the towel had been saturated with the nicotine and eau-de-Cologne mixture? As soon as Harleston cut himself he would naturally apply the towel to his face. This would account for the absorption of the poison by the cut. But how could it have been predicted that he would cut himself? Poisonous though nicotine might be, the mere dabbing of the unbroken skin with a solution of it would hardly be sufficient to cause death.

This point set Jimmy's mind afloat on a current of speculation. Nobody *habitually* cuts himself while shaving. He doesn't come down to breakfast every morning of his life with a gash across his face. He either learns to keep the razor in its proper path or he grows a beard. Harleston was accustomed to shaving himself. His familiar safety razor probably performed its task without accident at least nine times out of ten. This was a very mild estimate of the chances against Harleston cutting himself on any particular morning. And it was ridiculous to suppose that he could be provided with a poisoned towel every morning on the off-chance that he would cut himself sooner or later.

And yet there might have been a reason why Harleston should have cut himself on that particular morning. The odds against a man cutting himself with a familiar razor were pretty great. But suppose he were to use an unfamiliar razor for the first time? Every different make of razor requires a slight variation in the manner of its use. A man accustomed to one type might very easily make a slip with another. If Harleston had shaved himself with the razor so thoughtfully sent him by Novoshave Ltd., the odds against him cutting himself would have been considerably increased.

But he hadn't. That was just the trouble. The razor he had used was a Gillette which, judging by its appearance, was an old and trusty friend. How he had managed to cut himself with it was something of a mystery. Jimmy had heard the wound described in the course of the medical evidence at the inquest. It was a vertical cut, three-quarters of an inch long, on the right side of the face, close to the lobe of the ear. Now that Jimmy came to think of it, it seemed to him that it was rather a curious sort of cut to be sustained while shaving. In his experience, the cuts caused by razor blades were usually horizontal rather than vertical. That is to say, they were parallel to the edge of the blade. The reason for this being, no doubt, that they were caused by the blade not being properly secured in the holder. The edge of the blade was thus held at the wrong angle and cut the skin along a considerable proportion of its length. A vertical cut would appear to mean that only one point on the blade was out of adjustment, and that seemed to Jimmy rather extraordinary.

Another perplexing point was this. What had become of the Novoshave razor and shaving cream? These had evidently arrived by post on Saturday morning in the parcel described by Janet Harleston. Victor Harleston had unpacked his parcel. He had done so in the dining-room. There, the only receptacle for objects was the desk. Jimmy, in the course of his search that morning, had examined the desk so thoroughly that he felt convinced that the razor and shaving cream were not in it now.

What was Harleston likely to have done with them? Presumably he would neither have destroyed them nor given them away. His reputation for meanness suggested the alternative that he might have sold them. But when, and to whom? He had hardly had much opportunity before his death. On the whole, that alternative seemed most unlikely. They must be in the house somewhere. Unless, like the towel, they had disappeared. Things seemed to have an uncanny way of disappearing from that rather drab house in Matfield Street.

Jimmy felt impelled to further search. He and Hanslet between them had already turned the house upside down. Still, there might be some obscure corner which he had overlooked. Jimmy went to the superintendent's room.

'Do you mind if I go and have another look over that house in Matfield Street?' he asked.

Hanslet looked up from some papers at which he was working.

'You're welcome to look as much as you please,' he replied. 'And if you can find that infernal towel, I'll stand you an expensive drink. Here you are, take the keys.'

Jimmy let himself into the house and went upstairs to the bathroom. He tried to imagine how and where he would stand if he were about to shave himself. In front of the wash-basin, of course. There was a mirror conveniently fixed to the wall behind it. He would stand so, facing the mirror, and the light from the window would fall upon his face.

The window!

Jimmy stiffened suddenly. The various uses of a window had not occurred to him until this moment. Primarily, no doubt, windows were intended to admit light. But they had another use as well. They could be opened for the admission of air. And, once opened, things could be thrown out of them.

Jimmy went to the window, which was of the ordinary sash type. It opened readily enough at his touch. He put out his head. Beneath him was the untended plot of garden, completely overgrown with weeds and coarse rank grass.

Perhaps he had half-expected to find the missing towel there. But there was no sign of anything of the kind. A towel thrown out of the window would lie on the surface and not bury itself under the grass. But anything heavier would be hidden in the tangle. Jimmy decided that it might be worth while to go outside and look.

The only way into the garden was through a door in the basement and up a short flight of stone steps. This door was bolted and locked, but the key was on the inside. Jimmy tried the bolts and had difficulty in forcing them back. The key, again, turned rustily in its lock. It was evident that this door had not been opened for some considerable time. A quantity of rubbish had collected behind it and Jimmy had some difficulty in forcing it open. However, he succeeded at last, passed through the doorway, and up the crumbling steps.

Once in the garden he placed himself beneath the bathroom window. From this point he began his search. He examined the rough and tangled grass foot by foot. But he found nothing until he was nearly half-way across the garden. And then, about a dozen yards from the bathroom window he caught sight of a square brown object. He picked it up. It was a leather case, empty and bearing the word 'Novoshave' embossed in gold upon its lid.

The case was practically new, and had obviously not been lying out in the open for long. The letter from Novoshave to Harleston had mentioned a razor in a case. This undoubtedly was the case. But why, in the name of all that was wonderful, had it been thrown out of the window? And where was the razor which it had contained?

Perhaps the razor had followed the case in its inexplicable flight. Jimmy continued his search. Again he quartered the grass for some time without results. Then, almost at the farther end of the garden he caught a gleam of metal. This was the missing razor. The spot where it lay was nearly twenty yards from the house. It must have been flung out of the window with some considerable violence.

Very carefully Jimmy picked up the razor and carried it and the case into the house. Then, methodically, he searched the remainder of the garden, but no further discoveries rewarded him. He returned to the house, carefully shutting and locking the door leading to the garden. Then he proceeded to examine the razor. It appeared to be quite new. Nor could it have lain long in the garden, for the blade was free from rust. It bore the word 'Novoshave' and the trade mark of the firm. And it had evidently been used. The edge of the blade was clogged with a small quantity of thick brownish substance of the consistency of soft soap. And on the chromium-plated frame was a stain which Jimmy recognised as that of blood.

It was not long before Jimmy's imagination supplied him with a theory to account for what had happened. Harleston had decided to experiment with this new razor. Unfortunately, probably owing to some clumsiness on his part, he had cut himself at the first stroke. Impetuously, he had flung the razor out of the window and the case after it. He had finished his shave with the Gillette with which he was familiar. But that did not account for the disappearance of the towel. What in the world could he have done with that?

However, this find was sufficient for the moment, Jimmy

carefully wrapped up the razor and case, and took them back to Scotland Yard, where he showed them to Hanslet. The superintendent was puzzled, but at the same time impressed.

'You seem pretty successful at finding things, Jimmy,' he said. 'What do you suggest doing with these?'

'I'd like to know what that brown stuff on the razor is,' Jimmy replied. 'How would it be to send this little lot to Dr Grantham and the Home Office for analysis?'

Hanslet agreed to this suggestion, which Jimmy immediately carried out. He then returned to his own room. The question uppermost in his mind was this. How did the discovery of the razor affect, if at all, the theory of Janet Harleston's guilt?

He was quite ready to admit to himself that the girl interested him. Hanslet himself had doubts of her guilt. If she were a murderess, Jimmy thought, she was at the same time a superlative actress. At the inquest she had shown no signs of nervousness. She had managed to convey the impression that her half-brother's death was as great a mystery to her as to anybody else. And she had seemed considerably brighter than when Jimmy had seen her first. Of course, she had secured her independence and that might account for it. But if she had murdered her brother, would not her relief have been tempered by some fears for her own safety?

And yet it seemed extremely difficult to establish a theory which would account for her innocence. It occurred to Jimmy that she might have been the unconscious tool of Philip, but somehow the idea did not ring true. From what he had seen of the two, Jimmy had come to the conclusion that Janet had far more intelligence and initiative than her brother. In fact, Philip had struck him as a rather simple-minded individual. He might have had the will to commit a murder, but surely not the ability. And this, if it were indeed a murder, showed signs of ingenuity of a very high order.

It seemed that the superintendent's mind must have been running in a very similar channel. He called up Jimmy and asked him to come round to his room.

'Sit down,' he said, 'and listen to me. This case has got to be investigated very thoroughly, and it's a job that will take two of us. I've seen the Assistant Commissioner and he agrees that you shall help me. Now, I'm going to Lassingford first thing tomorrow morning. I want to make a few inquiries there. The reports of analysis will probably come in while I'm away. Look through them and see if they throw any fresh light upon the affair. And you'd better keep the key of that house in Matfield Street in case you want to make any further explorations.'

6

On the following morning, which was Wednesday, Jimmy went to Hanslet's room as soon as he arrived at the Yard. There he found the report from the Home Office analyst. This dealt with the various objects that had been submitted.

The first paragraph of the report dealt with the contents of the teapot found in Harleston's bedroom. This had been found to be an infusion of tea, heavily impregnated with nicotine. From the fact that the liquid was more greatly contaminated than the leaves, it seemed probable that the poison had been added after the tea was made. Next came the dregs of tea found in Harleston's cup. These also contained a percentage of nicotine. But in the latter case the proportion was higher than in the case of the tea in the pot. The analyst made the suggestion that further nicotine might have been added to the cup after the tea had been poured out.

The next article to be dealt with was the eau-de-Cologne found in Janet's bedroom.

This bottle contained a mixture of two liquids. The first was the cheaper type of eau-de-Cologne in which the solvent employed had been propyl alcohol. The second was nicotine which was present to the extent of rather over ten per cent. This percentage was rather greater than in the case of the tea.

The report then dealt with the coffee found in the dining-room. Neither the liquid in the pot nor the few drops remaining in Harleston's cup contained any trace of nicotine.

The contents of the stomach were then reported upon at length. Only a very slight trace of nicotine had been discovered here. This was consistent with the view that the nicotine had not been swallowed but absorbed through the skin. The nature of the contents was such as to suggest that the deceased had consumed nothing for several hours before his death but a quantity of tea and a quantity of coffee. The quantities in each case might be estimated at an ordinary cupful.

Lastly the report dealt with the deposit on the razor. This had been removed and analysed. It had been found to consist of a mixture of cold cream and glycerine. To this mixture had been added nicotine to the extent of rather less than five per cent.

The analyst had appended a note upon this. Cold cream and glycerine form the basis of many well-known commercial shaving creams. Particularly those which render unnecessary the application of soap. It is quite possible that the basis of this deposit is one of these to which nicotine has been added subsequently. The application of such a preparation to the unbroken skin would be very dangerous. If it were to come into contact with a cut or any form of abrasion under conditions which would allow of its absorption, the consequences would probably be fatal.

To Jimmy this note was full of significance. He remembered the letter from Messrs. Novoshave. They had presented Harleston with a razor and a tube of shaving cream. The razor had been found, but what had become of the cream?

He proceeded to elaborate the mental picture which he had already formed. Harleston had decided to try the experiment which the letter had suggested. He had done so thoroughly, using the cream as well as the razor. He had no doubt covered his face with the cream and then started to shave. The razor had cut him and he had flung it away. But the cream remained on his face in intimate contact with the wound. He had probably not troubled to wipe it off but had finished his shave with his old razor, by its aid.

Now if the cream had contained nicotine, Harleston's death was accounted for. But how had it happened that the nicotine had been present? Nicotine could hardly be a normal ingredient of Novoshave cream. Then somebody must have added it with a definitely homicidal purpose. Who could have had access to the cream between the time of its receipt by Harleston and the following Monday morning?

The razor, now freed of its deposit, had been returned. Jimmy examined it carefully. It seemed in perfect order and the blade was in its correct position. He drew the razor idly across a pad of blottimg paper. A fine sharp cut, running the whole length of the stroke, was the result. The razor had two cutting edges. He turned it over and repeated his experiment, with exactly the same results.

It seemed, then, that this particular razor was a remarkably dangerous weapon. Jimmy took a lens and examined the guard which protected the blade. He found that a minute notch had been cut in one of the ribs of the guard, and that the sharp edge of steel thus produced had been turned outwards. This operation, almost invisible to the naked eye, had been carried out on both sides of the razor. Anybody using it in its present state must certainly cut himself.

Things were becoming distinctly clearer, Jimmy thought. Harleston had been provided with a razor with which he would inevitably cut himself, and with shaving cream which would prove fatal if it came in contact with that cut. But who had provided them? It was fantastic to suppose that the firm of Novoshave should have designs upon the life of their accountant. The razor and cream must have been tampered with after despatch. The parcel containing them had been taken in by Janet during her half-brother's absence at his office. She alone had had access to it until his return. The contents of the parcel must have been in the house during Sunday when Philip had paid his apparently stormy visit. And the shaving cream, together with the towel with which Harleston had wiped his face, had disappeared.

The reason for their disappearance was now fairly obvious. They formed valuable evidence of the means by which Harleston had met his death. It was natural that the murderer should wish to destroy his evidence. Someone had entered the bathroom after Harleston had left it. They had taken the towel and the tube of shaving cream. They would, no doubt, have taken the razor as well. But Harleston's petulant gesture had prevented them. He had flung the razor and its case out of the window and they were not to be found.

But this reasoning, though perfectly logical, contained no

clue to the identity of the culprit. However, upon consideration, Jimmy thought that it tended to exonerate Janet. The
unknown individual had not contented himself with entering
the bathroom. He had gone into Harleston's room and poured
nicotine into the teapot and cup. He had also gone into
Janet's room and added the poison to her eau-de-Cologne.
His reason for doing so was easy to understand. He wished
to create the impression that Janet had poisoned her half-
brother by adding nicotine to his early tea.

If this exonerated Janet, it also exonerated Philip. It was
hardly conceivable that the latter should have laid a trail of
false clues directly pointing to his sister. There remained the
period when Janet had been absent from the house. According
to her, the stranger she had met on the doorstep had volunteered to go in and look after her brother. Had he done so,
he would have had an opportunity for traversing the whole
house. Was this stranger the murderer? And if so, how and
when had he found an opportunity of tampering with the
razor and shaving cream?

It seemed to Jimmy that Scotland Yard was faced with a
very pretty problem. The method of the murder might now
be established. But, if Janet and Philip were eliminated, the
search for the culprit would be beset with difficulties. His
motive was particularly baffling. Harleston might have had
few friends, but, on the other hand, he was not the type of
man to incur violent enmities. Nobody, apart from the
members of the family, could hope to gain anything by his
death. He seemed to have been too colourless an individual
to have furnished any motive for revenge.

Even supposing that the man seen by Janet on the doorstep were indeed the murderer, how was he to be traced?
She had no recollection of him and would be wholly unable

to identify him if she were to see him again. He had appeared for a moment and disappeared. Nor, in the course of his visit to Matfield Street, had he left any visible clue behind him.

There was one fairly obvious thing to be done. Jimmy had brought with him to Scotland Yard the torn slips of paper on which the letter from Novoshave had been written. These he had stuck together with transparent paper. He went to his own room, placed the letter in an envelope and started off for the offices of Novoshave Ltd.

Upon reaching them he asked to see Mr Topliss. After a short interval he was shown into a private office where a keen-faced middle-aged man greeted him.

'Well, Inspector,' he said sharply, 'what brings you here?'

'I'd like to ask you a few questions, if you've no objection, Mr Topliss,' Jimmy replied. 'In the first place, do you know anybody of the name of Victor Harleston?'

'Harleston,' said the other. 'Harleston. Why, yes, of course. He was the fellow who was here last week from Slater & Knott. They are our accountants, and they sent Harleston in to do our audit. Rather a surly sort of chap, I thought, but he seemed quick enough at his work.'

'Do you know his private address?' Jimmy asked.

'I haven't the slightest idea,' Topliss replied.

Jimmy withdrew the envelope and produced the letter. 'Then I should be glad if you would explain this,' he said.

Topliss read the letter with growing amazement. 'I can't explain it,' he replied. 'All I can tell you is that I never dictated this letter, nor did I sign it. The signature is not unlike mine, I'll admit, but if you compare it with the genuine article you will see for yourself at a glance that it's an obvious forgery.'

He took some letters from a tray on his desk and passed

them over. 'You'll find half a dozen specimens of my signature there,' he said.

Jimmy compared these with the signature of the letter to Harleston. There was a certain resemblance, but, even to his inexpert eye, it was plain that it had not been written by the same hand.

Mr Topliss picked up the letter and glanced through it for a second time.

'I can't make this out at all,' he said. 'The whole thing is nonsense from beginning to end. In the first place, our model K. razor is not yet ready. Delivery from the factory won't begin for another month or six weeks. And we aren't in the habit of distributing our goods gratis. We are quite capable of satisfying ourselves of the excellence of our products without seeking outside opinion. In any case, we should not be likely to set a high value upon the opinion of a man like Harleston.'

'The letter appears to have been written on your official notepaper,' Jimmy remarked.

'Yes, this is our notepaper right enough. But I don't suppose it would be very difficult for anybody to get hold of a sheet of that.'

'Who, besides the members of the firm, would be likely to know that this new model was in preparation?' Jimmy asked.

'That's just what I was wondering. We've kept the matter secret so far as possible, our idea being to spring a surprise upon our competitors. Of course, the factory staff know about it, and the people in the office here. But I don't see how any outsider could have got to hear of it.'

'Harleston was engaged upon your audit last week,' said Jimmy. 'I suppose it is not impossible that he should have learnt of the new model?'

'He's almost certain to have heard of it. But have you any reason to suppose that he wrote the letter to himself?'

'Not at present. The peculiar thing is that the letter was apparently accompanied by a razor and a tube of shaving cream. I've got the razor here and I'd like to show it to you. But I must ask you not to touch it on any account.'

Jimmy had brought with him the razor which he had found in the garden. He now produced it and laid it upon Mr Topliss' table. The latter glanced at it and laughed. 'That's not one of the new models,' he said. 'It's one of the present model J. which we have been marketing for three or four years. I can tell from the serial number that it is of very recent manufacture.'

'Would Harleston have been able to distinguish between models J. and K?' Jimmy asked.

'I don't see how he could,' Topliss replied. 'Nobody but myself in this office has ever seen the completed specimen of the new model.'

'Is there any means of tracing the hands through which this particular razor has passed?'

'I'm afraid not. The serial number is used for manufacturing purposes only. We do not invoice this to our customers, and the sales department keeps no record of the numbers. This razor might have been bought anywhere. I'm proud to say that our products are widely distributed throughout the country.'

'Would analysis of your shaving cream reveal the presence of cold cream and glycerine?' Jimmy asked.

Mr Topliss smiled. 'You mustn't expect me to reveal trade secrets, Inspector,' he replied. 'But I think I may tell you without being indiscreet that it would.'

'The formula does not by any chance contain nicotine, I suppose?'

'Nicotine! Good heavens, no. We are shaving experts, not tobacconists.'

After having extracted a promise from Mr Topliss that he would make inquiries in his office about the letter, Jimmy returned with it to Scotland Yard. His inquiries had had the results which he had expected. The letter was not genuine. Somebody had bought a Novoshave razor, and tampered with it. They had also bought a tube of shaving cream and poisoned this with nicotine. Then the letter had been written, the parcel made up, and both sent to Harleston.

Perhaps this way of looking at it appealed to Jimmy because it exonerated Janet and Philip. If the razor and cream were already dangerous when they reached Harleston nobody in his household was involved. But who could have been the writer of the letter? Harleston had certainly not written it to himself. And, according to Mr Topliss, any other person possessing the necessary knowledge must be in the employ of Novoshave Ltd.

Was it possible that Harleston had some enemy in that firm? Jimmy decided that he might as well pursue that line of inquiry. He made a second journey, this time to Chancery Lane, and secured an interview with Mr Knott. The latter, upon learning his identity, greeted him genially.

'You've come to talk about this unfortunate business of poor Harleston, I suppose?' he said.

'I have, and I should be very glad if you could help me, Mr Knott,' Jimmy replied. 'You told Superintendent Hanslet that Harleston had no connection with the firm of Novoshave beyond the audit, I believe.'

'That is so,' replied Knott. 'We have audited the accounts of Novoshave for several years. But, as it happens, this was the first year in which Harleston had been put on to that particular job. So far as I am aware, he knew nothing whatever about the firm, except of course, that they were among our customers.'

'How long was Harleston engaged upon this audit?'

'About ten days. I can tell you exactly if you wait a minute.' Knott picked up his diary and turned over the pages. 'Here you are,' he said. 'Harleston started the audit on Monday, the 7th of this month and finished on Thursday the 17th.'

'Was he engaged alone upon the audit?'

'No, he had one of our juniors with him. A fellow of the name of Fred Davies.'

'I wonder if I could have a word with Davies?'

'Of course, I'll send for him,' Knott replied readily.

He telephoned the necessary instructions, and in a couple of minutes Davies appeared. Knott introduced him to Jimmy, who began questioning him at once.

Davies' account was not very illuminating. He had been in Harleston's company during the whole time they had been working together at the offices of Novoshave Ltd. So far as he was aware, Harleston had had no conversation with any member of the staff, except the cashier and his assistant, and that only upon matters connected with the audit. Harleston had always been a taciturn sort of man who was not likely to go out of his way to talk to strangers.

'Could Harleston have discovered any irregularity in the books without your knowledge, Mr Davies?' Jimmy asked.

A new and rather fanciful theory had occurred to him. Perhaps there might have been a falsification of the books by some member of the firm. Harleston alone had discovered this. The culprit, seeing himself threatened with exposure, had removed Harleston before he could reveal his knowledge. The theory seemed far-fetched, and Davies' reply disposed of it.

'That's hardly possible,' replied the latter. 'Harleston and I were working in very close collaboration. We checked one another's figures throughout.'

'Do you know that Messrs. Novoshave are shortly about to put a new model razor on the market?' Jimmy asked.

'I remember seeing references to it in some of the documents we examined,' Davies replied. 'Since it did not directly concern us, I never thought about the matter.'

'Can you tell me the letter of the alphabet which was to be a sign to the new model?'

'No, I couldn't. Their present model is J. so presumably the new one would be K. But that's nothing more than a guess.'

'Were you on friendly terms with Harleston?'

Davies and his employer exchanged a smile. 'We got on all right,' the former replied. 'But I doubt anybody in the office could claim to be on particularly friendly terms with Harleston.'

'He might have invited you to his home?' Jimmy suggested tentatively.

At this Davies laughed outright. 'Nothing like that!' he exclaimed. 'Harleston never by any chance asked any of us to come and see him.'

'You are not by any chance acquainted with his half-sister, Janet Harleston?'

'I didn't even know he had a half-sister. I never once heard him mention his own affairs.'

There was nothing more to be learnt from Davies, and at a nod from his employer he left the room.

'I'm afraid it's very little use making inquiries about Harleston's private life here,' said Knott. 'Although he had been employed by us for the last fifteen or twenty years, we none of us knew anything about him. He never spoke about himself and repelled all advances in that direction. He appeared at the office punctually and disappeared as regularly when his work was finished. Where he spent the rest of his time we never took the trouble to inquire. Of course, I was aware of his private address, and once, in a burst of over-whelming confidence, he told me that he had a sister who kept house for him. Beyond that I know nothing whatever about his private life and I am quite certain that nobody else in this office knows even that much.'

'You are possibly aware that he had certain means of his own beyond his salary?'

'I always suspected it, though I never knew for certain. He never mentioned anything of the kind—in fact, he deliberately gave the impression that he had a hard struggle for existence. If he had money, I can't imagine what he spent it upon. Certainly not upon his fellow-men, of that I am quite certain.'

'I believe you gave him a bonus of a hundred pounds at the beginning of this year. Was there some definite reason for this, or was it merely a matter of routine?'

Knott smiled benignly. 'Hardly a matter of routine,' he replied. 'It has always been our custom to give a bonus to such of our clerks as have been with us fifteen years, and whose service has been in every way satisfactory. Purely as a mark of our appreciation, you understand. There was no question of anybody becoming entitled to this bonus. As a matter of fact, Harleston completed his qualifying period of service two years ago, but my partner, Mr Slater, then opposed the granting of the bonus in his case.'

'Was there any reason for his opposition?' Jimmy asked.

'Merely the fact that Mr Slater disliked Harleston. I really can't say why, but I believe they had a serious difference of opinion years ago, before I joined the firm. Mr Slater has now retired from active participation in the business and lives in the country. He never comes to the office now, and so far as I know, he and Harleston have not met since his retirement. Since their antagonism was no longer irritated by daily meeting, I brought up the question again this year, and was successful in getting Mr Slater's consent to the payment of the bonus.'

'Has Mr Slater any knowledge of Harleston's private affairs?'

'That I couldn't tell you. It is quite possible. If you want to ask him, you will have to go down to Torquay where he lives. I'll give you his address.'

Having obtained the address, Jimmy returned to Scotland Yard. He had made some slight progress and there was nothing more to be done until Hanslet returned.

7

Meanwhile, Superintendent Hanslet was having a day in the country. He had travelled by train to the nearest station to Lassingford, and walked the remainder of the distance. He had no difficulty in finding Hart's Farm and in assuring himself that Philip Harleston and his sister had returned there after the inquest. He did not make his presence known to them but repaired to the village inn, knowing, by experience, that this was the best place in which to acquire information.

He found the Plume of Feathers to be a pleasant little pub, not inconveniently overcrowded. In fact, when he entered, the only occupants of the bar were the landlady, a cheerful, elderly woman, and a single labourer, consuming a hunk of bread and cheese and a pint of cider. He ordered himself a drink and waited patiently to be drawn into their conversation.

The opening moves followed their usual course, the landlady taking the lead. Hanslet's part was merely to reply to her questions.

Yes, it was wonderful weather for the time of year though the wind was still a bit cold. No, he had never been to Lassingford before. He had merely come down from London for a country walk. That was the worst of living in town, one could never get enough exercise. Yes, he thought he might come down again in the spring when the fruit trees were in blossom.

The mention of fruit trees gave Hanslet his opportunity. 'There seems to be quite a lot of orchards round here,' he said innocently.

The landlady smiled benevolently. Londoners were so ridiculously ignorant. Surely everybody must know that Lassingford was the very centre of the fruit-growing district of Kent?

'Oh yes,' she replied, 'all the farmers here grow fruit. Apples and pears mostly. You'll have to go to the next parish if you want to see cherries and plums.'

Hanslet evinced a lively astonishment. 'What, do you mean to say that they grow nothing but fruit!' he exclaimed.

'There used to be hops as well, but they're mostly grubbed out now. Over at Hart's Farm, for instance, there used to be fifty acres of hops, but it's all planted with apples now.'

The subject had been reached earlier than Hanslet had dared to hope. 'That seems a pity,' he said. 'I prefer beer to cider, myself. Hart's Farm, you said. I wonder if I passed it in my walk?'

'If you came from the station, you must have walked right along the edge of it. It's a fair-sized place. Over two hundred acres of fruit.'

'Who does it belong to?' Hanslet asked idly.

'Old Mr Burrage, and it belonged to his father before him,' the landlady replied. 'They've made a lot of money out of the place, and that's a fact. But Mr Burrage is getting a bit past work now. He'll be nigh upon eighty, won't he, Sam?'

The labourer, thus appealed to, nodded his head. 'He'll be all that, missus,' he replied, somewhat indistinctly, since his mouth was full of bread and cheese.

'And so you see he's taken on a manager,' the landlady continued. 'Young Mr Philip Harleston. At least he's rather more than a manager, so people do say. Mr Burrage's sons didn't somehow take to farming. That was always a grief to the old man. So he offered a share in the farm for sale and Mr Harleston bought it. He became a sort of very junior partner as you might say. And now I hear that he's got a young lady staying with him.' The landlady paused, then added darkly, 'They do say that she's his sister.'

'Very charitable of them,' remarked Hanslet lightly. 'Nice job for a young fellow, I should think. Out in the open all day. I wish I'd had his chances when I was that age.'

'Oh, there's plenty of work with it. Out in all weathers from daylight to dark. There's more to be done to fruit trees than you might think. There's the washing and the spraying and the pruning and the picking. You won't never get a crop of apples if you don't look after the trees.'

'Bless my soul!' exclaimed Hanslet ingenuously. 'I always thought the things just grew. Now, all this washing and spraying you talk about. That must take a lot of time and labour, doesn't it?'

''Tis mostly done by machine nowadays,' the landlady replied. 'But still it does make a bit of work, there's no denying.'

'What do they wash and spray with? Just ordinary water?'

'Oh no, they use all manner of chemicals. Sam can tell you more about them than I can.'

Sam, who had now finished his meal, lighted a short clay pipe. He puffed at it vigorously for a few seconds before re-entering the conversation.

'There's a lot of different washes, depending on the time of year and what not,' he said. 'Tar oil, for instance, that they'll be using round about now. And then there's sulphur lime that some like to use a little later. And then there's nicotine. You have to be careful when you're using that.'

'I suppose at a place like Hart's Farm they use all these washes?' Hanslet suggested.

'Oh, you may be sure of that,' the landlady replied. 'There isn't much about fruit trees that old Mr Burrage doesn't know. And Mr Harleston, he's pretty quick to learn, so they do say. Last year between them they had a better crop than anybody else in the parish. Isn't that so, Sam?'

'Ay, that's so,' Sam replied. 'Clever young chap, that Mr Harleston. Spends all the time he can spare at the research station and picks up a lot of tips there, I don't doubt.'

'His time must be fairly well occupied,' Hanslet remarked. You don't see much of him in here, I suppose?'

'Oh, he comes in most evenings for a game of darts,' said the landlady. 'He likes company and I dare say he finds it a bit lonely in a place like this, coming from London as he did. It would never surprise me to hear that he'd taken up with some nice young lady. I should think he'd get tired of living in that cottage all by himself, with nobody but an old woman coming in to do for him in the morning, and she's stone deaf at that.'

'Doesn't he ever have any visitors?' Hanslet asked.

'Well, there was a gentleman in a smart car came in here some three or four weeks back and asked where Mr Harleston lived,' said the landlady. 'I told him, but Mr Harleston never said anything about the gentleman or who he was.'

'I mind I saw a car outside his cottage,' Sam put in reflectively. 'About the middle of the morning, it was. And not long before, I'd seen Mr Harleston away down at the farther end of the farm.'

'Then likely enough the gentleman missed him,' the landlady remarked. 'You never can tell where to find Mr Harleston. And unless you catch him when he comes home to dinner, you might spend your time looking for him.'

Hanslet glanced at the clock. The hands were pointing to ten minutes to one. The landlady's hint appeared to him a good one. He had gathered sufficient preliminary information for his purpose. The next thing was to interview Philip Harleston, and incidentally, his sister. There was every probability that he would now find them both at home.

He left the Plume of Feathers, and retraced his steps to the cottage, which he had already located. He knocked at the door, which was opened by Janet, who seemed surprised but not perturbed on seeing him.

'Is your brother Philip at home, Miss Harleston?' the superintendent asked.

'He's just come in,' she replied. 'We're going to have lunch in a minute or two. Perhaps you'd like to join us, Mr Hanslet?'

'Thanks very much, but I won't do that,' Hanslet replied. 'I'll just sit and talk to you both while you have your meal.'

A few moments later, Philip entered the room. Seen here

in his own environment, he made a better impression than he had done at Scotland Yard. In his breeches and gaiters, he looked the typical young farmer, energetic and capable. He greeted the superintendent quietly, and glanced from him to his sister, as though awaiting an explanation of this visit.

Hanslet hastened to supply it. 'It's about Mr Victor Harleston,' he said. 'What arrangements are you making about the funeral?'

'Oh, Mr Mowbray is doing all that,' Janet replied. 'I asked Philip what we'd better do, and he said we'd better leave it to him. We heard this morning that he'd arranged the funeral for Friday and of course we shall go up to it.'

'Will your half-brother's death make any difference to you financially?' Hanslet asked.

Janet and Philip glanced at one another, but again it was the former who replied.

'Philip and I shall share father's money, which up till now Victor has always had. I have no idea how much my share will be, but I have always understood that it will be quite enough for me to live upon.'

'What have you thought of doing, now that your half-brother is dead, Miss Harleston?'

'Oh, I shall stay here with Philip,' she replied unhesitatingly. 'I always meant to do that sooner or later, as soon as Philip could afford to have me.'

'When would that have been if your half-brother had lived?'

It was Philip who answered this question. 'Not for another couple of years. You see, my position is this. My father bought a tenth share of this farm from Mr Burrage and gave it to me. The agreement was that I should eventually manage the farm at a salary of three hundred a year, and of course, I take a tenth share of the profits. But, since I shouldn't be much good as a manager until I had thoroughly learnt the job, I was to have no salary for the first seven years. And those seven years will not be up until the Christmas after next. As soon as I began to draw my salary I was going to bring Janet down here.'

'You would rather live here than in London, then, Miss Harleston?' Hanslet suggested.

'I'd rather live with Philip than with Victor. Poor Victor was always so terribly mean. He couldn't help it, I suppose. It was just natural to him. He hated giving me money and I had to scrape what I wanted for myself out of the house-keeping allowance. If it hadn't been for Philip who's been awfully good to me, I shouldn't have a rag to wear.'

'I used to argue with Victor about the way he used to treat Janet,' Philip put in. 'But it wasn't a bit of good. He always said that if she didn't like it, she could go away but that, if she did, she needn't expect any help from him. Mr Mowbray told me that under the terms of the Trust he was only bound to provide her with a home. Of course, my father meant by that that he should look after her properly. But, as Janet says, Victor was so infernally miserly that he wouldn't spend a penny more than he was bound to.'

'Then in many ways your half-brother's death is a relief to you, Miss Harleston?' Hanslet said quietly.

'Well, yes, I suppose it is,' she replied. 'Somehow I never expected it to happen. I imagined myself slaving for him for another two years and becoming a burden upon Philip. Of course, I'm sorry, but it's no use my pretending that I'm broken-hearted.'

'It may sound a callous thing to say about one's half-brother,' Philip remarked. 'But I can't feel the slightest regret for Victor's death. I don't think there's anybody in the world who will miss him in the slightest.'

'Well,' said Hanslet cheerfully, 'you two young people will be happier, from what I can make out.' He got up from his chair, walked to the window, and stood for a moment or two looking out. 'You've got a lot of fruit trees to look after here,' he said.

'Oh yes, there's plenty to do,' Philip replied. 'What with one thing and another we're at work upon them most of the year round.'

'You have to wash and spray them and that sort of thing, don't you?'

'Yes, it all takes time and it costs money. But it pays in the end. If you give the trees proper attention, you get a heavier crop and a better quality.'

Hanslet turned from the window and sat down again. He had been given an arm-chair beside the fireplace, and from it he could see the faces of the brother and sister as they ate their lunch. 'You use nicotine for spraying, don't you?' he asked casually.

Janet, by far the quicker of the two, was the first to see the implication. 'Nicotine!' she exclaimed. 'Why, that's what the doctor was talking about at the inquest.'

'Yes, Miss Harleston, your brother died of nicotine poisoning,' Hanslet replied gravely.

Janet turned slowly towards Philip, a look of horror in her eyes. She said nothing, but Hanslet had no difficulty in reading her thoughts. From that moment he felt convinced of her innocence. She knew nothing whatever about the nicotine—of that he was certain. But, for the first time, a terrible idea had flashed into her mind. Philip had always been anxious to release her from her bondage.

With a muttered excuse she got up and hurriedly left the room.

Hanslet was relieved at this. He felt that Philip would be easier to deal with, without his sister at hand to prompt him. He repeated his question in a slightly different form.

'You are in the habit of using nicotine, are you not, Mr Harleston?'

By this time Philip's duller brain had perceived the purport of the question.

'Yes, we use nicotine on the farm, among other things,' he replied half-reluctantly.

'You are aware that nicotine is a very powerful poison?'

'Yes, of course, we have to take special precautions when using it.'

'Do you purchase the nicotine as you require it, or have you a stock on hand?'

'We buy as much as we think we shall want for the season's spraying but there's usually a certain amount left over.'

'Have you any on hand at the present time, Mr Harleston?'

'Yes, three or four small tins, I think.'

Hanslet frowned. 'That is rather a vague answer,' he said. 'In the case of a dangerous substance like that I should expect certain obvious precautions to be taken.'

'Oh, we take precautions all right,' Philip replied. 'The stuff is kept in an outhouse behind this cottage which is always locked and I'm the only person who keeps the key. I superintend the mixing of the wash when it's wanted.'

'Do you keep any record of the stock in hand?'

'Certainly. I keep a book in which I enter the amount purchased and the amount used.'

'I should like to see that book, Mr Harleston.'

Philip got up from the table unhesitatingly. He went to a

cupboard in the corner of the room and from it extracted an ordinary account book. This he handed to the superintendent, 'I think you'll find it clear enough,' he said.

Hanslet had no difficulty in understanding the entries, which were neatly kept. He read them through and then turned to Philip.

'As far as I can make out, this is the position,' he said. 'At the beginning of last year you had five tins of nicotine in stock. Twelve tins were purchased during the year and thirteen issued. That should leave you with a balance of four in hand now. Is that correct?'

'Yes, that's right,' Philip replied. 'I remember now there are four tins in the store.'

'I should like to see those four tins,' said the superintendent.

Philip went to the cupboard a second time. From a hook within it he took a key. 'If you care to come along I'll show them to you,' he said.

They went out of the cottage by the back door, immediately beyond which was a lean-to shed. The door of this shed was secured by a stout chain and padlock. Philip inserted the key and the padlock opened easily. He opened the door and Hanslet was at once aware of a faint odour of rank tobacco. There were some steel drums on the floor and he pointed to these.

'Is this the nicotine?' he asked.

'Oh no,' Philip replied. 'That's merely tar oil. Harmless enough, but I keep it in here for convenience. Those are the tins of nicotine, up on that shelf. Hullo!'

He went up to the shelf and stared at it, scratching his head in perplexity. Then he began to look anxiously round the shed, searching the floor and peering behind the drums. Hanslet smiled grimly but made no comment, for on the shelf were three tins of nicotine only.

Philip abandoned his search after a minute or two. 'I can't make it out,' he said in the tone of a puzzled child. 'There are only three tins here, and there ought to be four. And I'll swear there were four on that shelf when I last looked at it.'

'Curious,' said Hanslet quietly. 'When did you last look at the shelf, Mr Harleston?'

Once again Philip scratched his head. 'I couldn't tell you exactly,' he replied. 'Not for the last few weeks certainly. You see, we've done no washing since the autumn and I had no occasion to come in here. But I know those four tins were on the shelf then.'

Hanslet stepped up to the shelf and inspected it for himself. He saw that a good deal of dust had found its way into the shed, and lay thickly upon the tops of the three remaining tins. The shelf beside them was also heavily coated. But in one place, close to the last tin of the row, was a circular patch where the dust lay far more thinly. This had evidently been where the fourth tin had stood. Further, the relative thinness of the dust deposit showed that it must have been removed fairly recently.

'Well, Mr Harleston, how do you account for this?' Hanslet asked after a long silence.

'I can't account for it,' Philip replied. 'Somebody must have got in and taken it.'

'But I thought you told me that you were the only person who had a key of the padlock,' Hanslet insisted.

'So I did. That's just what I can't understand. I certainly didn't take the tin.'

'It certainly appears somewhat remarkable,' said Hanslet. 'Where do you usually keep this key?'

'In the cupboard from which you saw me take it just now. I always keep it there.'

'Does anybody but yourself know where it is kept?'

'I don't think so. Nobody but the charwoman ever comes into the cottage, and I don't suppose she's bothered to look into the cupboard. Besides, I always lock it when I go out. It contains the accounts of the farm and I shouldn't like anybody prying into them.'

Hanslet examined the padlock and the chain. These showed no signs of having been forced at any time. The shed was solidly constructed and had no window. The only means of entrance to it was the door. Whoever had removed the missing tin had certainly done so by unlocking the padlock.

It hardly seemed to Hanslet worth while to ask any more questions. The two stood there in silence, Hanslet staring intently at Philip's troubled face.

It was very quiet out here at the back of the cottage. In the still air the sounds of the countryside, though distinct, were yet very faint. The shrill voice of a child playing somewhere in the distance. The rumble of a lorry dying away upon the high road. The not unmusical note of a saw-bench apparently leagues away. The superintendent heard all these with his sub-conscious brain. His whole conscious attention was concentrated upon the young man before him.

Hanslet, though by no means a profound psychologist, had learned something of the workings of the human conscience. He saw in Philip a weak character who had been goaded into crime by the praiseworthy motive of freeing his sister from her bondage. And he knew the limits of endurance of which such a character was capable. Up to a point Philip might defend himself. His imagination, seeking desperately for some way of escape, might invent answers to the most searching questions, but the point at which his defence must surely break down was now reached. Hanslet, the stronger character, held all the cards. He had discovered the disappearance of the tin of nicotine. He knew the use to which the poison had been put. In the face of his imperturbable silence, Philip must find it impossible to maintain a show of innocence.

It was typical of the situation which leads to breakdown and confession. Momentarily Hanslet expected the wild outpouring on Philip's part. He could even foreshadow the lines which it would take—a bitter recital of his sister's wrongs, followed by a stumbling description of the crime. And then a frantic attempt at self-justification. He had not meant the poison to be fatal. He had only meant to frighten Victor. Anything, any improbability which would save him from disgrace and the gallows.

But the expected confession did not come. Philip seemed paralysed into speechlessness. Hanslet felt almost sorry for him, as the hunter may feel sorry for the game which has provided him with a good chase. A kindly word might help him.

'Come now, Harleston,' he said encouragingly. 'Haven't you anything to tell me?'

'I can't understand it, I can't understand it,' Philip repeated helplessly.

His wits had deserted him at this critical juncture, Hanslet thought. It would perhaps be best to leave him alone for a while—alone with his conscience and with Janet. The two would be powerful auxiliaries in the cause of justice. His conscience would give him no peace. His sister, whose manner had left Hanslet in no doubt of the suspicion that had suddenly been born in her, would be a constant reproach to him.

Abruptly and without a word, the superintendent turned away. He walked rapidly away from the cottage to the local police station, where he arranged that the watch upon Philip and his sister should be redoubled. Then he caught the first train back to London.

At the Yard he found Jimmy waiting for him. The latter was full of his discoveries, to the account of which Hanslet listened with the closest attention. He made Jimmy repeat the most important points and then, twirling a pencil in his fingers, and staring fixedly out of the window. 'I think that pretty well settles it,' he said at last in a tone of suppressed triumph.

'I'd like to know what you think about it,' said Jimmy tentatively.

'I dare say you would,' Hanslet replied. 'What would you say if I told you that I've found out where the nicotine came from?'

Jimmy felt a thrill of apprehension. He knew well enough where Hanslet had spent the day. Without being fully conscious of it, he had come to regard himself as the champion of Janet and, so, indirectly, of Philip. But he felt that it would be ridiculous to allow the superintendent to perceive this.

'I should say you had done a pretty clever piece of work,' he replied diplomatically.

'Oh, I had a pretty good idea from the first where to look,' Hanslet said. 'I paid a visit to that farm of Philip Harleston's. He admitted that he used nicotine for his fruit trees. I made him show me the stuff and he was forced to admit that he could not account for one tin of it which was missing.'

Jimmy could not escape the significance of this.

'It looks as though Philip must have had a hand in it,' he said slowly, and then hesitatingly, he added, 'Do you think his sister was in the plot?'

'No, I don't,' Hanslet replied emphatically. And at this reply Jimmy felt a spasm of relief, as though in some inexplicable way a burden had been removed from his own mind.

'I'm hoping that the fellow will make a clean breast of it,' Hanslet continued. 'I believe he will. If he doesn't I shall make it my business to tackle him again. As long as he keeps on saying nothing but "I don't understand," things will be a little difficult for us. It is the most difficult of all defences to break down. And I don't at present see how we're to connect the nicotine which has disappeared from Hart's Farm, with the nicotine which caused Victor Harleston's death. I'd rather like to put that point before the Professor. He might be able to think of some dodge. I'll tell you what, I'll ring him up and ask him if we may go round this evening. And if he says yes, I'll take you with me.'

8

Hanslet had no difficulty in obtaining the required permission. He and Jimmy arrived at Westbourne Terrace shortly after nine o'clock that evening. They were shown into the study where they found Dr Priestley, Oldland and Merefield. Their host seemed to be in what for him would be described as a genial mood. He greeted them both courteously and expressed pleasure at renewing the acquaintance with Jimmy.

'Well, Superintendent,' he said, 'to what do I owe the pleasure of this visit?'

'I'd like your advice, Professor,' Hanslet replied. 'We've got a lot further with the Harleston case since I saw you last. Jimmy here has made a very interesting discovery in Matfield

Street and I've made an equally interesting one at Lassingford. I'd like to tell you.'

But Dr Priestley interrupted him. 'You know my preference for accounts at first hand,' he said. 'Perhaps Inspector Waghorn will give us an account of his discovery in his own words.'

Thus encouraged, Jimmy told his story. He described the finding of the razor and its case. He gave a summary of the report upon the various objects submitted for analysis. Finally he repeated the conversation he had had with Mr Topliss of Novoshave and Mr Knott of Slater & Knott. Not forgetting, in the latter case, the statement of Harleston's colleague Davies. He observed, not without a certain nervousness, that Harold Merefield at a nod from his employer was making notes of his remarks.

When he had finished Dr Priestley nodded, but made no comment. He merely glanced at Hanslet. 'It is your turn now, Superintendent,' he said.

Hanslet described his visit to Hart's Farm and his discovery that a tin of nicotine was missing from there. But, unlike Jimmy, he was not content with a bare recital of the facts. 'It's as clear as it could be,' he continued. 'Neither Philip Harleston nor his sister made any pretence of sorrow for their half-brother's death. In fact, they practically admitted that they were jolly glad he was out of the way. And as soon as I mentioned nicotine, the girl tumbled to it at once. Philip was too stupid to realise what I was after at first, but when I insisted upon looking at his stock of nicotine he simply fell to pieces. I'm expecting to hear every moment that he's made a full confession.'

'An expectation in which you possibly may be disappointed,' remarked Dr Priestley acidly. 'Since you are convinced of this young man's guilt, I fail to see where my advice can be of service to you.'

'In this way, Professor,' Hanslet replied, in no way daunted by Dr Priestley's tone. 'As you say, he may not confess yet awhile. I'm not sure he isn't too stupid to realise that he's cornered. And I want to know if you have any suggestion how to trace the nicotine from Hart's Farm to Matfield Street.'

Oldland, who had hitherto listened in silence, laughed softly.

'That's asking a good deal, isn't it?' he said.

But Dr Priestley paid no attention to him. 'Before offering any suggestion, I should be interested to hear the theory which you have formed, Superintendent,' he said.

'Well, it's fairly obvious what happened, I think,' Hanslet replied. 'Philip was dissatisfied with the way Victor treated Janet. He and Victor had already had words about it, but apparently to no effect. He's rather a weak-minded individual, in my opinion. Criminals, I find, usually are. He thought it would be an excellent plan to get Victor out of the way. Janet and he would inherit the money and everybody would live happily ever after. But, like so many murderers, he forgot the police have an inconvenient habit of inquiring into suspicious deaths.

'Having once decided to remove Victor, the means of doing so must have been fairly obvious to him. He had access to any amount of nicotine, and, as he admitted to me, he knew that it was a very dangerous poison. The nicotine was normally employed in destroying bugs on fruit trees. Surely a far better use for it would be in the removal of Victor.

'But how was Victor to be induced to take the stuff? From my experience of that pot of tea the taste and smell would put anybody off. The intended victim would detect it, if it were mixed with his food or drink. So, then, he thought of another dodge. I'm surprised that so stupid a man should have shown so much ingenuity. I rather suspect that somebody else must have put him up to it.'

'Then surely that somebody was an accessory before the fact?' Dr Priestley inquired mildly.

'Oh yes, I dare say,' Hanslet replied. 'But that isn't the point at the moment—it's the principle I'm after. Philip went into the first convenient shop, where he bought a Novoshave razor and a tube of shaving cream. He typed out the letter to Victor and put this in a parcel with his purchases. And then . . .'

Hanslet, catching Dr Priestley's eye, stopped abruptly. The latter eyed him severely. 'But this letter, I understand, was written on the headed paper of Novoshave Ltd.,' he said.

'That's right, Professor,' Hanslet replied. 'I've got the letter here. Perhaps you'd like to see it.'

He produced the letter from his pocket and handed it to Dr Priestley, who read it through. 'How do you account for Philip Harleston's possession of this headed paper?' he asked.

'Easily enough,' Hanslet replied triumphantly. 'Victor had several sheets of it in his desk.'

But Dr Priestley seemed not yet satisfied. 'There is another difficulty to be surmounted,' he said. 'Inspector Waghorn has told us that the production by Novoshave Ltd. of the new pattern razor has been kept a secret. How should Philip Harleston have known of this new pattern and of the letter of the alphabet to be assigned to it?'

Hanslet evaded a direct answer to this question. 'That objection applies to anybody outside the firm of Novoshave,' he said. 'It's a thousand pities that the paper in which the parcel was wrapped has escaped us. I wouldn't mind betting that we should have found the Lassingford post-mark upon it. But I'm getting a bit ahead of myself. Before Philip packed up his parcel he played tricks with the contents. Jimmy has told you how the razor had been treated so that Victor would be certain to cut himself with it. The shaving cream was contained in an ordinary tube. All Philip had to do was to squeeze the cream out of the tube, mix the nicotine with it and put it back again.'

'Here, hold on a minute, Mr Hanslet,' Oldland exclaimed. 'It would be easy enough to squeeze the cream out of the tube, but how the dickens do you suppose he got it back again?'

Hanslet chuckled. 'And you an experienced motorist, Doctor?' he replied. 'But I'll admit that point puzzled me for a bit. I haven't tried it for myself, but I think it could be done this way. You get an ordinary motor car grease gun and fit it with an adaptor which you could screw on to the end of the tube. Then you squeeze out the cream, leaving the tube flat. You fill the grease gun with the mixture of cream and nicotine, screw the adaptor on to the tube and then use the gun in the ordinary way. The cream would be forced into the tube until it was as full as it was before.'

Dr Priestley nodded approvingly. 'Yes, I think the operation could be carried out in that manner,' he said.

'Victor received the parcel when he came home to lunch on Saturday,' Hanslet continued. 'He opened it and no doubt he read the letter. Sooner or later he would try the suggested experiment. He was the sort of man who would not neglect a razor and a tube of shaving cream which he had secured for nothing. We know that he tried the experiment on Monday morning and that it proved fatal to him.'

'That theory is to some extent conjectural,' Dr Priestley remarked. 'In spite of the most meticulous search neither you nor Inspector Waghorn have succeeded in finding either the tube of shaving cream or the towel used by Victor Harleston that morning.'

'Because they have been deliberately removed,' Hanslet replied. 'Somebody was anxious to remove all traces of how the murder had been carried out and to substitute false clues. The false clues were meant to suggest that Victor had been poisoned by drinking nicotine in his early tea. This, of course, would throw suspicion upon Janet, but Philip may be too much of a fool to have seen that. His idea, I have no doubt, was to suggest that Victor had put some nicotine in himself and so committed suicide.'

Both Dr Priestley and Oldland looked incredulous, but the superintendent proceeded.

'However that may be, it was essential that the real evidence should be made to disappear. The tube of shaving cream, if found, would have given the game away. The towel would certainly be smeared with it, and would be just as compromising. The razor, having been tampered with, would have afforded a valuable clue. Therefore it was necessary to remove these things. The shaving cream and towel were still in the bathroom, but Victor, apparently in a fit of temper, had flung the razor out of the window. And that bit of irritation on his part will probably hang his murderer.'

'It is not clear to me, Superintendent, whom you suspect of having removed these things,' said Dr Priestley coldly.

Hanslet hesitated. Since he had become convinced of Janet's innocence, the difficulty of this point had not escaped him. 'I'm not quite sure,' he said. 'It seems to me that there are two possible explanations. The first is this. Philip may have told his sister some cock-and-bull story. For instance, that he meant to play a practical joke on Victor. He had sent him a razor with which he would be certain to cut himself. Her part in the joke was to remove the apparatus before Victor had time to look round and ask questions. She went up to the bathroom while Victor was dressing, found the towel and the shaving cream, but of course, couldn't find the razor.'

'Not a very convincing theory,' Dr Priestley observed. 'It appears to me to involve several contradictions. One of these will be sufficient as an example. Miss Harleston told Inspector Waghorn that she had not been into the bathroom since her brother had shaved himself. At the same time she made this statement she had no idea that the cut on his face had any connection with his death. Why then, should she not have admitted that she had removed the towel and the shaving cream?'

'I'm not altogether wrapped up in that theory myself, Professor,' Hanslet replied. 'And yet the alternative seems almost fanciful. It brings in the man whom Janet Harleston saw on the front doorstep. We have absolutely no confirmation of that man's existence.'

Oldland put in a word. 'She mentioned him to me quite independently, you must remember.'

'Well, let's suppose for the moment that he did exist,' said Hanslet. 'In that case we must assume that he was Philip's accomplice. According to Janet Harleston, he told her that he was a friend of her brother's. She appears to have assumed that he meant a friend of Victor's, but he might easily have meant that he was a friend of Philip's. Taking advantage of her absence, he went upstairs to the bathroom and abstracted the towel and shaving cream. At the same time, he put the nicotine into Victor's tea pot and cup and also into Janet's eau-de-Cologne. Having done that, he cleared off before Janet returned.'

'I prefer your second theory, Superintendent,' said Dr Priestley.

'I don't see how else you can account for his actions. If he was not an accomplice, he must have acted independently. And if he acted independently he must have been the murderer. In that case, can you suggest any imaginable motive for the crime?'

'The motive of a crime is often the last particular to be ascertained,' Dr Priestley replied. He picked up the letter, which until then had remained upon his desk. He read it through once more very carefully and then turned it over. He immediately perceived the pencil notes on the back of it, and these he studied with great deliberation. 'I take it that you have observed these figures, Superintendent?' he asked.

'Oh yes, I've seen them,' Hanslet replied. 'Somebody seems to have made a calculation on the back of the letter. Mr Harleston probably. Just a casual note of no particular importance.'

Dr Priestley gave expression to one of his rare smiles. 'It is difficult to say what may or may not prove to be of importance,' he said. 'This calculation, as you have no doubt perceived, involves comparatively large sums of money. Rather more than one would expect Victor Harleston to have at his disposal. I find it difficult to believe that they can be notes of his personal income.'

'There's no reason to suppose that they are. Harleston was an accountant, you must remember. He may have made these notes in connection with some audit that he was conducting.'

'That may be so,' said Dr Priestley. 'But none the less, I believe that these notes would be worthy of your attention.

When, and under what circumstances, were they made? Since we are bound to assume that this letter accompanied the parcel, they must have been made after its receipt.'

'That may be so,' Hanslet agreed. 'But I can't see that they can have any possible connection with his death.'

'Even if they have not, they may indicate what was in Victor Harleston's mind shortly before his death,' Dr Priestley replied. He turned suddenly towards Jimmy. 'What is your impression, Inspector?' he asked.

Jimmy could find no answer to this sudden question. 'I'm afraid I haven't given the figures much thought, sir,' he replied.

Curiously enough this rather lame answer seemed to satisfy Dr Priestley. He relapsed into silence, his eyes fixed dreamily upon the ceiling. Abruptly he seemed to awake from his lethargy. 'What do you think about it, Oldland?' he asked.

'I hardly know what to think,' Oldland replied. 'There seem to me to be so many inexplicable points about the case, whatever theory one may adopt. About that missing tin of nicotine, Mr Hanslet. You saw the remaining three tins. What size were they?'

'Oh, about as big as a tin holding fifty cigarettes,' Hanslet replied.

'A tin that size would hold the dickens of a lot of nicotine,' said Oldland thoughtfully. 'Enough to poison a good-sized parish. Now what on earth would Philip Harleston have wanted with such a quantity? If I had been Philip, this is how I should have set about the business. I should have opened one of the tins and taken out a couple of teaspoonfuls, which would have been quite enough for my purpose. I should have replaced these with an equal quantity of oil, and then shut up the tin again. Then, when you came to examine the book and the nicotine in stock, everything would have appeared correct.'

Despite Oldland's glance in his direction, Dr Priestley made no comment. After a slight pause, the former continued. 'I should be inclined to attach considerable importance to the disappearance of a whole tin. A couple of teaspoonfuls, I said. Why, a few drops of the pure alkaloid would have been sufficient. The other evening Priestley mentioned the case of Count Bocarmé. I don't know whether you happen to be familiar with the details of that case, Mr Hanslet?'

'I'm afraid I'm not,' Hanslet replied shortly. 'We haven't time at the Yard for historical research, you know.'

'I wasn't familiar with it myself until I looked it up yesterday evening,' said Oldland. 'A brief account of my researches may be of interest, in the light of Victor Harleston's death. Or perhaps you'd rather tell the story, Priestley?'

Dr Priestley shook his head and Oldland continued.

'The case occurred in France in the year 1851. The people concerned were these, Count Bocarmé, his wife the countess, and her brother. The brother's name was Gustave. It is rather curious that a brother and sister should have been concerned in this case, too.

'To Gustave had been left the greater part of his father's fortune. He had a weakly constitution and was probably tuberculous. As a boy he had had a leg amputated. The count and countess seemed to have expected that he would die young, in which case his fortune would have reverted to the countess. But instead of showing any signs on any early decease he flourished exceedingly. And, to the consternation of his sister and brother-in law, he proposed to get married.

'This was a bit of a blow to the happy couple. The count was very much in debt and his only hope of extricating himself from his trouble was the reversion of Gustave's fortune to his wife. On the evidence there seemed to be very little doubt that they conspired to murder Gustave. It transpired that the count's mother had her suspicions. She warned Madame Bocarmé that her husband was up to no good, but the countess seemed to have disregarded this. Since she herself would benefit her disregard was not unnatural.

'She seems, however, to have tried other expedients before embarking upon murder. She tried to break off Gustave's engagement by writing anonymous letters to him concerning his fiancée. Since this rather clumsy method failed, she seemed to have agreed with her husband that Gustave's death was the only way out of the difficulty. The plan having been decided upon, the next thing was to put it into execution. One fine day Gustave was invited to the count's chateau to dine. The countess' behaviour on that occasion seems to leave no doubt of her complicity. She arranged that the children and their governess should have their dinner in the schoolroom. She sent the servants out, saying that she and her husband could wait upon themselves. In the course of the trial, her husband asserted that it was she who actually administered the poison.

'In any case, Gustave did not survive the dinner. The subsequent inquiry established the fact that he had, while alive, taken some substance which had had a corrosive effect on the soft palate, tongue and stomach. Moreover, his face was scratched and bruised. This was taken to indicate that he had put up some sort of resistance. A significant fact was that the count's hands showed evident signs of having been deeply bitten and his nails showed traces of blood under the white.

'The proceedings of the police were what the newspapers

nowadays would term sensational. A chemist named Stas identified the poison found in the body as nicotine. The police exhumed and examined a number of bodies of animals buried in the garden of Bocarmé's château, and found nicotine in them all. It was proved that the count had studied, in Belgium under a false name, the effects of nicotine poisoning, and that two flasks of liquid extract of nicotine known to be in his possession at the time of the murder had disappeared. In order to show the virulence and the rapidity of the action of the poison, Stas himself tried nicotine on three dogs, each of which died in under three minutes.

'The theory advanced by the prosecution was that the nicotine had been forcibly poured into Gustave's mouth. It was significant that his crutches, without which he was unable to move, were missing. The count, who appears to have been a pretty poor sort of creature, declared that his wife was responsible for their disappearance. They had been resting beside Gustave's chair, and since some of the poison had been spilt upon them, his wife had taken them away and burnt them.

'The jury do not appear to have placed much reliance on Bocarmé's words. He was condemned to death. His wife, either for sentimental reasons or because the evidence against her was not conclusive, was acquitted. How much poison Gustave swallowed, will, I suppose, never be known. But it was asserted at the trial, as Priestley mentioned the other evening, that his death occurred within five minutes of the administration of the poison.'

'Thanks, doctor,' said Hanslet warmly. 'There are a good many points of interest in what you have told us. The parallel between Count Bocarmé and Philip Harleston seems fairly close. Bocarmé had studied the effects of nicotine poisoning.

Philip had no need to study it. He knew all about nicotine, since he was familiar with its use. That seems to me to be additional evidence against him.'

'The more he knew about the effects of nicotine, the less likely would he have been to abstract the whole tin,' Oldland replied. 'It was, when you come to think of it, the most senseless thing to do. At any moment, the police might inspect his books and compare it with the nicotine in stock. Even if he thought it wiser to take a whole tin, rather than abstract some of its contents, he could easily have falsified his book. Instead of this, he seems deliberately to have fabricated clues against himself.'

Dr Priestley resumed his part in the conversation. 'You told us, I think, Superintendent, that the shed in which the nicotine was kept showed no signs of having been broken into. On the other hand, the door of this shed was secured by an ordinary padlock. Our experience tells us that it is a perfectly simple matter for anybody to secure a key which would open such a fastener.'

'I know, Professor,' Hanslet replied. 'The possibility exists that some individual outside the Harleston family opened the door and pinched the tin of nicotine. I'll go so far as to admit that that removes the doctor's objections. A casual thief would not risk opening one of the tins in the shed and abstracting some of its contents. He would pocket the whole tin and clear off. But I simply can't imagine the existence of any such outside person.'

'Perhaps you will explain why,' Dr Priestley suggested.

'I'll try. To begin with, I'll repeat what we know about Victor Harleston. He was a man with no friends. He never invited his colleagues to his home. He seems to have been very reticent about his private affairs. In fact, nobody but the members of his own family were in any way intimate with him. This seems to me to dispose of the idea of a murderer outside the family. Look at the knowledge that such an individual must have possessed. He must have been aware that Victor had a half-brother Philip, who was a fruit farmer and had nicotine in his possession. The exact place in which that nicotine was kept must have been known to him. In addition, there is the knowledge revealed by the contents of the letter. The fact that Mr Harleston had been engaged upon the audit of Novoshave Ltd. The fact that that firm were about to produce a new model razor. The letter of the alphabet which was to be assigned to that model. It seems incredible to me that anyone person should have known all these things with the exception of Philip and Janet. I won't insist upon the lack of motive, Professor.'

Dr Priestley seemed still unconvinced. 'I appreciate your difficulties, Superintendent,' he said. 'But the reasons for your insistence upon Philip Harleston's guilt fail to impress me. I do not for a moment assert his innocence. But were I a member of the jury empanelled for his trial, I could not conscientiously give an opinion in favour of his guilt upon the evidence which you have adduced.'

'I know, Professor, that's just my difficulty,' Hanslet replied. 'That's really why I came to see you this evening.'

'I can offer no suggestions,' said Dr Priestley curtly. 'You have a preconceived theory of Philip Harleston's guilt. Your theory may be correct. You have ascertained certain facts and these facts appear to support it. But as the history of these obscure cases has so frequently demonstrated, it is necessary to ascertain all the facts before coming to a definite conclusion. Because, so far, you have been able to ascertain nothing of Victor Harleston's past history, you assume that no such history exists. He may have had relations with individuals whose interest it is to keep silent. He may have engaged in enterprises of which the records have not yet been discovered. My advice to you is to question everybody with whom he was in any way connected. Incidents in his past life which may account for his murder may thus be revealed. And, if you personally have no time for such patient investigation, I should recommend you to employ Inspector Waghorn as your deputy.'

II

Clues in Abundance

1

Hanslet and Jimmy parted upon leaving Dr Priestley's house. But, as they went their respective ways, the mind of each was still occupied with what he had heard. And perhaps the parallels of the Bocarmé case were uppermost.

These parallels appealed to each in a different way. To Hanslet the relationship of the characters involved were of great interest. Here were a husband and wife who had conspired together to murder the latter's brother. Well, in this Harleston affair, there were a brother and sister who had conspired together to murder their half-brother. The analogy seemed fairly close. And, looked at in the right way, it might prove instructive.

One of the superintendent's misgivings had been the relationship existing between the suspect and the murdered man. It seemed incredible that two decent people should conspire to murder a brother, even a half-brother. Their motive was easy to understand, but to Hanslet it had seemed doubtful whether that motive would ever have goaded them into murder.

But now, Oldland's account of the Bocarmé case had supplied a precedent. Here were two people, rather more than respectable, one might even say distinguished. Titled people, in fact, and Hanslet had a great respect for titles, even foreign ones. Yet they had certainly conspired to murder the countess' brother under peculiar conditions of brutality. In the face of this precedent, one could not argue about natural affection, blood being thicker than water, and all that sort of thing. Philip Harleston might be supposed to have murdered his brother with as little compunction as the count had murdered Gustave.

Philip was the culprit—there could be no shadow of doubt about that. It was all very well for the Professor and Oldland to theorise. Nobody knew better than Hanslet that the case against Philip was by no means proved. But, if one set Philip aside, where was one to look for a substitute? The difficulty of finding any other person with sufficient information as to Victor Harleston's affairs was insuperable.

Except, of course, Janet. That morning Hanslet had been convinced of her innocence. He now began to ask himself the reason for this conviction. The only answer he could find caused him to frown in displeasure. It had been a psychological, not a practical reason. That flash in her eyes when the subject of nicotine had been introduced. But then, all women were born actresses. How could the Superintendent be sure that her apparent horror had been genuine? He comforted himself with the thought that, sooner or later, he would contrive to force a confession from Philip. And that confession, carefully checked, would probably settle for good and all the question of Janet's guilt. Having reached that point he went to bed and promptly fell asleep. His familiarity with the perplexities of detection was such that no problem, however obscure, had any longer the power to keep him awake.

Jimmy was not so fortunate. He, too, had returned to his quarters considering the Bocarmé case and its application to the present affair. He was overjoyed at the indirect compliment which Dr Priestley had paid him. It showed that the old chap had appreciated his efforts, perhaps even his methods. Well, he would do his best to deserve his good opinion. He certainly would not allow himself to be caught napping, as he had been in that unfortunate Threlfall affair. With this spur to his ambition, Jimmy prepared to give his imagination full scope. The Bocarmé case, as expounded by Oldland, had impressed him enormously. The characters concerned in it seemed to offer fascinating study. He determined to attempt some psychological reconstruction of the crime.

To begin with the victim, the ill-starred Gustave. Jimmy saw him as a rather fretful invalid, hobbling about on the crutches rendered necessary by his amputated leg. He had inherited his father's fortune, and he probably guarded his inheritance with considerable care. The future of his inadequately dowered sister must have been something of a problem to him. His delight when she married a man with the name and position of the count was probably proportionately great. Whether or not he had contributed to her dowry Jimmy had no idea. But, once married, the responsibility for her was no longer his but her husband's. He saw no reason to finance the happy couple. He certainly was not prepared to put his hand in his pocket to pay the husband's debts.

And then there was that matter of his health. He had always been regarded by himself and others as delicate, and perhaps this had grown upon him. Very likely he had made himself out to be more of an invalid than was actually the case. Jimmy had met people like that. They liked to be petted and fussed over. Very likely Gustave's chief topic of conversation had been his indifferent health. A man of means with only one leg and a delicate constitution would attract a lot of sympathy.

But perhaps he had not considered the reaction upon his sister and her husband. Gustave, with his complaints and his crutches, had convinced them that he already had one foot in the grave. They expected his early death. Poor Gustave! It was very tragic that he should have to die so young. But, after all, one must try to make the best of things. Perhaps it would be a mercy if his sufferings were ended. And, well, a healthy couple were better fitted to enjoy the money than a crippled weakling.

But Gustave's hypochondria was miraculously cured. He met a girl, an impalpable and pathetic figure in the background of the tragedy. He suddenly realised that he was not so ill as he had always thought and been encouraged to think. The determination possessed him to be fit, as fit as a man with only one leg can be. He proposed to the girl and she accepted him. After that, for Gustave the future must have taken on a very different aspect. With a wife beside him, he might even become a useful member of society. It was reasonable to suppose that he would have children to whom he would leave his money. Gustave, on the night of his dinner at his brother-in-law's chateau, was probably no longer the querulous invalid.

Then came his sister, the countess. Jimmy saw her as an

ambitious, designing woman. From the first she has been ashamed of her plebeian origin and had determined to capture a title. Among her assets was Gustave's notorious ill-health. Anyone could see that he would not live very long. And then the money came naturally to her. Why, she could almost offer any man who married her a post-dated cheque.

With the appearance on the horizon of the count, she saw a way of realising her ambitions. She was not likely to have been deceived as to his character or position. He might be a spendthrift, perhaps deeply in debt. His reputation in consequence might be none too savoury. But that hardly mattered, with Gustave's money in prospect. He was a count, that was the main thing. And Madame la Comtesse had no doubts as to her ability to maintain her new dignity.

Perhaps she received small subsidies from Gustave. Trifling loans to be repaid when her husband had extricated himself from his difficulties. The repayment of these loans need not be considered. Gustave could not hang on indefinitely. And then she would hold the purse strings. The count's affairs could be settled as cheaply as possible, and there would be a comfortable balance with which to support a state worthy of her position.

And then the bomb burst. Gustave appeared one fine day with incredible and devastating news. He felt better than ever before in his life. And, with a self-satisfaction which must have sent a chill of horror to his sister's heart, he announced that he was about to get married.

The subsequent conversation between husband and wife would have been instructive could one but have heard it. Probably there was as yet no whisper of assisting Gustave's exit from this world. The immediate problem was the marriage. At all costs, it must be prevented. Once Gustave was married, his sister's expectations vanished into thin air. But what was to be done? Gustave probably possessed the characteristic obstinacy of the invalid. It was no good trying to persuade him that a man with his disabilities ought not to get married. He simply would not have listened. No doubt it was the countess who hit upon the subtler method.

So she set to work upon the anonymous letters. Jimmy could almost imagine their contents. Clever insinuations against the character of her brother's fiancée, torturing to a man whose powers of observation were necessarily limited. But the countess expended her wit to no purpose. Gustave, inspired by love, or perhaps merely obstinacy, persisted in his intended marriage.

Then came the point which appealed most fervently to Jimmy's imagination. The insinuations having failed, more drastic measures must be undertaken. But which of them had first suggested murder? Jimmy thought it had probably been the countess. He believed that she possessed more intelligence than her husband, who was merely a tool, though a willing one, in her hands. Had she whispered at last that if Gustave would only die before his marriage, all would be well?

Once the suggestion had been made, the crime developed between them, furtively, in fugitive allusion. Gustave's constitution was notoriously delicate. He had to be careful what he ate, lest his food should disagree with him. Suppose he should take something which would disagree with him so violently that the disagreement would be fatal? Acting on her hint, the count went off to Belgium to study poisons and their actions. The countess, no doubt, remained at home, enthusiastically helping her brother in the preparations for his marriage.

The count returned, equipped with the poison which he

had chosen. It was a simple matter to stage the setting of the crime. Gustave was invited to dinner. It was to be a purely informal affair, a *dîner à trois*, as befitted the members of a family. It would be an opportunity to discuss the wedding, the honeymoon, a thousand intimate details. The children would be in the way, they and their governess should dine in another room. The servants, too, would be a hindrance to conversation. The three of them would be much happier waiting upon themselves. Gustave would enjoy himself better so.

Jimmy saw the mind of the countess in these preliminaries. The necessary domestic arrangements would come naturally to her. Her plan succeeded, as she had known from the first that it must succeed. Gustave, once in that fatal dining-room, was at her mercy. Then came the crucial point. Which of them had actually administered the poison?

Jimmy's recent experiences had enlarged his knowledge of nicotine. As the instrument of a poisoner it had its advantages and disadvantages. Its advantages lay in the fact that a comparatively small dose would be almost immediately fatal. Its disadvantages lay in its taste and smell. Nobody whose taste was not atrophied would willingly consume it, however carefully it might be disguised. If Gustave were to be dosed with nicotine, the administration of that dose must necessarily be forcible.

The scene was easy enough to picture. The actual moment had been prearranged between the count and countess. Probably when a fresh course was to be served. Gustave, having only one leg, would not be much use at removing plates and dishes. He would naturally remain in his chair while the host and hostess busied themselves between the table and the sideboard. Unobserved by Gustave, the count poured some of his poison from a bottle into a spoon. The countess watched him, then she approached Gustave, laid her hands upon his arms and whispered some affectionate sisterly message into his ear. Gustave found himself pinioned. And at that moment the count appeared before him with the spoon. With his free hand, his brother-in-law pushed his head back and forced his mouth open. Gustave might bite and struggle as he pleased. In his disabled condition, he was no match for the two of them. The countess watched him die with a satisfaction that she took no trouble to conceal. It was in keeping with her character, as Jimmy had imagined it, that she should have had the presence of mind to perceive the traces of the poison spilt on the crutches and to destroy them.

Finally, Bocarmé himself, a sorry character from many points of view. That he had married the countess for love seemed to Jimmy very doubtful. He had, no doubt, ascertained very early in their acquaintance that her father was a rich man. That Gustave would inherit his money was a temporary inconvenience, nothing more. Gustave's expectation of life was obviously not very great. He would die, and his sister would inherit the money. The prospect must have afforded considerable satisfaction, not only to Bocarmé, but to his creditors as well.

Once married, Bocarmé must have regarded his brother-in-law with considerable impatience. His debts were increasing and his creditors growing more clamorous. And yet this confounded cripple with his perpetual complaints lived on from day to day. He probably blamed the countess for misrepresenting the case. It gradually became apparent to him that he had made a bad bargain. The announcement of Gustave's intended marriage was the last straw. Even then, Jimmy thought, the count had not considered murder as a profitable speculation. He probably had no inconvenient scruples where crime was concerned. But his imagination did not rise to the commission of a murder expeditiously and safely. No doubt it was his wife who inspired him.

The idea once implanted in his mind he set to work. His researches in Belgium convinced him that nicotine would be the best substance for his purpose. He secured a supply and undertook a series of preliminary experiments on the domestic animals. But even at this stage he must have committed some blunder. His mother somehow became suspicious. Perhaps the inexplicable decease of the cats and dogs seemed ominous to her. At all events, she conveyed a warning to the countess that something sinister was in the wind. The countess, knowing her husband's intentions only too well, allowed this warning to pass unheeded. She probably satisfied her mother-in-law with some facile explanation, and almost certainly she warned her husband to be more careful.

Bocarmé's character had been completely revealed at the trial. He had been as ready to commit murder as he had been to run into debt, so long as his own safety was not menaced. He had been sufficiently under the influence of his wife to carry out her designs and to accept her assurance that nobody would ever find out. But when he found himself in the dock he relapsed into panic. In a frantic attempt to save his own head, he threw all the responsibility upon his wife. It was probably correct that she had been the instigator of the crime. But to assert that she had poured the poison into her brother's mouth, in the face of the evidence of his own bitten hand, must have seemed rather futile. In any case, there was nothing to choose between them. They were both equally guilty. How the countess had come to be acquitted was a mystery beyond Jimmy's comprehension.

Thus Jimmy pictured to himself the principal actors in the Bocarmé case. As in the case of Hanslet he had been immediately struck by the relationship between them, and the possible application of that relationship to the Harleston family. But his examination of the analogy went further than the superintendent's. He could see in Gustave a distinct likeness to Victor Harleston. Each had possessed money which, in the case of his death, would pass to his sister. Gustave, as Jimmy imagined him, had not been a very enlivening companion. Victor, it was pretty plain, had been not only mean, but a petty tyrant as well. Gustave had had no particular affection for Bocarmé, as Victor had none for Philip.

Was there also a parallel between Bocarmé and Philip? Jimmy fancied that he could trace one. Bocarmé, not over-intelligent, easily led by his wife. Philip, no doubt an excellent fruit farmer, but not nearly so quick as his sister. But here the parallel ended. Bocarmé's motive had been a purely selfish one, to free himself from debt. Philip's motive, supposing him to have been the criminal, had been chivalrous and unselfish. He had murdered his half-brother in order to free his sister from an intolerable situation.

So far, Jimmy's imagination travelled easily enough. Up to this point the path had been impersonal and detached. But now he found himself faced by a dark and forbidding country which he hesitated to enter. His logic had led him to the point which he had so long evaded. The vision of Janet Harleston was clear, almost inconveniently clear, in his memory. It was, of course, ridiculous to suppose that there could be anything in common between her and the Countess Bocarmé.

Jimmy's usually firm mouth twitched with irritation. It was ridiculous, he told himself. Janet could be no more to him than a figure in the case. As such she must be viewed dispassionately. But no man in his senses after talking to her could believe her capable of deliberate murder.

Yes, that was all very well. But a recollection of one of the superintendent's remarks crossed Jimmy's mind. 'We're all bound to form our own opinions,' Hanslet had said. 'But they cut no ice until we are in a position to support them by proof. A personal belief in innocence or guilt won't convince a jury. And the sooner you get that firmly into your head, my lad, the better.'

Try as he would, Jimmy found it impossible even to speculate upon the possibility of Janet's guilt. He could get no further than the reiteration of the phrase, 'A girl like that couldn't do such a thing.' Philip, if he had been the culprit, must have acted entirely without her knowledge. The Bocarmé analogy broke down. In this case, it had been the man, and not the woman, who had taken the initiative. But was Philip's apparently simple mentality capable of the ingenuity which had been displayed? Jimmy, from what he had seen of him, was decidedly of the opinion that it was not.

So, by a different route, he arrived at the dilemma which confronted Hanslet. If neither Janet nor Philip were guilty, who was the murderer? Jimmy fully appreciated the difficulties. Who in the world was there who could have had either the motive or the opportunity, let alone both? The man seen by Janet on the doorstep? But that suggestion merely completed the vicious circle. Jimmy was quite prepared to believe Janet's statement. In her panic at her brother's sudden illness she had not been in a state to observe the man with any attention. The only impression that she had carried away had been that he had said that he was a friend of her brother. If she had considered this statement at all, she had assumed that the man meant that he was a friend of Victor's. But that, from all accounts of Victor's aloofness from his fellow-men, seemed improbable. The only other construction that could be put upon the words was that he was a friend of Philip's.

If that was the case his presence at the critical moment seemed to drive another nail into Philip's coffin. Philip himself could not enter the house to destroy the evidence. He would be seen and recognised by his sister and awkward questions would be asked. So he commissioned a friend who was unknown to Janet to do it for him. This friend, in his enthusiasm, exceeded his instructions. He secured the towel and the shaving cream, and poured nicotine into the remains of Victor's early tea. So far so good. But then, just to improve appearances, he added nicotine to Janet's eau-de-Cologne. Or perhaps by so doing he had sought to avert suspicion from Philip. Philip, having murdered Victor for Janet's sake, would never have laid a clue which would cast suspicion upon her.

Jimmy felt his thoughts growing a trifle confused. It was by now long past midnight. He undressed and went to bed, but unlike the superintendent, found himself wholly unable to sleep. After a long struggle he was bound to admit to himself that it was the image of Janet's face, the sound of her voice in his ears that was keeping him awake. With something of a shock he realised that he was no longer the impartial police officer. He had become, in spite of himself, Janet's advocate.

This would never do. He switched on the light again and reached out for the pencil and pad of paper which stood beside his desk. Resolutely he bent his thoughts to a more methodical reasoning. What clues were there which could usefully be followed up?

Jimmy, recalling the conversation at Dr Priestley's house, thought that he could think of one or two. The missing tin of nicotine, to begin with. Here again was a parallel with that confounded Bocarmé case. Before the murder of Gustave, Bocarmé had been known to possess two flasks of nicotine; after the event, these flasks had disappeared. Before the murder of Victor, Philip had admitted having four tins of nicotine in his store. One of these had now disappeared.

But Oldland's argument that Philip would not have taken a whole tin, but only a small portion of its contents, had impressed Jimmy. Even if he had taken the tin from the store, he would have put it back again after he had used as much of its contents as was necessary. Hanslet's statement showed that the store, being secured by a very ordinary padlock, could easily have been entered during Philip's absence about the farm.

There was evidence, though of the vaguest, that some time before Victor's death Philip had had a visitor who had called upon him in a car. It seemed probable that he had not seen this visitor, since he was at some distance from his cottage when the latter called. Had the visitor taken advantage of this to enter the store and remove a tin of nicotine? In that case, it would be reasonable to suppose that the visitor and the man seen by Janet on the doorstep were one and the same.

Suppose that some stranger had stolen the nicotine, what would he have done with the tin after he had extracted sufficient from it for his purpose? This, Jimmy feared, would be an unprofitable line of inquiry. He certainly would not have kept it as a souvenir. He would have thrown it away, or at all events disposed of it in such a way that it could not be traced to him. But the history of crime showed that nearly all criminals permit at least one act of carelessness. Bocarmé was an excellent example. He had allowed it to be known that he had nicotine in his possession and he had in some way aroused his mother's suspicions. Might not Victor's murderer have done something equally thoughtless? Perhaps there were people who knew that he had nicotine in his possession. Perhaps, even, he had retained the tin, confident that it would never be discovered. There was, Jimmy decided, just a faint chance that this clue might prove helpful. He made a first entry on his writing pad. 'Tin of nicotine.'

What else was there? Obviously the letter purporting to have been written by Mr Topliss of Novoshave to Victor. Jimmy remembered that Dr Priestley had displayed considerable interest in the figures scribbled on the back. Were they the work of Victor? It would be easy enough to secure specimens of Victor's figures and compare them. But even if Victor had written them, what possible light could they throw upon his death? Nevertheless, Jimmy added to his notes the words 'pencilled figures.'

So much for the clues that existed. Were there any more to be found? Dr Priestley had insisted upon the necessity for exploring Victor's history. How was that to be done? Janet and Philip could be questioned, of course, but their statements might be prejudiced. Mr Knott had mentioned his partner, Mr Slater, who lived at Torquay. Would an interview with him be worth while? Jimmy, thinking that it might be, determined to suggest it to Hanslet. He made a third note on the paper, 'Mr Slater.' This done he switched off the light once more and made a final effort to sleep. In time he succeeded.

2

Hanslet and Jimmy met next morning at Scotland Yard.

'Good-morning, Jimmy,' said the superintendent. 'I hope you enjoyed the edifying conversation you heard yesterday evening? Well, what about it? Are you convinced now that Harleston did it?'

Jimmy hesitated. 'I hope you won't mind if I say that I'm not altogether sure,' he replied.

'Mind!' exclaimed Hanslet. 'Of course I don't mind. You're fully entitled to your own opinion. But if he didn't do it, who did? Tell me that?'

'I wish I could tell you,' said Jimmy. 'But I thought of something last night. What about having a chat with Mr Slater of Slater & Knott? There's just a chance that we might find out something about Victor's past life.'

Hanslet grinned. 'Lives at Torquay, doesn't he?' he said. 'Charming place, I believe. But I'm too busy for a jaunt to the seaside on the off-chance of picking up a piece of gossip. You can run down if you like, but don't waste more time than you can help. The solution of our problem is to be found nearer London than Torquay, I fancy.'

Having thus obtained the necessary permission, Jimmy travelled down to Torquay. He sought out the address which Mr Knott had given him and found it to be a substantial villa on the outskirts of the town. He rang the bell, presented his card, and asked for an interview with Mr Slater. With very little delay this was granted. He was shown into a comfortably furnished dining-room, and a few moments later Mr Slater joined him.

He was rather a fine looking old gentleman, Jimmy thought. His age appeared to be between seventy and eighty, and from the groping movements of his hands, as though he were feeling his way, it was easy to guess that his sight was nearly gone. He steered himself to an arm-chair, and peered through his very powerful glasses in Jimmy's direction.

'Inspector Waghorn?' he asked.

'Yes, sir,' Jimmy replied. 'I hope I'm not intruding. I should be glad to know what you can tell me of Victor Harleston, who was a clerk in your firm.'

Mr Slater nodded. 'Ah yes,' he said deliberately. 'The poor fellow died very suddenly, did he not? Knott wrote to me about it. I can no longer read letters for myself but my daughter reads them to me. The infirmities of old age, Inspector. I never took to the boy from the first, though I knew his father well.'

This sounded promising. 'You knew his father, sir?' Jimmy prompted.

'Yes, I knew Peter when his first wife was alive, before Victor was born. I was only a clerk then, and glad to pick up odd shillings in my spare time. So I used to help small tradesmen with their accounts. That's how I met Peter Harleston. He was a very good business man in his way. I believe he died worth quite a lot of money.'

'Of which Victor had a life interest, I understand?'

'Yes, under certain conditions. He had to provide for his half-sister. Queer chap, Peter. He wouldn't leave his money outright, in case his children should spend it. He needn't have had any fears about Victor, though. I never met either of the other two, so I can't say.'

'In spite of Victor's income he was content to remain as a clerk in your firm?' Jimmy suggested.

'I don't suppose the income amounts to very much nowadays. Trustee securities don't give the yield they used to. Still,

I dare say Victor had between £400 and £500 a year of his own. He had his sister to keep, and I suppose he thought that wasn't enough for the two of them.'

'How did Victor come to join your firm, Mr Slater?' Jimmy asked.

'I took him on at his father's request. Peter Harleston told me that his son had shown some aptitude for figures and I advised him to train him as an accountant. I said that if he passed his examinations I'd give him a trial. He seemed satisfactory enough, so he stayed on. Long after I had given up helping Peter with his accounts, he and I remained friends. Not personal friends exactly, for I never went to his house. But he would drop in at the office sometimes, and ask my advice. For instance, I helped him to purchase a share in a fruit farm for his other son, Philip. That was the week before I retired from business, I remember.'

'I gather, Mr Slater, that you were not particularly attracted to Victor Harleston,' Jimmy suggested.

The old man smiled. 'I can't say that I was,' he replied. 'He never took the trouble to make himself attractive, if the truth is known. But it wasn't exactly that. So long as my clerks are efficient, that is all I ask of them. Very early in my association with Victor, I caught him out in what can only be described as a mean trick. That was a long time ago and I needn't go into details. It will be enough to say that Victor had found a means of defrauding his colleagues of a few shillings, no more. Had it been anybody else, I should have discharged him on the spot. But since the amount involved was so small, I allowed my friendship for his father to influence me. I gave Victor a pretty severe talking to and there it ended.'

'His conduct was satisfactory after that?'

'There was no fault to be found with his conduct in the office. As an accountant, he was thoroughly to be relied upon. But I thoroughly disliked his attitude at the time when his father bought his brother Philip a share in Hart's Farm. He did everything he could to oppose the scheme. In fact, he very nearly persuaded his father to abandon it. His contention was that very little money had been expended upon finding him a job, and that it was not fair that Philip, the younger brother, should be unduly favoured. I imagine that Victor knew that he would inherit a life interest in his father's estate and he disliked the idea of any spending of the capital.'

'You were not in favour of his receiving a bonus from the firm, I believe?'

'I most certainly was not,' Mr Slater replied emphatically. 'Our custom has been to grant bonuses only in exceptional cases. For instance, where the recipient has carried out some particularly difficult piece of work, or that his domestic affairs involve a considerable strain upon his income. Neither of these conditions applied to Victor Harleston. When Mr Knott approached me on the matter some weeks ago, I was disinclined to agree to his suggestion. Victor Harleston had been with the firm for some years, it is true. But his services have been no more valuable than those of his colleagues. He had nobody to support but his sister, and for this purpose he had a private income of his own. However, Mr Knott was very insistent and at last I agreed, though reluctantly, I confess.'

'You were not in any way influenced by your personal dislike for Victor?' Jimmy asked rather diffidently.

'Not in the least. In fact, it was because Mr Knott might imagine that was my reason that I finally consented. I hope I am sufficiently impartial to give credit where credit is due; without being swayed by my personal feelings. And entirely between ourselves, Inspector, I had another reason for my hesitation.'

'May I be allowed to know that reason, Mr Slater?'

Mr Slater hesitated. 'Well, I suppose one may safely confide in a policeman,' he replied. 'My failing eyesight was the reason for my retirement from the business. I found that I was becoming very little use in the office, and my oculist warned me that persistence in my work might result in total blindness. He strongly urged me to retire and to live in some pleasant seaside place such as this. I felt compelled to follow his advice. An arrangement was made whereby Mr Knott took over the active management of the business and I became a sleeping partner. I have never visited the office since the day of my retirement. However, I still keep in touch. Mr Knott comes here at frequent intervals to see me. In fact, I am expecting him this evening.

'At the time of my retirement the business was extremely flourishing. But I am sorry to say that since then it has steadily gone downhill. I do not mean to suggest that my retirement is in any way the reason for this. It is due entirely to economic conditions, and perhaps, to the growing competition in our profession. This being the case, I considered it hardly a fitting time to grant bonuses to employees who had no earthly need of them.'

Mr Slater, once started, became positively garrulous. 'There's no question of the firm being in a critical condition,' he continued. 'Profit diminishing steadily from year to year, that's all. I'm not concerned for myself. There'll be plenty to last me to the end of my days. But I should like to leave my son and daughter-in-law well provided for. I bought this house for them, you know.'

Naturally Jimmy didn't know. But he said nothing. He had

already learnt a golden rule. If you are interviewing anybody, and they show a disposition to talk, do not on any account interrupt them. In spite of the apparent irrelevance of the remarks, there is always the chance of picking up something which may be useful. So he merely nodded and Mr Slater continued.

'I hope you'll stop for a cup of tea, Inspector, and meet Gavin and Winifred. I'm sure you'd like them both. Gavin's a very clever artist. Paints pictures, you know, and very good they are. But his luck's been against him since quite a lad, poor boy. He sends his work up to the Academy every year, but somehow the hanging committee don't appreciate it. Gavin himself says it's because he won't pander to their ideas. I don't know, for I'm not an expert in the sort of figures he paints. The only figures I know anything about are the ones you write down in books.'

Mr Slater chuckled at his very mild joke and Jimmy followed his example. To the latter it seemed that they were getting on excellently. He was not greatly interested in Gavin and his art, but eventually, he thought, the conversation must take a more informative turn.

'Gavin always wanted to be a sailor,' Mr Slater went on reminiscently. 'But when he was nine he had a terrible accident. He was thrown out of a dog-cart and the wheel passed over him and broke both his legs. The fool of a doctor who attended him bungled things, with the result that he was lamed for life. It nearly broke my wife's heart. He was our only child and naturally she was devoted to him.'

Jimmy uttered a sympathetic murmur, but Mr Slater hardly heeded him, so set was he on his subject. 'Of course, that put an end of all Gavin's prospects of going to sea. In fact, for a long time it was doubtful whether he would ever be able to use his legs again. It was a terrible blow to the poor boy, and for years we found it very difficult to interest him in anything. However, he used to amuse himself with a pencil and paper, and a friend of mine who happened to watch him one day said that he had a definite gift for sketching. So he went to an art school and since then he seems to have found a definite occupation in painting. I don't mind telling you in confidence, Inspector, that his efforts have not hitherto proved very remunerative. That's why I want to leave as much money as possible behind me when I die.'

Mr Slater paused. When he continued, it was plain that he was talking rather to himself than to Jimmy. 'Yes, it was a good move to buy this house. It suited all of us. You see, there's the studio for Gavin to play about in, and plenty of nice people in the town for Winifred to know; I'm happy enough with them. As happy as I should be anywhere, going blind and with nothing to do. And they're very good to the old man. He lives with them and pays the bills. No, no, it isn't that. They're good children, good children. But it'll be a relief to them when the old man breathes his last. I know that though they've never dropped a hint in word or deed . . .'

Rather to Jimmy's relief, Mr Slater's musings were inter-ruped by the opening of the door and the entrance of a hard-featured and expensively-dressed woman. She glanced rather haughtily at Jimmy. Mere policemen were obviously beneath her notice.

'Tea's ready, father,' she exclaimed sharply.

'Thank you, my dear, thank you,' Mr Slater replied. 'Let me introduce you to Inspector Waghorn of Scotland Yard. This is my daughter-in-law, Winifred, Inspector.'

Winifred Slater acknowledged the introduction with a curt nod. Mr Slater continued.

'We were just having a little chat, my dear. About poor Victor Harleston, you know. You remember reading to me Knott's letter about him? A very sad affair, very sad indeed.'

'Well, you'd better come along and have your tea now,' she said. And without wasting any more words, she went out, leaving the door open behind her.

'I think we'd better go in to tea,' said Mr Slater, rising laboriously from his chair. 'Winifred doesn't like to be kept waiting. We always have tea in the studio and you'll have an opportunity of seeing Gavin's work.'

Jimmy hesitated. He was not particularly anxious to see Gavin or to inspect the masterpieces so consistently rejected by the Academy. But his train back to London did not leave for another hour and he thought that he might as well remain as far as possible in Mr Slater's good graces. He might have need of him again on some future occasion.

So, Mr Slater leading the way with those peculiar groping gestures of his, they passed through the house into the studio. Here they found Winifred Slater already seated at the tea-table. Standing before an easel under the north light was a heavy, thick-set man, whom Mr Slater introduced with evident pride as 'My son, Gavin.' Jimmy glanced at him curiously. He was wearing an apron, much bedaubed with paint. His features had a malicious cast about them, Jimmy thought, as though he had a grievance against the world. Rather a bad-tempered looking chap, but then his infirmity and his constant disappointments might account for that.

The walls of the studio were covered with large canvases, no doubt the work of Gavin's brush. Jimmy was no art expert. He liked pictures or disliked them because they did or did not appeal to him. But he felt in agreement with the judgment of the Hanging Committee. Gavin seemed to excel in the portrayal of people of unusual shape in impossible positions. And his sense of colour made even Jimmy blink.

Gavin came across the room and greeted him superciliously. As soon as the man moved his lameness became apparent. But apart from that he seemed fit enough. In fact, he was a powerful sort of chap, Jimmy thought. An ugly customer to tackle, in spite of his game leg. He was not greatly taken by either him or his wife. It flashed through his mind that Mr Slater's life with them was probably not quite so contented as he tried to make out.

Tea was rather an uncomfortable meal. Neither Gavin nor Winifred seemed to have anything particular to say. It was left to Mr Slater to drone on about the amenities of Torquay and its neighbourhood. Nothing further of any possible interest to Jimmy transpired. He was relieved when the time came for him to leave the house and make his way to the station.

On his way back to London he made notes of his conversation with Mr Slater. On reading them through he resigned himself to the conviction that he had wasted his day. He had learnt nothing of any interest. Mr Slater had merely confirmed what everybody else had said. Victor Harleston had been an unpleasant sort of person and would not be greatly missed. But, under modern conditions, people don't get murdered just because they are unpopular. In his search for an alternative motive, Jimmy felt that he had drawn completely blank. It was discouraging. But Jimmy had learnt that the detective must explore many blind alleys before he finds the true thoroughfare.

His final thought was one of sympathy for Mr Slater. 'Poor old chap,' he muttered. 'I wouldn't live with that couple for anything you could offer me.'

3

It was not until next morning that Jimmy and Hanslet met again. The superintendent listened to Jimmy's account of his visit to Torquay with obvious impatience. At the end of it he snorted disdainfully.

'I could have told you before you started that you wouldn't learn anything,' he said. 'There's nothing more to learn. We know the whole story. All we want now is proof, and that I mean to find before I'm very many days older. Look here, this is Friday, the day on which they are going to bury Victor Harleston. Philip and Janet will attend the funeral, of course. You'd better go too, and keep an eye on them.'

'You're not expecting the coffin to sweat drops of blood in their presence, are you?' Jimmy asked.

'What the devil are you talking about?' replied the superintendent, whose knowledge of ancient superstitions was not so extensive as Jimmy's. 'I want you to keep an eye on those two young people. Detain them for an hour or so after the funeral on any pretext you like. I don't want them back again at Lassingford too soon. I'm going down there myself, while they're both out of the way, to have a look over that cottage of theirs. There's just a chance that I may find something which will give us what we want.'

So Jimmy took up his position outside the cemetery. He saw the procession arrive and noticed that there were only four mourners. Janet, Philip, Mr Mowbray and a fourth, whom Jimmy recognised as the young clerk, Davies, to whom he had spoken in Mr Knott's office. The latter obviously was representing the firm of Slater & Knott. Jimmy waited until the mourners should return. He had no desire to be present at the graveside.

He had not very long to wait before they came out. He stepped forward and Janet immediately recognised him.

'Why, there's Inspector Waghorn!' she exclaimed.

The others looked at him with varying degrees of interest. Philip seemed fairly surprised. The lawyer glanced at him shrewdly, but made no remark. Davies nodded towards him as if in recognition of their acquaintance.

Janet, however, approached him impulsively and drew him aside.

'Why are you here, Mr Waghorn?' she asked with something like terror in her voice.

'Merely out of curiosity, Miss Harleston,' Jimmy replied as gently as he could.

She shook her head impatiently. 'It's something more than that, I know,' she said. 'Listen, Superintendent Hanslet came down to see us yesterday. He suspects Philip of—of having something to do with Victor's death.'

Jimmy felt a sharp stab of pity at the sound of her voice. He could guess what lay beneath this rather obvious statement. Hanslet might suspect her brother. That was his affair. What tortured her was that she did not know whether to suspect him herself or not.

'He found some nicotine missing from Philip's store,' she continued. 'You don't believe he had anything to do with it, do you, Mr Waghorn?'

Jimmy could find no answer to this appeal. He felt an insane desire to comfort her. It was on his lips to say, 'My dear, I know well enough that you had nothing to do with it and I don't see that anything else matters.' But such a speech would be unpardonable on the part of an Inspector of Police. His official reply sounded bald and unconvincing.

'I am sure you will understand, Miss Harleston,' he said.

'Until your brother's death is satisfactorily explained everybody connected with him must be, to some extent, under suspicion.'

A look of profound discouragement came into her eyes. It was clear that she had hoped for something, no matter what, which would have helped to set her own doubts at rest. She turned away as though to rejoin the others. But Jimmy had been told to detain her and for once his duty coincided with his inclination.

'Are you going back to Lassingford at once, Miss Harleston?' he asked.

'No,' she replied, 'not until the six o'clock train. Mr Mowbray wants us to go back to his office with him. There are lots of things to be settled.'

Jimmy felt strangely disappointed. If she and Philip were going to the lawyer's office, Hanslet's requirements would be satisfied. The lawyer would have the pleasure of her company instead of himself, that was all. And Jimmy had thought out all manner of schemes for spending an hour or so with her. She interested him, it was no good pretending that she didn't. In a professional way, of course. A most instructive type to study. Well, the opportunity had been deferred. He went back to Scotland Yard feeling that the day was somehow less bright than it had been. And once there he plunged with unusual energy into a mass of routine work.

Hanslet returned from Lassingford also disappointed, but for quite another reason. He had searched the cottage from attic to cellar but had found nothing that could possibly throw any light upon Victor Harleston's death. He had half hoped that he might have found the remains of the tin of nicotine hidden away in some obscure corner. But this hope had failed him and he was proportionately irritated. He seemed to think that Jimmy ought to have confronted Philip at the funeral, and extorted some sort of statement from him.

'You're a damned sight too gentle with these folk,' he grumbled. 'The velvet glove is no use in a case like this. What you want is the iron hand. Show them that you know that one or the other of them did it and that you don't mean to give them any peace until you can prove which it was. Make their lives a burden to them till they give in in sheer desperation. That's the way to handle them, my lad. You watch me and I'll show you. I'll give that young rogue a few yards more rope and then I'll go for him properly.'

Hanslet's irritation caused Jimmy no surprise, for he fully understood the reason of it. It is one thing for a police officer to suspect a given individual of a crime, but quite another for him to bully the suspect into a confession. English judges, rightly or wrongly, look upon an extorted confession with grave dislike. They may even refuse to allow such a statement to be given in evidence. Hanslet counted upon a confession to secure conviction. But that confession, to be of any use, must be made voluntarily. He felt that, sooner or later, Philip's resistance would break down. But it galled him to have to wait. His temperament was not that of the cat which waits patiently for hours at the mousehole. It was rather that of the ferret who goes into the burrow after the rabbit.

The weekend passed without any further development. But on Monday morning at about eleven o'clock, a messenger brought Jimmy a card. It bore the name of Mr Fred Davies of Slater & Knott, accountants.

Jimmy wondered what on earth Davies could want with him. However, that was soon discovered. 'Show him in,' he said.

Davies entered the room rather diffidently. 'Er—good-morning, Inspector,' he said nervously.

'Good-morning, Mr Davies,' Jimmy replied heartily. 'I saw you on the day of Mr Harleston's funeral, I think. Sit down. You'll find that chair pretty comfortable.'

He asked no question as to his visitor's errand, thinking it best that he should explain it himself. Davies sat down and fidgeted uneasily. The rather chilling air of Scotland Yard seemed to depress him. 'Have a cigarette,' said Jimmy carelessly, handing him his open case.

The gesture seemed to reassure Davies. The interview was not to be so formal as he had feared. He took a cigarette and lighted it at the match which Jimmy struck for him.

'Thanks,' he said gratefully. 'Yes, I was at the funeral. The chaps at the office thought somebody ought to go and they chose me. And it's the same today. They knew that I'd met you and as we'd made up our minds to speak to the police, they said that since I knew you, I'd better come and talk to you about it.'

This was not very explicit. 'I'm very glad you came, Mr Davies,' replied Jimmy. 'If I can help you in any way, you've only got to ask me.'

'That's very good of you,' said Davies. 'I expect you'll laugh at me when I tell you what it's all about. We're worried because Mr Knott hasn't been to the office since Thursday and nobody seems to know where he is.'

'What steps have you taken to find him, Mr Davies?' asked Jimmy quietly.

'I'd better tell you all about it from the beginning. Mr Knott left the office at lunch-time on Thursday, saying that he was going down to Torquay to see Mr Slater and would probably not be back until Friday afternoon. There's nothing unusual about that. He often goes down to see Mr Slater, and stays the night.'

'However, Mr Knott did not come back on Friday. During the afternoon, some urgent correspondence came in which required his personal attention. The chief clerk thought that Mr Knott might have decided to spend the weekend at Torquay and sent a telegram to Mr Slater, and an answer came back that Mr Knott had left for London by the first train that morning.'

Jimmy nodded. He remembered that Mr Slater had told him that he expected Mr Knott on Thursday evening. 'Where does Mr Knott live?' he asked.

'He has rooms in the Temple, at Crozier Court. The chief clerk went there as soon as he received Mr Slater's telegram. But Mr Knott was not there and the rooms were shut up. And nobody had seen him since Thursday morning. Mr Knott is a bachelor and lives alone.'

It struck Jimmy that a bachelor might absent himself for the weekend without all this fuss being made.

'Don't you think it probable that he'll turn up in the course of the day?' he asked.

'Well, I hope so,' Davies replied. 'But it's most extraordinary that he should have kept away like this. He expected the arrival of this correspondence that I mentioned. Before he went away he told the chief clerk that he would be back without fail on Friday afternoon. It's most unlike him to stay away from the office without letting anybody know where he is. We are beginning to wonder if anything can have happened to him.'

'You were quite right to come and see me, Mr Davies,' said Jimmy. 'I'll set about making inquiries at once. To begin with, I shall want an accurate description of Mr Knott and if possible a photograph.'

'There's a very good photograph of him at the office,' Davies replied. 'It was taken last year at our annual dinner.'

'Then I think I'll go back with you and fetch it. By the time we get there there may be some news.'

Jimmy accompanied Davies to the offices of Messrs. Slater & Knott. He thought it as well to get some confirmation of the Davies' story, and asked for an interview with the chief clerk, but this gentleman, whose name was Grant, had nothing to add to the account which Jimmy had already heard. Mr Knott had told him personally, just before his departure, that he would be back by Friday afternoon, without fail. Since then he had had no word from him.

Jimmy was shown the telegram which had been received from Mr Slater. It was brief and to the point. 'Knott left here for London 7.20 yesterday morning.'

'Mr Knott expected to have urgent affairs to attend to on his return, did he not?' he asked.

'That is so,' replied Grant. 'He expected the arrival of some very important correspondence on Friday morning. It concerned one of our most prominent clients and Mr Knott had made an appointment for that gentleman to come here at three o'clock that afternoon in order to discuss it. The gentleman arrived and waited for half an hour. But Mr Knott did not turn up nor have we heard anything of him since. It is extremely awkward, for the matter is one which must be settled without delay.'

Under these circumstances, Knott's non-appearance seemed inexplicable. Jimmy examined the photograph which was produced for him, and recognised it as an excellent likeness. Grant and Davies between them gave him a detailed description of Knott's appearance and of the clothes which he was wearing when he was last seen. Armed with these and the photograph he returned to Scotland Yard. Here he drafted a circular for distribution to all police stations.

After what he had learnt, it seemed to him unlikely that Knott's absence from his office was voluntary. If he had left Torquay at seven-twenty in the morning, he should have reached London some time before noon. On arrival he would proceed direct to Chancery Lane or to his rooms in Crozier Court. Apparently, however, he had done neither of these things. He might have met with an accident of some kind, either in the train or after its arrival at Paddington. Jimmy telephoned to the station and was assured that the seventwenty from Torquay on Friday morning had arrived without incident. Jimmy repeated his inquiries at the various London hospitals without effect. Nobody of the name of Knott or answering to the description given by the inspector had been admitted during the past week.

Jimmy's next step was to report the matter to Hanslet. Since Knott was remotely connected with the Harleston case, it seemed the proper thing to do. But the superintendent was not much impressed. 'He'll turn up all right,' he said. 'But we want to know where he is, for we shall want him as a witness as soon as we bring Philip Harleston before the magistrates. You'd better run down to Torquay again, and see if you can find out anything about him there.'

So Jimmy paid a second visit to Mr Slater and was received with the latter's habitual courtesy. He explained the purport of his visit. Mr Slater seemed very much perturbed.

'Dear me,' he said, 'that's very annoying. The business cannot carry on without Mr Knott's personal supervision. Grant, the chief clerk, is a very good fellow, but he cannot be expected to take charge at a moment's notice like this. Do you think that Mr Knott can have met with an accident, on his journey back to London?'

'I can't obtain any news of such a thing having happened,' Jimmy replied. 'You are sure that he left here by the seven-twenty train on Friday morning?'

'Well, I didn't see him off, of course,' said Mr Slater. 'I don't get up so early as that nowadays. But that's what he told Gavin he meant to do when they were chatting together on Thursday evening. He didn't say anything about it to me. I expected him to catch the same train as he usually does—the ten-thirty.'

'He had an appointment for three o'clock at the office on Friday. Perhaps that was the reason why he took the earlier train?'

'It may have been. He told me about that appointment—in fact, he asked my advice about the line he should take. If he handled the matter properly, it should prove a source of considerable profit to the firm. I sincerely hope that it will be possible to postpone it until Mr Knott reappears.'

'Mr Knott gave you no hint that he did not mean to return to the office on Friday?'

'Certainly not,' replied Mr Slater emphatically. 'On the contrary, he told me how necessary it was that he should be there. I had suggested that he should stay the weekend with us as he sometimes does, but he explained that it was absolutely impossible. There was another reason which made it necessary for him to be back in London on Friday. He had a large sum of money with him which he had to hand over to one of his business friends before six o'clock.'

'You mean that he had the money with him while he was here, Mr Slater?' Jimmy asked.

'Yes. The money was in notes of various denominations. He counted them in my presence while we were alone together. The total, to the best of my recollection, was £750.

When he counted the notes he returned them to an envelope, which he put in his pocket.'

'Have you any idea of the source of this money? Or of the person to whom it was to be paid?'

'Very little. Mr Knott told me that it was a personal matter of his own and had nothing to do with the firm. I formed the impression that he had the opportunity of buying some shares or other upon exceptionally favourable terms. He definitely told me that the matter must be concluded by six o'clock on Friday afternoon. I saw him last at nine o'clock on Thursday evening. It is my habit to retire to bed at that hour. But I expected to see him again at breakfast on the following morning. However, Gavin told me that he had left by the seven-twenty.'

The fact that Knott was carrying a large sum of money with him when he disappeared seemed to Jimmy to put a new complexion on the situation. And so far, there was no evidence that he had actually left Torquay by the seven-twenty. Mr Slater had merely taken his son's word for it. It was obvious that the matter required further investigation.

'I wonder if I might have a few words with your son, Mr Slater,' he asked.

'Certainly,' replied Mr Slater without hesitation. 'He's at work in the studio, I expect. You know your way. Perhaps you would like to go there and see him.'

Jimmy took advantage of this invitation. He went into the studio and found Gavin still at work before the easel. He turned his head as Jimmy entered the room.

'Hullo, Inspector,' he said ungraciously, 'you here again?'

'Yes,' replied Jimmy shortly. 'I'm trying to get news of Mr Knott. He hasn't been seen since he was down here last Thursday.'

'I thought there must be something up when they sent that telegram from the office,' said Gavin easily. 'What's happened to him? Not done a bunk with the firm's money, I hope.'

The mention of the word 'money' gave Jimmy his cue.

'You were aware that he had a large sum of money with him when he was here?' he asked quickly.

'Not I,' Gavin replied. 'I know nothing whatever about high finance. That's the Governor's affair, not mine.'

He seemed impatient to end the conversation, for he turned back to the easel as though to resume his painting.

But Jimmy meant to get to the bottom of this affair. Already he had a vague suspicion, too utterly fantastic to be encouraged. He had taken a dislike to Gavin at first sight and he told himself that this must have something to do with it.

'I'm afraid I shall have to trouble you a little longer, Mr Slater,' he said coldly. 'When did you last see Mr Knott?'

'Why, when he went to bed on Thursday night, of course. You don't suppose that I took the trouble to get up and shake his hand at seven o'clock in the morning, do you?'

'What time did he go to bed?'

'Oh, soon after eleven I think it was,' replied Gavin impatiently. 'We sat in here and drank whisky after dinner. The Governor always clears off at nine or soon after. Winifred wasn't with us, she was out at a bridge party somewhere.'

'So that you and Mr Knott were alone from soon after nine till soon after eleven?'

'Yes, that's right. Swapping yarns and drinking. Knott's not a bad fellow. He's usually got one or two amusing stories up his sleeve. I'm always glad to see him, so long as it's not too often.'

'When did he tell you that he meant to go back to London by the seven-twenty?'

'Oh, while we were together here after dinner. He said that he'd forgotten to tell the Governor that he would have to go by that train and asked me if it would be all right. I offered to ring for the maid and tell her to call him early. But he said it didn't matter. He didn't want to disturb anybody. He knew his way about the house and could let himself out. As for breakfast, he could get that on the train.'

Jimmy considered this for a few moments. It was not, on the face of it, improbable. Knott was a frequent visitor to the house and could behave informally. He knew from experience that it took less than ten minutes to walk to the station. If he had left the house a few minutes after seven he would have been in plenty of time for his train. There was a chance then that he might have been seen.

'What time in the morning do the servants get up?' Jimmy asked abruptly.

The other shrugged his shoulders. 'How should I know?' he replied. 'I don't run the house. You'd better go and ask them. And, if you haven't noticed it for yourself, I am bound to mention that I have a job of work to do.' He turned his back on Jimmy as though to conclude the interview. Jimmy decided to take advantage of his discourteous invitation. He left the studio and set out to explore the back premises.

His arrival there caused something of a flutter. He found the cook and housemaid sitting together over a cup of tea, and in a few words he explained the reason for his intrusion.

'I'm awfully sorry to butt in like this,' he said apologetically. 'I only want to know if anybody saw Mr Knott leave the house on Friday morning.'

The two women glanced at one another sharply. The cook shook her head forebodingly.

'There now, I always said that it wasn't natural,' she said.

'What wasn't natural?' asked Jimmy politely.

'Why, what Lizzie here told me she found after the gentleman had gone,' replied the cook.

Lizzie was apparently the housemaid. But Jimmy was not to be drawn off at a tangent like this. If there was any mystery in Knott's departure from the house, he wanted to get his facts in proper order.

'Mr Knott is supposed to have caught the seven-twenty train to London on Friday morning,' he said. 'Did either of you see him leave the house by any chance?'

Both shook their heads and Lizzie replied. 'He must have gone before I was up and about, sir, and that was a quarter to seven. I went to call him at eight o'clock, like I always do when he stays here, and I found—'

She stopped abruptly, as though afraid of divulging her information. But Jimmy encouraged her.

'What did you find, Lizzie?' he asked.

'Why, that Mr Knott had got up and gone, sir,' she replied stubbornly.

'Come now, Lizzie,' said Jimmy reprovingly. 'It's no use trying to hide anything from me. It might make things unpleasant for you, you know. What else did you find when you went to call Mr Knott at eight o'clock?'

Thus cautioned, Lizzie decided to make a clean breast of it.

'Why, sir, I found a patch of blood as big as a saucer on his top sheet, sir,' she replied in an awestruck voice.

'Where is that sheet now?' asked Jimmy quickly.

'In the washing basket, sir, waiting for the laundry man who calls tomorrow.'

Jimmy thanked his stars that he had not delayed his visit to Torquay. Knott's disappearance was becoming more sinister with every new point ascertained. 'The bed had been slept in, I suppose?' he asked.

'Oh yes, sir,' Lizzie replied. 'And there was another funny thing about it. The pillow case had gone and I couldn't find it anywhere.'

'Have you found it since?'

'No, sir, it's clean gone. I told Mrs Slater about it and she said that it didn't matter. Mr Knott must have taken it to wrap something up in. He'd be sure to post it back, she said.'

'Mr Knott brought a suitcase with him when he came, I suppose?'

'Oh yes, sir. He dressed for dinner on Thursday. But his things had all gone and the suitcase too, when I went into his room.'

Jimmy decided not to pursue his inquiries any further for the present. He asked Lizzie for the bloodstained sheet and when she had brought it he secured a sheet of brown paper and wrapped it up in a parcel. He then left the house, taking this with him, and proceeded to the local police station.

Here he found the superintendent, to whom he unfolded his story. 'I don't altogether like the look of it, sir,' he said. 'Nobody saw Knott leave that house. And the blood on this sheet, taken with the fact that the pillow case is missing, seems to me rather significant.'

The superintendent looked grave. 'We know something about this Mr Gavin Slater,' he said. 'He's made himself a nuisance to us more than once. Since he has been here he has made himself notorious. For instance, he's got drunk in nearly every pub in the town, until there are very few places that will serve him. The trouble with him is that he gets violent when he's in drink. Not long ago he created a disturbance in the main street and when the constable went up to see what was the matter he wanted to fight him. Master Gavin got so obstreperous that the man had no option but to bring him here. We put him in the cells for an hour or two, but we didn't charge him, out of regard for his father, who is a most respectable person. Since then, I fancy, he takes his drink at home, and a very good thing too. As for this Mr Knott of yours, you'd better leave us to make a few inquiries.'

On the following morning Jimmy learnt the results of these inquiries. On the previous Friday there had only been six passengers by the seven-twenty train. Of these, not one of them in any way resembled the description of Knott. This, of course, was not conclusive, for, after such an interval, memories of the railway officials could not be relied upon implicitly.

The superintendent, whose name as Jimmy had learnt was Latham, was inclined to take a serious view of the matter.

'I don't like the look of things,' he said. 'Gavin Slater is capable of anything when he is drunk. He may be lame, but that doesn't prevent him getting about as much as he wants to. And, as you may have noticed, he's a pretty powerful sort of chap. The missing man, you say, had a large sum of money on him. I think we ought to make further inquiries as to what happened at Mr Slater's house on Thursday night.'

Jimmy thought so, too. He and the superintendent went to the house and were admitted by Lizzie. It was Jimmy who had suggested that they should first interview Winifred Slater, and Lizzie told them that she was in the drawing-room writing letters. She showed no surprise when they were announced.

'Oh, have you come again!' she asked petulantly. 'If you're inquiring for Mr Knott, I'm afraid that I can tell you nothing whatever about him. I only saw him for a moment on Thursday evening. I went out very soon after he came.'

'What time did you return?' the superintendent asked.

'Oh, soon after midnight,' she replied. 'Mr Knott had gone to bed by then.'

'Did you find anybody waiting up for you?'

Her lips curled disdainfully. 'Only my husband,' she replied. 'And he could hardly be described as waiting for me. He was fast asleep and snoring on the sofa in the studio.'

'You will forgive my reverting to an unpleasant subject, Mrs Slater. It is common knowledge that your husband occasionally indulges rather too freely in alcohol. Do you think it probable that he had done so on Thursday evening?'

She shrugged her shoulders. 'Since he was asleep it is difficult to say. But there was a broken tumbler on the floor and an empty decanter of whisky on a table close beside it. Anyway, I took the usual precautions.'

'And what were those, if I may ask, Mrs Slater?'

'Oh, I went up to our room and locked the door. I always do when Gavin's like that. A bed is kept made up for him in his dressing-room, and he can sleep it off there.'

'You heard or saw nothing more of your husband after you had gone upstairs?'

'Nothing whatever. I didn't see him again until he came down to breakfast next morning, looking very much the worse for wear.'

'Were you surprised when Mr Knott did not put in an appearance at breakfast?'

'Not particularly. Mr Knott's comings and goings are no affair of mine. He only comes down to see my father on business. But I remember that my father asked where he was and Gavin told him that he had gone by the early train. My father seemed to think this natural and said something about his having an appointment in London.'

'The housemaid drew your attention to the fact that the pillow case was missing from the bed in the room which Mr Knott had occupied?'

'Yes, she did. But I should hardly suspect Mr Knott of stealing the household linen. He probably took it away with him for some reason and will eventually send it back.'

'You saw that there was a patch of blood on the upper sheet?'

'Yes, but I didn't pay much attention to it. Mr Knott might have had an attack of nose-bleeding in the night.'

The superintendent and Jimmy left the room together. Lizzie had told them that Gavin was to be found in the studio. They went to seek him and found him extended on the sofa. A half-empty glass of whisky was beside him and his appearance suggested that after Jimmy's interview with him on the previous evening, he had imbibed with considerable freedom.

However, he sat up at the sound of their entrance and glared at them malevolently.

'Hallo, two of you this time!' he exclaimed. 'This damned house is getting overrun with inquisitive policemen. What is it now?'

'You and I have met before, Mr Slater,' said the superintendent warningly. 'We don't want any nonsense, understand that. You will kindly answer the questions which we shall put to you. To begin with, we want you to recall the events of last Thursday evening. Yesterday, you told Inspector Waghorn that you and Mr Knott spent the evening in this room alone. Do you still adhere to that statement?'

'What do you mean?' replied Gavin belligerently. 'Of course

we did, since the Governor had gone to bed and Winifred was out.'

'You talked together until about eleven o'clock, when Mr Knott went to bed? Is that correct?'

'Yes, that's right. I won't swear to the time exactly but I think it was soon after eleven.'

'You had a few drinks together before Mr Knott went to bed?'

'Yes, one or two. But Knott is always a slow drinker. I don't suppose he had more than a couple.'

'And you finished the decanter after he had gone upstairs?'

'I dare say. I don't see what it's got to do with you, anyhow. You can't stop a man drinking as much as he likes in his own house.'

The superintendent did not allow himself to be put out. 'The decanter was found empty in the morning, and one of the tumblers broken on the floor. I suggest that you drank more than was good for you that evening, Mr Slater.'

'Well, what else was there to do?' replied Gavin aggrievedly. 'I couldn't persuade Knott to sit up. He said he had to make an early start and wanted a good night's rest, first. And I thought I'd better sit up and wait for Winifred. Rotten for the girl to come home and find nobody about.'

'And did you greet Mrs Slater when she returned?' the superintendent asked.

'Well no, to tell the truth, I didn't. I began to feel sleepy and thought I'd just have a nap on this sofa before she came in. And when I woke up it was after four o'clock, the fire had gone out, and it was infernally cold.'

'What did you do then, Mr Slater?'

'Oh, just crawled upstairs. I didn't want to disturb Winifred, who I knew must have been in bed long ago. So I went into my dressing-room, lay down, and was very soon asleep. Since you make such a point of it, I don't mind confessing that I had a devilish thick head when I woke up again.'

'When was that?' asked the superintendent sharply.

'When they brought me a cup of tea. About eight o'clock, I suppose.'

'Now, Mr Slater, I want you to be very careful how you answer this question,' said the superintendent impressively. 'Did you see Mr Knott again after he had gone to bed about eleven o'clock?'

'No, of course I didn't,' replied Gavin indignantly. 'What should I want to go barging into his room for?'

'You are perfectly sure of that?' the superintendent persisted.

At this the limits of Gavin's patience seemed to be exhausted. He rose to his feet and stood there for a moment or two confronting them. 'Do you think I'm a liar?' he exclaimed wrathfully. 'If you do, you can get on without any more help from me. I'm not going to stay here to be bullied by any damned policeman.'

He limped to the door and banged it behind him. They heard his halting step pass through the hall and then another bang as the front door closed behind him. Jimmy glanced apprehensively at the superintendent, but the latter only chuckled.

'It's all right,' he said, divining Jimmy's thoughts. 'I've already told off one of my chaps to keep an eye on him. He won't go very far, don't you worry. No further than the nearest pub that will serve him. And, now that we've got this room to ourselves, it might pay us to have a look round.'

But before carrying out this suggestion, Superintendent Latham sat down on the sofa which Gavin had just vacated.

'Let's get our ideas in order, Inspector,' he said. 'We've both got at the back of our minds that Gavin Slater may have murdered this man Knott for the money he is said to have about him. He seems to have had plenty of opportunity and the money is the obvious motive. They may have quarrelled, of course. Gavin Slater, as you may have noticed, is a very easy person to quarrel with. Do you know of any other reason why he should have wanted to kill Knott?'

'I don't,' replied Jimmy. 'If he did kill him, it was very short-sighted policy on his part. Knott is, or was, his father's partner, and his death would very seriously upset the business which is, indirectly, Gavin Slater's sole support.'

'A drunken man wouldn't think of that,' the superintendent replied. 'That sum of money, £750, I think you said, would obscure the perception of everything else. I imagine him sitting here after Knott had gone to bed, drinking glass after glass of whisky, and thinking of the money. The first questions to ask ourselves are these. If he killed him, how and when did he do it? The blood on the sheet and the missing pillow case seem to stare us in the face, don't they?'

Jimmy, while listening, had been examining the room with more attention than he had yet devoted to it. He caught sight of an unfamiliar object hanging on the wall among the canvases. Upon closer examination, he found it to be a curved knife, apparently of Eastern origin, with a jewelled handle and enclosed in a sheath. There were several objects of various kinds hanging on the walls. They had probably been used at various times by Gavin as models for his artistry. But this, Jimmy noticed, was the only weapon among them.

He pointed it out to the superintendent. 'Do you think we ought to examine that, sir?' he asked.

The superintendent chuckled. 'Go ahead, Inspector, this is

your case, not mine,' he replied. 'I'm only here to give you countenance. Have a look at it by all means.'

Thus encouraged, Jimmy set to work. He took out his handkerchief, and, wrapping it round his fingers, unhooked the knife from the wall, holding it by the extreme tip of the sheath. He then laid it upon the nearest table. 'I wonder if you'd mind lending me your handkerchief, sir,' he asked.

'Scotland Yard performing its duties according to textbooks,' the superintendent replied. 'Yes, here you are.'

With two handkerchiefs, Jimmy was able to grasp the tip of the knife with the other. As he drew his hands apart, the knife came out of the sheath.

'I'd like you to have a look at this, sir,' said Jimmy in a tone of suppressed excitement.

The superintendent got up from the sofa and strolled across the room. In silence the two of them gazed at the blade of the knife. Nearly the whole of its surface was covered with a dark incrustation. The superintendent's face darkened.

'I don't altogether like the look of that,' he said significantly.

'It's suspiciously like blood,' Jimmy replied. He returned the knife to its sheath and then looked round the room. He caught sight of the half empty glass of whisky which still stood on the floor beside the sofa. This he picked up, still using the handkerchief, and poured its contents into a convenient flower-pot. Then he put it on the table beside the knife.

The superintendent nodded approvingly. 'Good dodge, that,' he said. 'The glass is pretty sure to show a good imprint of Gavin's fingers. If you find the same print on the hilt of the knife, things will look a bit ugly for him. You've done pretty well, so far, Inspector. But I shouldn't rest on your laurels yet. You may make further discoveries.'

Jimmy laughed. 'I'll try, sir,' he replied. He walked round

the studio examining carefully every inch of it. He stopped before an oak chest and raised the lid. It was full up to the brim of garments of various shapes and gaudy colours. Jimmy lifted them out one by one, examining them as he did so. They were all of exotic origin, and Jimmy recognised some of them from the figures in the canvases. He laid them in a pile on the floor until the chest was almost empty. And there, right at the bottom, he found a pair of striped silk pyjamas. He took out the lower half first and examined it. Upon it was sewn a tape embroidered with the name E. Knott.

Then he proceeded to examine the top half. He held it out by the sleeves for the superintendent's inspection. In the left breast, just above the pocket, was an incision about an inch long. And round this incision the silk was stained with blood.

Neither Jimmy nor the superintendent made any comment. The former put the pyjamas aside and piled the rest of the garments back into the chest. Then he continued his examination of the studio. But no further discovery rewarded him.

'You've found enough to be getting on with, I should think,' the superintendent remarked. 'If you like to take these exhibits up to the Yard, I'll keep an eye on things this end. Of course, the next thing to do is to search for the body. It's not in this room, that's pretty obvious. And I don't suppose it's lying about anywhere inside the house. But there's a pretty big garden outside. I think that's where we ought to start. I'll get a squad of men on to it straight away.'

'I'd like a word with Lizzie before I go back to the Yard,' Jimmy said. The superintendent nodded.

'Quite right,' he replied. 'If you ring that bell over there, she'll probably appear.'

Jimmy tried the experiment with success. Lizzie came in and looked inquiringly from one to the other. Jimmy picked up the lower half of the pyjamas. 'Do you recognise these by any chance, Lizzie?' he asked.

Lizzie's face brightened immediately. 'Oh yes, sir,' she replied. 'They're the pair I took out of Mr Knott's suitcase and laid on his bed the night he was here.'

'You're quite sure of that, Lizzie?'

'Oh yes, sir. You see they're silk and such a lovely colour I shouldn't be likely to forget them. Neither Mr Slater nor Mr Gavin wear silk pyjamas.'

'What sort of a suitcase did Mr Knott bring with him?'

'Quite a big one, sir. And it was one of that kind you can make bigger if you want to.'

'A Revelation, I expect. Quite a big one, you say. Can you give me any idea how big?'

Lizzie looked about her. 'About as big as the top of that table, sir,' she replied at length.

Jimmy took a tape-measure from his pocket and measured the table she pointed out. The top of it proved to be twenty-eight inches by eighteen. Quite a sizeable suitcase for a man to bring with him for only one night.

'Did you unpack this suitcase, Lizzie?' he asked.

'Yes, sir,' Lizzie replied. 'I unpacked it before Mr Knott went up to dress for dinner.'

'What did you find in it?'

'Nothing beyond what he wanted for the night, and his evening clothes, sir.'

'Did you call Mr Gavin on Friday morning?'

'Yes, sir, I took him up his cup of tea as usual at eight o'clock. But he wasn't in bed, sir. That is, he wasn't undressed.'

This sounded a more promising line of inquiry. 'Tell us exactly what you saw when you went into Mr Gavin's room,' Jimmy said.

Lizzie tittered. 'Well, sir, I saw that he'd had one of his bad evenings. He was lying on the bed with the eiderdown thrown over him. He'd taken off his coat and boots and hung them on the floor. I picked up the coat and put it on a chair, and took the boots down to be cleaned. And they were all wet, as if he'd been out in the rain.'

Superintendent Latham looked up sharply.

'There was no rain here on Thursday night,' he said. 'And the ground was quite dry.'

But Lizzie stuck to her point. 'Mr Gavin's boots were soaked through, sir,' she replied. 'And cook will tell you the same for I showed them to her.'

'Where are those boots now, Lizzie?' Jimmy asked.

'I put them back in Mr Gavin's room after I'd dried them, sir. I expect they're there now.'

'Run up and see, there's a good girl. And if you find them bring them down here.'

'I'd like to know how those boots got wet,' said the superintendent when Lizzie had departed on her errand. 'It was dry as a bone here all last week. She's an intelligent girl, is Lizzie. I expect there are plenty more questions you will like to ask her.'

Before Jimmy could reply Lizzie returned with the boots. They were an old, rather heavy pair, and as Jimmy took them from her he uttered an exclamation. 'Why, they're still damp.'

'I noticed that, sir,' Lizzie replied. 'I can't understand it, for they were quite dry when I put them up in Mr Gavin's room.'

'Has he used them since?'

'Not to my knowledge, sir. At least he hasn't put them out to be cleaned.'

'Sea-water, perhaps,' said the superintendent. 'The sea is

quite close to this house, you know. And if anything is soaked in sea water, it takes a long time to get the salt out of it. And while the salt is there it's bound to feel damp.'

'I expect that's it, sir,' said Jimmy. Then, turning to Lizzie, 'Mr Gavin had dressed for dinner on Thursday evening, I suppose?'

'Oh yes, sir. And he still had his evening clothes on except the coat when I called him.'

'Then he certainly wasn't wearing these boots. He would have been wearing a pair of light shoes. What became of them, Lizzie?'

'I don't know, sir. Now I come to think of it, I haven't seen them since that evening.'

'You were the first person about the house on Friday morning, Lizzie,' said Jimmy. 'You went into the hall, I expect. Did you notice if the front door was bolted on the inside?'

'I'm afraid I didn't, sir. But it never is. I did notice though that there were some wet patches leading from the front door to the foot of the stairs. I could see them on the polished floor.'

'What sort of patches, Lizzie?'

'Why, as if someone had walked across the hall in wet boots, sir. I got the mop and rubbed them off at once.'

Jimmy smiled. Lizzie's mind was that of a housemaid rather than that of a detective. Not that it made any difference. The marks would have disappeared by this time in any case. 'Did you come into this room at all?' he asked.

'Yes, sir. I came in here to dust round while the family were at breakfast. And there was a broken tumbler lying on the floor.'

'You cleared that away, of course,' said Jimmy. 'I think that's all we want to know for the present, thank you, Lizzie.'

She left the room and Jimmy turned to the superintendent. 'I'd like your opinion on this, sir,' he said.

The superintendent shook his head. 'Too early to give an opinion yet,' he replied. 'All I'm prepared to say at the present is that it seems unlikely that Knott left this house alive. I'll have a look round here and see what I can find. Meanwhile you'd better take those exhibits up to the Yard and get the experts' opinion upon them. You needn't be afraid of anything happening to Gavin Slater while you're gone. I'll make myself responsible for him.'

4

Jimmy reached Scotland Yard that afternoon. He had brought with him from Torquay a parcel containing the bloodstained sheet, the knife and sheath, the tumbler which Gavin Slater had used, and the pair of boots secured by Lizzie. These he handed over to the experts for examination. Then he sought out Hanslet and gave him a detailed account of his adventures.

Hanslet listened attentively, and when Jimmy had come to an end he gave him a nod of approval. 'You seem to have managed that business pretty well,' he said. 'What is your theory on the facts at present available?'

'I tried to reconstruct the affair as I came back on the train,' Jimmy replied. 'I'm inclined to accept as correct the statement of Mr Slater senior and of Lizzie. I'm not so sure of Mrs Slater, and I don't put the slightest reliance upon what Gavin Slater told us.

'According to Mr Slater, Knott arrived at the house on Thursday, shortly after I left it. He and Mr Slater had a conversation before dinner. In the course of that conversation it was revealed that Knott had in his pocket a sum of money amounting to £750 in notes. Mr Slater actually saw these notes. He and Knott were alone at the time. Knott had an important appointment in London at three o'clock on Friday afternoon. That is confirmed from other sources. I have found by looking at the timetable that if he left Torquay by the ten-thirty he would have arrived in London in time to keep that appointment. This was apparently his intention, since he said nothing to Mr Slater about leaving earlier.

'After dinner Mr Slater retired to bed early, as is his usual custom. He is an old man. His eyesight is very bad and, as I noticed in talking to him, he is slightly deaf. He would not be likely to hear or see anything unusual which might happen in the house after he went to bed. Mrs Slater states that she was out that evening and did not return till about midnight. Her statement in this respect can easily be verified.

'Mr Slater having retired, Knott and Gavin Slater went into the studio. For what happened after that we have only Gavin's statement. It is probably correct that they sat and talked and had a few drinks together. But I do not believe for a moment that Knott expressed his intention of leaving by the seven-twenty next morning. That, I feel pretty sure, is an invention of Gavin's to account for Knott having left the house before he was called by Lizzie.

'What happened in the studio on Thursday evening I can only conjecture. But I imagine that Knott made some reference to the money he was carrying about with him. What else may have passed between them I don't know. But eventually, I think, Knott went upstairs, leaving Gavin in possession of the studio. His wife states that she found him there extended on the sofa when she returned about midnight.

'But I don't think that on this occasion Gavin was as drunk as he pretended. I think he waited where he was until his wife was safely in bed. Then he prepared to act. He removed his shoes and then took down the knife from the wall. Having unsheathed it, he crept upstairs to Knott's room.

'Now, we have to remember the state of that room when Lizzie entered it next morning. She found a patch of blood on the upper sheet and the pillow-case missing. I found Knott's pyjamas subsequently in the chest in the studio. The gash in those pyjamas, and the blood on the upper sheet, suggest to me this. When Gavin entered the room, Knott was asleep and lying on his back. Gavin stabbed him with the knife he was carrying, in the region where he imagined the heart to be. Upon withdrawing the knife blood spurted from the wound. This accounts for the stain on the upper sheet and on the pyjamas. Gavin understood that he must prevent any further flow of blood. He took off the pyjamas and threw them aside. He then whipped off the pillow case, made a wad of it, and placed it over the wound so that it would absorb the blood. Then he searched the room until he found the envelope containing the money.'

Jimmy paused and looked inquiringly at Hanslet. 'Does that sound right so far?' he asked.

Hanslet nodded. 'It doesn't sound far wrong,' he replied. 'But at this point your friend Gavin is confronted by the murderer's bugbear. He had to dispose of the body. How did he manage to do that?'

'Superintendent Latham had an idea that he may have buried it in the garden,' Jimmy replied. 'I'm not sure that he's right. We have the wet boots and the wet marks in the hall, both found by Lizzie. These certainly suggest that Gavin went out some time during the night and got his feet wet.

But how? The weather was quite dry that night. Even though there was dew on the grass in the garden, that would not have made the boots as wet as all that. The only explanation I can think of is that Gavin went down to the sea and perhaps waded into it for a short distance.'

'Carrying the body with him?' remarked Hanslet incredulously.

'Carrying the body with him, but not in its original state. Knott had brought with him an unusually big suitcase. Gavin may have found that it exactly suited his purpose. I think he must have carried the body downstairs and out of the house. Here, in some secluded spot in the garden, he dismembered it, perhaps with the knife he had already used. And that was where the suitcase came in. He packed the parts of the body into it and carried them down to the sea. He may have made two or even more journeys. He threw the limbs and trunk into the water and finally the suitcase as well. Then he returned to the house to tidy up. And it was on this occasion that he made the marks in the hall noticed by Lizzie.

'He put the knife back where it came from. I'm not quite sure what he did with the clothes and other things brought by Knott. He may have thrown them into the sea with the body, or he may have burnt them in the studio fire. But the pyjamas, for some reason, he did not destroy. He put them at the bottom of the chest, perhaps thinking that they would never be found, or perhaps intending to dispose of them on some future occasion. He also destroyed his own evening shoes, for the reason, I suppose, that some blood had been spilt upon them. Like the nicotine on the crutches in the Bocarmé case, that Oldland was telling us about.'

Hanslet frowned. The Harleston case was still unsolved

and he did not care to be reminded of it. 'Never mind that,' he said sharply. 'Get on with your own story.'

'Gavin's next move was rather a clever one. Under the circumstances, he couldn't very well provide himself with an alibi. So he set to work to create the impression that he had got drunk and incapable that evening. He smashed the glass on the floor in the studio. He then went up to his own room and lay on his bed for Lizzie to find him in the morning. I fancy that the condition in which she did find him was not altogether unfamiliar to her. Later he invented the story of Knott's departure by the seven-twenty to account for his disappearance. This story was accepted without question. Gavin counted upon no inquiries being made until some days after the crime, and as it turned out he was correct.'

'Well, that's a very pretty theory,' said Hanslet. 'From what you tell me, it's probably correct. But you can't very well charge Gavin Slater with murder until you've found the body, or at least some part of it. The local people are looking after that, you say? But you can't stop with your hands folded while they're doing it. What steps do you propose to take?'

'Well, I'd like your advice upon that,' Jimmy replied. 'It seems to me that the first thing to do is to establish the motive. I'd like to make quite sure that Knott actually had that large sum of money with him. So far we only have Mr Slater's word for it. I don't doubt him in the least, but his sight is none too good, and what he took to be notes might have been something very different. It seems to me rather curious that Knott should have taken £750 down to Torquay only for the purpose of bringing it back again. I think I'll slip round now to Slater & Knott's office and make inquiries. I've just time to get there before they close.'

Hanslet agreed to this, and Jimmy made his way to

Chancery Lane. But Mr Grant, the chief clerk, could give him no information. 'It seems to me very unlikely that Mr Knott would have carried so much money in his pocket,' he said. 'Unless, of course, he meant to dispose of it in some way at Torquay.'

This suggested an idea to Jimmy. 'Mr Slater, I understand, shares in the profits of the business,' he said. 'How are these usually paid to him?'

'By cheque, twice a year in July and December,' Grant replied. 'Never, under any circumstances, in notes. I cannot imagine any reason why Mr Knott should convey money to his partner in that way. In fact, I think that you must be suffering under some misconception, Inspector.'

Jimmy asked for the name of Mr Knott's bank, but it was too late by now to make inquiries there that evening. He returned to Scotland Yard, not without misgivings. Hitherto he had had no doubts of Mr Slater. That old gentleman seemed to him the very personification of honesty. Now it seemed possible that he had fabricated the story of the £750. And, if that was the case, Jimmy's neat theory of motive vanished into thin air. On the other hand, what could Mr Slater have had to gain by making such a statement? The disappearance of Mr Knott promised to be just as puzzling as the death of his clerk, Victor Harleston.

Was there any connection between the two occurrences? This question had been at the back of Jimmy's mind ever since he had heard of Knott's disappearance. So far, there was absolutely nothing to show any such connection. But, after all, Knott had been Harleston's employer. Was it possible that they had shared some mysterious secret between them? And if so, had this secret been so menacing to the Slater family that they had determined upon a double murder? This was a line of speculation which afforded Jimmy food for thought for the remainder of the evening.

Next day he received the report of the experts upon the exhibits which he had submitted to them. The first object to be dealt with was the sheet. The report stated definitely that the stain upon it was caused by human blood, and was now some five or six days old. Further, the blood in question belonged to No. 1 of the four classes into which human blood has now been sub-divided.

In the case of the pyjamas, the report stated that the stain on these indicated human blood of class one, and was apparently of the same age as that on the sheet. The encrustation on the knife was also human blood of class one. The leather of the boots was impregnated with salt, suggesting that they had been soaked in sea-water.

Even more convincing in Jimmy's eyes was the final section of the report. This dealt with the further examination of the knife and of the glass. On the hilt of the knife it had been possible to develop very satisfactory impressions of the four fingers of a right hand. Impressions almost equally distinct had been found on the sheath. These latter were of the thumb and finger of a left hand. The report described the position of these marks and proceeded to draw conclusions. 'The relative positions of the prints found on the knife and sheath are distinctly suggestive. The impressions of the right-hand fingers on the hilt of the knife are in a line parallel to the axis of the blade, with that of the first finger nearest the end of the hilt. The impression of the thumb is not visible, though on the opposite side of the hilt to the finger impressions are those of part of a palm. This would suggest that the hilt was grasped in the right hand with the thumb overlapping the fingers. This would be the natural way in which to hold a knife with which it was intended to deliver a stab. The impressions of the left hand on the sheath are not so distinct. This would suggest that the sheath had not been grasped so firmly as the hilt. The position of the prints on the sheath suggest that this was held in the left hand while the knife was either withdrawn from it or thrust into it with the right.'

The tumbler submitted for examination had also given favourable results. 'Here again have been found the prints of the four fingers and thumb of a right hand. Upon comparing these prints with those upon the hilt of the knife, we have no hesitation in reporting that they were made by the same individual hand.'

Good enough, Jimmy thought. The various items in this report bore out his theory in every respect. There could now be very little doubt that Gavin Slater had murdered the unfortunate Knott. But it would be a nuisance if Superintendent Latham and his men failed to discover some essential part of the body. Jimmy, who in his spare time had taken to perusing works on criminology, was well aware of the danger of taking proceedings for murder in the absence of the corpse. He was familiar with the notorious Campden case, in which a mother and her two sons were hanged for the murder of a gentleman who turned up bright and smiling some years later.

Having read the report, Jimmy went to the bank of which he had been informed that Mr Knott was a customer, and interviewed the manager. The latter, upon the production of Jimmy's credentials, agreed to answer his questions to the best of his ability. It transpired that Mr Knott had visited the bank on the previous Thursday morning. He had then asked to be informed of the amount of the balance standing to his personal account. Upon being told that this was in the neighbourhood of £800, he had written a cheque for £750, stating that he had a payment to make of this amount on the following day. When he was asked how he would like the money to be paid, he replied that he would like it in notes of £20 or less. The cheque was therefore paid with thirty-five £20 notes, three £10 notes and four £5 notes.

Jimmy, as a matter of routine, took the numbers of these notes. He then made a few tactful inquiries about Mr Knott's account. He learned that it was Mr Knott's habit to allow it to accumulate until it reached a considerable amount. He would then purchase securities approximately to the extent of this amount. These purchases had sometimes been made by cheque, but on several previous occasions he had drawn comparatively large sums in notes. The transaction of the previous Thursday was therefore, not unprecedented.

Jimmy went back to Scotland Yard to digest this information. So far as the money was concerned, Mr Slater's statement was fully substantiated. Where was that money now? That was the question. He rang up the police at Torquay, gave them the numbers of the notes, and suggested that they should make inquiries at the local banks. He learnt, in return, that nothing further had been discovered having any bearing on the crime.

The next step was to explore Mr Knott's rooms in Crozier Court. Jimmy obtained the necessary authority and, armed with this, went to the Temple. He had very little difficulty in effecting an entry, as he found that the porter possessed a duplicate key.

Mr Knott's rooms were most comfortably furnished. They contained everything which might be expected in a bachelor's quarters, and in addition a varied collection of books, suggesting that Mr Knott was a reader of catholic tastes. The appearance of the room suggested that their occupant had intended to leave them for no more than a few hours. A morning newspaper, bearing the date of the previous Thursday, was lying open on a table. Beside it was a memorandum pad on which was scribbled a note in pencil. This read: 'Ring up for car to meet train at Paddington Friday.'

A very thorough exploration of the room revealed nothing unexpected. A small cash box caught Jimmy's eye, and some further search revealed the key to fit it. But upon opening the box, he found it empty, except for a cheque book in which only the counterfoils remained. Finally, Jimmy satisfied himself that there was no money concealed about the place. Unless Mr Knott had handed over the money to some other person before he left London, he must have taken it with him to Torquay.

As he returned the key to the porter, the note on the memorandum pad recurred to his memory. 'Do you happen to know if Mr Knott owned a car?' he asked.

'Yes, he's had a car for the last few years,' was the reply. 'He keeps it in a garage in Norfolk Street.'

Jimmy sought out this garage and renewed his inquiries there. He learnt that Mr Knott owned a car which he used mainly at weekends. Sometimes, however, he would take it out in the course of the week. 'Last Thursday for instance, he rang us up,' said Jimmy's informant. 'He asked us to take the car round to Paddington Station and to meet him there at quarter past two on Friday.'

'Did you do this?' Jimmy asked.

'Oh yes, we sent the car round all right. But Mr Knott didn't turn up. The man waited for an hour or more then brought the car back here. And we haven't seen or heard anything of Mr Knott since.'

As Jimmy went back to Scotland Yard, he congratulated himself that everything was running smoothly. The statement which he had obtained at the garage was particularly instructive. The ten-thirty from Torquay arrived at Paddington at two-fifteen. It was perfectly clear that at the time Knott left London he had intended to return by that train. It seemed unlikely that anything should have occurred while he was at Torquay to make him change his mind. His decision to return by the seven-twenty was, therefore, a fabrication of Gavin Slater's. His reason for making this false statement was only too obvious.

Jimmy, during his course at Hendon, had been taught that method plays a very important part in successful detection. He had learnt a certain doggerel rhyme which now recurred to his memory.

'What was the crime? Who did it?
When was it done? And where?
How done? And with what motive?
Who in the deed did share?'

Not very inspiring poetry, perhaps. But, all the same, of considerable assistance to the methodical detective. He proceeded to apply it to the present case.

What was the crime? Presumably the murder of Mr Knott. Presumably, because the most convincing proof of murder was up to the present missing. That proof would be the whole or part of Mr Knott's dead body. But murder seemed to be the only possible theory to account for Mr Knott's disappearance. That his disappearance was not of his own volition, was proved from several separate sources. He had intended to return to London in time for his appointment at three o'clock on Friday afternoon. It was by now certain that he could not have been overtaken by any accident or sickness. Forcible detention seemed out of the question. Murder alone could account for his continued absence.

Who did it? There could be only one answer to this question. Gavin Slater. The fingerprints on the hilt of the knife were in themselves almost sufficient testimony. But even if they had not been found the gravest suspicion must have fallen upon him. Though it was conceivable that one of the other occupants of the house might have delivered the blow, none of them had the physical strength to remove the body.

When was it done? Between midnight and seven o'clock on Friday morning. That is, if Mrs Slater's statement was to be relied upon. Her husband would hardly have ventured to act before her return, in case she should interrupt his proceedings. In any case, it had been done after Mr Knott had gone to bed, for he was wearing his pyjamas when the blow was inflicted.

Where? In the room occupied by Mr Knott at his partner's house. There was no question about that. The blood on the sheet was sufficient evidence.

How done? With the knife found in the studio. The blood on this, on the sheet, and on the pyjamas, all belonged to the same class. This, though not conclusive proof, was extremely suggestive. Jimmy had already ascertained that the slit in the pyjamas was the same length as the width of the blade of the knife.

With what motive? To secure the £750 which Mr Knott had with him. This seemed the only reasonable motive. The alternative was that Gavin Slater, notoriously aggressive when in liquor, had fastened some drunken quarrel upon Knott. But in that case surely he would have attacked him at once, downstairs in the studio. He would not have waited until he had gone upstairs and undressed. Unless, upon taking more drink after Mr Knott's departure, his grievance had become magnified. He might then, after brooding upon it, have gone up with the knife in his hand. But, on the whole, the motive of robbery seemed the more tangible.

Who in the deed did share? This point did not appear to Jimmy quite so easy to answer as the rest. The murder might have been the work of Gavin Slater alone. No trace of the complicity of anyone else had yet been found. It seemed incredible that his father should connive at the murder of his partner. To Mr Slater, it would appear like killing the goose that laid the golden eggs. But Jimmy was not so sure of Winifred Slater. She had not made by any means a favourable impression upon him. She might have assisted her husband in carrying out the deed. There was at present no proof or even suggestion of this. But Jimmy determined to keep the possibility in mind.

With Hanslet's consent, Jimmy returned to Torquay that evening. As soon as he arrived there he went to see Superintendent Latham. He showed him the expert's report and told him of the results of his own further investigations. Then he ventured to put the question upon which everything depended. 'Have you had any luck with the body, sir?' he asked.

The superintendent shook his head. 'Not up to the present,' he replied. 'We have searched the garden very thoroughly. The body has not been buried there, of that I am pretty certain. But there are several places where it might have been cut up and where a bucket or two of water would have washed all the stains away. My own idea from the first was that the body had been thrown, either whole or dissected, into the sea. The fact that Gavin Slater's boots were soaked with sea-water seems to support that. Now from the end of the road in which Mr Slater's house stands, a path leads down to the rocks. I'll show you the place in daylight tomorrow. That seems to me the most likely route to be taken by anybody in the house who wished to throw something into the sea. So I have concentrated on that particular point, and my men are making inquiries for anybody who might have passed that way during Thursday night or early Friday morning.

'I've also been talking to an intelligent fisherman, who sometimes puts down lobster-pots off those rocks. He tells me that between two and six on Friday morning there would have been a very strong tide running at the spot. Anything thrown from the shore between those hours would be swept out to sea. Before or after then, however, the tide would be setting inshore, and anything that did not sink fairly soon would probably be cast up somewhere on the shores of the bay. I'm having inquiries made all along the coast and it's just possible we may hear of something.

'So much for the body. But I've got a very definite piece of news for you from another direction. As soon as I got the numbers of those notes I sent them round to the banks. Not very long ago I had a message from the manager of one of them. A five-pound note bearing one of the numbers had been paid in to his branch on Saturday morning by the landlord of the Rose and Crown. The Rose and Crown is quite a small pub at the opposite end of the town to Mr Slater's house.

'The bank manager informed me that it is the landlord's custom to bring his takings to the bank every Saturday morning. Last Saturday there was only one five-pound note among his money, so he will probably remember who he took it from. Would you like to go and see him? My car's outside, and I can run you to the Rose and Crown in a few minutes.'

Jimmy jumped at the offer, and they set out. The landlord of the Rose and Crown seemed somewhat perturbed at the sight of the superintendent, but upon being assured that his visit had nothing to do with any breach of the licensing laws, he regained his usual complacency. The superintendent introduced Jimmy to him. And Jimmy got to work without delay.

'You paid a five-pound note into the bank last Saturday morning, I believe?' he asked.

'Yes, I did,' the landlord replied. And then, in some concern, he added, 'there wasn't anything wrong with it, was there?'

'No, the note was right enough,' Jimmy said. 'We've been wondering where you got it from, that's all.'

'It won't take long to tell you that. There aren't many of my customers that carry five-pound notes about them. It was Mr Slater. You know him, I expect, Superintendent, by his limp. He often comes in here of an evening for a drink.'

'You know him quite well by sight then?' Jimmy asked.

The landlord smiled. 'Well enough to be able to swear to him, sir,' he replied. 'I dare say it would be no secret to the Superintendent that Mr Slater's apt to be a nuisance. There's been times when he's come here that I've had to refuse to serve him. But he was all right when he gave me that note, and I thought he seemed quieter than usual.'

'When did he give you the note?' Jimmy asked.

'Last Friday evening. I know that, for it was the evening before I went to the bank. If it hadn't have been I mightn't have had the change in the house. Mr Slater came in by himself at about half-past six and ordered his drink. A double-whisky and splash as usual. And when he put his hand in his trousers pocket he found he hadn't enough to pay for it. So he took out a note case, and there was a five-pound note in that. "Sorry, but this is all I've got," he said. I said I could change it for him and that's how it happened.'

Jimmy and the superintendent left the Rose and Crown. The latter looked at his watch. 'Half-past nine,' he said. 'The Slater family will have finished their dinner. What about it?'

'Yes, I think we'd better pay Gavin Slater a visit, sir,' Jimmy replied. 'We needn't say anything of our suspicions. I should just like to ask him casually where he got that note.'

They drove to the house and were admitted by Lizzie. Mr Slater senior had gone to bed and Gavin and his wife were in the studio. 'You needn't trouble to announce us, Lizzie,' said the superintendent. 'We know our way, and we'll go through.'

They opened the door of the studio to find Gavin at work on a canvas and his wife sitting on the sofa reading a magazine. Gavin turned round, stared at them angrily for a moment and then flung his brush and palette upon the floor.

'Damnation!' he exclaimed. 'I thought I made it clear yesterday that I'm sick of the sight of you infernal policemen. What is it now?'

'Only a question which can be answered very briefly, Mr Slater,' Jimmy replied.

'Well, out with it,' Gavin growled. 'And then perhaps you'll clear out for good and leave us in peace.'

'Did you change a five-pound note at the Rose and Crown last Friday evening, Mr Slater?'

'I changed one there one day last week, but I won't swear that it was Friday. It's not an offence to change a five-pound note, is it?'

Jimmy disregarded this question. 'Can you tell us how you acquired that five-pound note?' he asked.

'Yes, I can. On the evening that Knott was here he and I sat together for a bit after dinner, as I've already told you. He told me that he would have to go back to London by seven-twenty in the morning. Then he took out his wallet and looked inside it. He found that the smallest change he had was a five-pound note, and said that might be a nuisance on the train. He asked me if I could change one for him, and I told him that I could. So he took an envelope from his pocket and drew a lot of notes from it. I don't know how many there were, for I didn't take the trouble to count them. From this lot he took a five-pound note and gave it to me. I gave him four pound notes and two ten-shilling notes in return. And that's how I came by the note, if it's any satisfaction to you.'

'Thank you, Mr Slater,' said Jimmy gravely. And without further ceremony, he and the superintendent left the house.

'So Master Gavin knew that Knott had that money on him,' the superintendent remarked significantly as they re-entered the car.

'Yes, and he was shrewd enough not to attempt to lie about it a second time,' Jimmy replied. 'But I don't suppose his story of Knott having asked him to change the note is true. He invented it to account for his possession of the note. It hadn't occurred to him that the numbers might be traced. He won't attempt to change any more of them, that's pretty certain.'

'He won't get the chance if we have any luck with the body,' said the superintendent. 'I'm sorry for his poor old father, though. It'll be a terrible blow to him.'

They reached the police station to find an excited sergeant

awaiting them. 'I've got a chap here that says he saw Mr Gavin Slater early on Friday morning, sir,' he said, addressing the superintendent.

'Good!' exclaimed the latter. 'Who is the man?'

'He's a chap from the gas-works, sir. I knew that some of their men had to be at work by six, so I went along there and made inquiries. And I found this man, who always passes along the end of the road where Mr Slater lives about a quarter to six. You'll like to hear him for yourself, sir. He's waiting here now.'

The superintendent nodded approvingly. 'Yes, I'd like to hear him,' he replied. 'Send him along to my room.'

A few minutes later the man appeared, escorted by the sergeant. He gave his name and address and then told his story. He remembered starting from home as usual at twenty minutes to six on Friday morning. He could distinguish Friday from the other days of the week since it was pay day. He reached the end of the road in question about a quarter to six. It was then dark, but not absolutely so, as the morning was clear and there was a moon. As he approached the end of the road, a man crossed in front of him. The distance between them was not more than a few yards. The man was thick-set and walked with a decided limp. He was carrying some large object in his right hand. He could not swear that the object was a suitcase, but it was a bag of some kind. From the manner in which the man was carrying it, it appeared to be very heavy. The man increased his pace when he saw that he was observed, and disappeared along the path leading towards the sea. It was too dark for him to see the man's face, but the limp was very noticeable.

The superintendent put a few questions, then dismissed the man. He turned to Jimmy. 'If the man with the suitcase was Gavin, as in all probability it was, the time he was seen becomes of importance. He was, no doubt, carrying the remains of Mr Knott with the intention of throwing them into the sea. He could have done so two or three minutes after he was seen. That means he disposed of them before six o'clock. The tide then would carry them out to sea. The chances of their being picked up are infinitesimal, I'm afraid. And we can't very well drag the whole English Channel on the chance of coming across them. Well, we've done enough for tonight, I think. If you like to come round in the morning I'll take you along that path and show you the rocks.'

Jimmy went to bed that night feeling that the case against Gavin Slater was conclusive. It would be for his superiors to decide upon the next step. Probably they would decide to wait for a little, in the faint hope that some part of the body would be discovered. Even if it were not, there was surely sufficient evidence to justify Gavin Slater's arrest?

Next morning Jimmy and the superintendent walked along the path which led to the rocks. At this time of the year it was unfrequented, and they had the place to themselves. The path ran for two or three hundred yards between fences and was not overlooked. It descended by an easy slope to the rocky shore. There was no beach here, but only a series of more or less flat rocks mostly covered with seaweed. The tide, the superintendent pointed out, came up nearly to the foot of the path.

'You see how it is,' he said. 'Anybody who didn't mind getting their feet wet could walk over the rocks until they came to the edge of them, and then throw anything into comparatively deep water. And that I'll be bound is what Gavin Slater did.'

It was obviously useless to look for traces so long after the event. The tide would have washed everything away long ago. They returned to the police station, where they found a further piece of information awaiting them.

This time it was a young constable who had a story to tell. He had been sent to interview a pawnbroker in the town with regard to some goods which were believed to have been stolen. He had inspected the pawnbroker's stock and had noticed an exceptionally large expanding suitcase. He had made inquiries about this, and had been told that it had been pledged on the previous Monday morning with some other goods. Thinking it better not to pursue the matter further, he had left the shop and reported to the sergeant on duty.

'Excellent,' said the superintendent. 'I should like to see that suitcase for myself. I know the shop well enough. Shall we go along there now, Inspector?'

It seemed to Jimmy a forlorn hope. How Mr Knott's suitcase could have found its way to a pawnbroker's seemed difficult to imagine. However, he agreed to the superintendent's suggestion and they set off.

The pawnbroker greeted the superintendent with some suspicion. The matter of the stolen articles was causing him some annoyance. He had had a constable poking about that morning, and now here was the superintendent himself. He seemed distinctly relieved when the superintendent began to question him about a suitcase.

'You had a suitcase brought in here last Monday, I understand,' he said. 'I'm rather interested in suitcases just now, and I'd like to have a look at it, if you don't mind.'

The pawnbroker reached up to one of his shelves and lifted down the object in question. He put it on the counter. It was made of compressed fibre and looked rather the worse for wear. But it was undoubtedly an expanding suitcase, and upon the lid of it were stamped the initials 'E. K.'

Jimmy produced a steel measuring tape and measured the lid of the case. He found it to be twenty-seven inches by seventeen. And this corresponded pretty closely with Lizzie's guess.

The suitcase was empty and was lined with some white material. Traces of mould were visible on this and Jimmy found that it was distinctly damp to the touch. But what struck him most was that there were several dark stains upon the interior. It was impossible to tell in the present state of the case what had caused these stains.

'Was this case empty when it was brought to you?' the superintendent asked.

'No, sir,' the pawnbroker replied. 'There were some clothes and things in it. The lady who brought it said—'

'Never mind what the lady said. Bring along the other things and let's have a look at them.'

The pawnbroker disappeared into the back of his shop, to return a few moments later with a miscellaneous collection, which he laid out for the superintendent's inspection.

Jimmy passed them rapidly in review. A dinner jacket, waistcoat and a pair of black evening trousers. A white shirt, very limp indeed, and a collar, also very limp. A small leather box containing a black evening tie, some studs and links. A pair of patent leather shoes from which the shine had almost entirely disappeared. A safety razor in case which Jimmy recognised as a Novoshave. A sponge bag containing a shaving brush, a stick of shaving soap, a tooth brush, a tube of tooth paste and a nail brush. A pair of silver-backed hair brushes, bearing the initials 'E. K.' A small clothes brush. A silver cigarette case. A bunch of keys. A pair of black silk socks.

As the pawnbroker laid these things out, he fingered them suspiciously.

171

'I can't make it out, sir,' he said. 'These things were perfectly dry when I put them away, and now they seem all damp.'

'Yes, they're damp enough,' the superintendent replied, exchanging a significant glance with Jimmy. 'Now, then, what was the name of the lady who brought them to you?'

'It was Mrs Puddlecombe, of three Hunter's Rents. I've done business with her before, and I've always found her a most respectable woman. I asked her where she got the things, and she said that a gentleman who knew her husband . . .'

'That'll do,' the superintendent interrupted curtly. 'We'll hear for ourselves what Mrs Puddlecombe has got to say about it.' He bundled the various articles into the suitcase, which he shut and fastened. Then he carried it out to the car, Jimmy following him.

A short drive took them to Hunter's Rents, a row of dilapidated cottages in a mean street. The superintendent hammered on the door of number three, and after an interval a blowzy-looking woman appeared, and stared at her visitors with a hostile expression. 'Well, and what might you be wanting?' she asked.

'We are the police, and we want a word with you, Mrs Puddlecombe,' the superintendent replied.

'I'm sure I don't know what you can want with me,' she exclaimed defiantly. 'I ain't done nuffing wrong that I knows of.'

'Nobody's suggesting that you have,' replied the superintendent sternly. He opened the door of the car and produced the suitcase. 'Have you ever seen this before?' he asked.

The woman appeared suddenly confused. 'Why, it's just like one my husband brought home on Friday evening,' she exclaimed ingenuously.

The superintendent nodded. 'All right,' he said. 'Now let's

go into the house. I don't want the neighbours to hear all we've got to talk about.'

Rather reluctantly she led them indoors. The house was untidy and not particularly clean. She ran her apron over a couple of chairs in the front room as an indication to her visitors to sit down.

'Now then, Mrs Puddlecombe,' said the superintendent briskly. 'On Monday morning you pawned a suitcase containing some clothes and other things. Where did you get it from?'

'I came by it honest enough, if that's what you mean,' replied Mrs Puddlecombe indignantly. 'My husband's a casual labourer. Takes jobs here and there as he can get them. And the things was given him by a gentleman for whom 'e'd been doing a bit of gardening.'

The superintendent shook his head. 'It's no good talking to me like that,' he said. 'I know perfectly well where the suitcase and its contents came from. What I want to know is how they came into your hands, and I'll trouble you to tell me the truth. If you don't you may get yourself and your husband into serious trouble.'

This seemed to take the wind out of Mrs Puddlecombe's sails. She had apparently never imagined that her statement might be doubted. But she made one more attempt at evasion.

'My husband didn't steal them, if that's what you're thinking,' she said.

'I'm not suggesting that he did,' the superintendent replied patiently. 'I want to know where he found them, that's all.'

She shrugged her shoulders as though to disclaim responsibility. 'I told Bert he'd better keep the things, in case there was a reward offered. You won't do anything to him if I tell you, will you, sir?'

'Not if you tell us the truth,' the superintendent replied.

This reassured her. 'Well then, sir, it was like this, you see,' she said. 'My 'usband's got a job over at Paignton. 'E goes over there on 'is bike every morning and comes 'ome at night. The road runs along by the beach, and as he was coming 'ome on Friday he noticed something at the edge of the water. 'E got off 'is bike and went down to 'ave a look and found that blessed suitcase with a lot of things inside it. 'E emptied the water out of it, put it on 'is bike and brought it 'ome. As soon as I set eyes on it I saw it was no good until we had got it dry. So we put the suitcase and all the things in front of the kitchen fire. They weren't properly dry till Monday morning and then Bert said that as they were no good to us, I'd better take them along to the pawnbroker's and get what I could on them.'

'You know very well that you ought to have taken them to the police,' replied the superintendent sternly. 'However, we'll say no more about it this time.'

He and Jimmy drove back to the police station. There they examined the suitcase and its contents in detail. Jimmy's attention was concentrated upon the stains on the lining of the former. He pointed these out to the superintendent.

'We shall have to get the experts to say whether that's blood or not, sir,' he said. 'If it is, I think that we can account for the disposal of the body.'

'I have hopes, since this lot has been found, that parts of the body may be washed ashore as well,' the superintendent replied.

Jimmy hesitated. It was never good policy to disagree with one's superiors. But Superintendent Latham was an essentially reasonable man and it was not likely that he would resent a suggestion.

'I'm not so sure about that, sir,' said Jimmy. 'This is what I imagine must have happened. Gavin Slater cut up the body and carried it to that place we were at just now, using the suitcase for the purpose. He may have found it necessary to make two or even several journeys. When he had disposed of the body he packed Mr Knott's clothes into the suitcase and made a final journey to throw suitcase and all into the sea. He was seen upon one of his journeys about a quarter to six. If that was his last journey with the remains of the body, all these would have been thrown into the sea before six o'clock. In that case, they would have been carried by the tide away from shore. But it must have been after six when he threw in the suitcase, and that accounts for it having been washed ashore.'

'Very likely you're right,' said the superintendent. 'But in any case I shan't abandon hope. Now, I expect you want to get back to the Yard and show that suitcase to the experts. If anything else turns up, I'll let you know at once.'

5

'I shall be very glad to hear anything that Inspector Waghorn may care to tell me,' said Dr Priestley genially.

Hanslet and Jimmy were sitting in Dr Priestley's study on the evening of the day after the discovery of the suitcase. It had been Hanslet's suggestion that they should call upon the Professor. 'I'd like to hear his views upon an arrest for murder in the absence of the body,' he said. 'I'll ring him up and tell him that you've got a queer case on hand. He'll let us go round unless he's busy with one of his scientific puzzles. Why he spends so much time on what nobody but himself can understand, is more than I've ever been able to make out. It keeps his mind occupied, I suppose.'

Dr Priestley had agreed to receive them, and they went to Westbourne Terrace at the usual hour—nine o'clock.

'Here we are, Professor,' Hanslet had said. 'I think you'll be interested if you listen to this queer story that Jimmy has managed to unearth.'

Encouraged by Dr Priestley's favourable reply, Jimmy launched into an account of Mr Knott. He told the story exactly as it had developed under his own eyes, being careful to omit no essential detail. Once more he noticed that, at a sign from Dr Priestley, Harold Merefield took notes as he proceeded.

Dr Priestley listened with his usual inscrutable expression. 'A very curious chain of circumstances,' he said when Jimmy had come to the end of his story. 'Curious in more ways than one. I gather from your remarks, Inspector, that you have no doubt that Gavin Slater was the murderer of Mr Knott?'

'There doesn't seem to be much room for doubt, sir,' replied Jimmy guardedly.

'No, perhaps not,' said Dr Priestley mildly. 'You assume that the motive for the murder was robbery?'

'It looks very like it, sir. We know that one of the notes issued to Mr Knott was changed by Gavin Slater. The remaining notes have not been found, but no doubt Slater has secreted them in some secure place.'

'One of the remarkable factors of the case concerns what has and has not been found,' Dr Priestley replied. 'However, we may put that aside for a moment. What connection do you imagine to exist between the disappearance of Mr Knott and the murder of Victor Harleston?'

'That's just what's been puzzling me, sir. It is a very

remarkable thing that a clerk and his principal should be murdered within three or four days of one another.'

'It is indeed remarkable. But it becomes still more remarkable if you attribute the motive of robbery to the murder of Mr Knott. Have you any reason to suppose that any member of the Slater household knew in advance that Mr Knott would have a large sum of money in his possession during his visit to Torquay?'

'I don't very well see how they could have known, sir,' Jimmy replied.

'Then this second murder must have been entirely unpremeditated. Gavin Slater must have become aware of his visitor's possession of the money after his arrival at Torquay. He thereupon acted immediately, or as soon as he considered it safe to do so. How can you connect these circumstances with the murder of Victor Harleston?'

As usual Dr Priestley had laid his finger upon the weakest link in the chain. Jimmy began searching for a suitable reply, but Dr Priestley continued without waiting for it.

'If you maintain that Mr Knott was killed in order that his murderer might secure his money, you are immediately faced with a remarkable coincidence. I do not propose to discuss coincidence now. Your experience, Inspector, must already be sufficient to have taught you that coincidence plays a very large part in crime and its detection. But in this particular instance the appearances are so improbable that I am loath to credit them.

'Let us express this coincidence as simply as possible. On Monday the 21st, Victor Harleston, a clerk in the employ of Messrs. Slater & Knott, was murdered. You will permit me to remark that the motive for that murder is not yet definitely established, will you not, Superintendent?'

'It depends what you mean by "established," Professor,' Hanslet replied. 'I'm not yet in a position to prove that Philip Harleston murdered his half-brother in order that his sister might inherit his money, but I don't think that an intelligent jury would have any doubts upon the matter.'

'Even the verdict of an intelligent jury does not establish logical proof,' Dr Priestley replied. 'You are at liberty to adhere to your theory of motive. It only makes the coincidence more glaring. On Thursday, the 24th, Victor Harleston's principal, Mr Knott, goes to stay with his partner at Torquay. During the course of his visit, he is murdered by his partner's son, for the sake of the money which he has with him. His death, then, has no connection, however remote, with that of Victor Harleston's. It is really most remarkable that two men so closely connected for many years should be murdered within such a short period for totally different motives.'

'Well, what's the answer, Professor?' asked Hanslet expectantly.

'That is for you to discover,' replied Dr Priestley tartly. 'If I may offer a suggestion, it is this. That you should in both cases revise your opinion as to the motive.'

'And how do you propose that we should set about doing that?' Hanslet asked.

'By seeking fresh facts in both cases and trying to interpret those facts in their true light. It may assist you to understand my meaning if you will allow me to put a few questions which seem to be pertinent. In the first place, Inspector, how did Mr Knott reach his partner's house on Thursday evening? Did he walk from the station, for instance?'

'I didn't inquire, sir,' replied Jimmy incautiously. 'It didn't seem to matter, since his presence in the house was definitely established.'

'As you gain experience in criminal investigation, you will learn that every detail matters,' Dr Priestley replied. 'Now, that question brings me back indirectly to a remark I made just now. The contrast between what has been found in this case and what has not. We will suppose, since Mr Knott was carrying a large suitcase, that he took a taxi from the station to his partner's house. The taxi-driver might possibly remember how his fare was dressed. But we may assume, I think, that he was wearing an overcoat of some kind and almost certainly a hat. Where are these?'

Up till now, Jimmy had felt thoroughly satisfied with his conduct of the case. He had kept an eye upon all the essentials, and only the discovery of the body was wanting to complete his theory. But suddenly he felt that he had acted like the most inexperienced beginner. His only consolation was that Superintendent Latham had also overlooked the point.

'I don't know, sir,' he replied rather shamefacedly.

'Because it did not occur to you to inquire about them. You were so concerned with what you did actually find that you neglected to consider what you had not found. Yet negative results are frequently as important as positive results.

'Let us examine the negative results in this case a little more closely. They may help to elucidate the very puzzling question of motive. You assume, I suppose, that Gavin Slater packed the suitcase with Mr Knott's personal belongings, and disposed of these in order to create the impression that he had left Torquay by the seven-twenty train?'

'Yes, sir. When the household found that Mr Knott had gone with his baggage they would have no suspicion.'

Dr Priestley smiled gently. Jimmy had fallen into his trap. 'Have you any reason to suppose that Mr Knott travelled to Torquay in a dinner jacket?' he asked.

It took Jimmy some seconds to realise the implication of this remark. 'What a fool I am!' he exclaimed at last. 'I never thought of that.'

'It is not always easy for the imagination to recall articles which should be present and are not,' said Dr Priestley. 'The housemaid stated, I understand, that Mr Knott dressed for dinner on Thursday evening. That expression implies that he took off the suit of clothes that he was wearing when he arrived and put on evening dress. Where is the suit in which Mr Knott arrived? Where are his underclothes? Where are the shoes he wore during the daytime? They were not apparently packed by the murderer in the suitcase. Yet why should he have omitted these items?'

'I had an idea, sir, that Gavin Slater might have burnt Mr Knott's clothes in the studio fire. There is a big stove there, very suitable for the purpose.'

'He may have done so. Yet why should he have burnt some of Mr Knott's possessions and thrown the rest into the sea? He appears in more than one instance to have employed a curious process of selection.'

Hanslet thought it time to come to the rescue of his subordinate. 'I think I can account for the points you've just raised, Professor,' he said. 'My idea is this: This man Slater packed everything he could find into the suitcase. The suit which Knott wore during the day, his underclothes, his overcoat and his hat. He then carried the lot down to the sea and chucked it in. It is cast up on the beach, where it is found by the inquisitive Puddlecombe.

'This honest labourer takes the suitcase home and examines its contents. Some of these he can find a use for, others he cannot. A dinner jacket and a pair of evening trousers, for instance, could be of no possible use to him. But the suit, the overcoat, the hat and the underclothes, all these would come in admirably for Sunday best. So he puts them aside and sends his wife to the pawnbrokers with the rest. That sounds pretty reasonable, doesn't it?'

'Reasonable enough,' Dr Priestley replied. 'I would point out, however, that a rather more thorough investigation on the spot would have cleared up this point. But, in any case, evidence of the process of selection to which I have referred still remains. The pillow case was taken from the room occupied by Mr Knott, and yet the bloodstained sheet was left. Mr Knott's clothing was disposed of in one way or another, either by burning or by being thrown into the sea. And yet his pyjamas, gashed apparently by the knife stroke which killed him, were retained and hidden at the bottom of a chest. These preferences seem to me most remarkable. Have you formed any theory to account for them?'

'I haven't sir,' replied Jimmy uneasily. 'As regards the pyjamas I can only suppose that Gavin Slater preferred to hide them where he thought nobody would ever find them, than to take any risks in the disposing of them.'

'Very little risk would be involved in burning them,' Dr Priestley replied. 'I maintain the facts that are at present ascertained are incapable of the explanation which you have put upon them. But since the investigation is by no means concluded, no doubt fresh facts will be brought to light. You mentioned, I think, that the interior of the suit-case was stained. Has the nature of these stains been ascertained yet?'

'We submitted the case to the experts, sir, and their report came in this afternoon,' Jimmy replied. 'In spite of the immersion of the case in sea-water they have found it possible to identify the stains as being due to human blood; the stains were caused no doubt by the portions of the dismembered body carried in it.'

'Have you considered what would happen to dismembered portions of a human body thrown into the sea?'

'In this case, sir, I have,' Jimmy replied. 'The tide would sweep them out to sea, if they were thrown in before six o'clock on Friday morning.'

'That is only correct up to a point. The specific gravity of the human body is slightly greater than that of sea-water. A man floats mainly by virtue of the air contained in his lungs and other cavities. If the air is removed from these cavities and they become filled with water, the body will sink. A dismembered limb, for instance, would sink slowly when thrown into the sea. During the time it was sinking, the tide would sweep it away, certainly. But it would ultimately come to rest upon the bottom at no very great distance from the place where it was thrown in.'

'I'm afraid that won't help us much, sir. If the limbs reached the bottom, there would not be much of them left by now. The local fishermen are accustomed to set their lobster-pots in that very spot and lobsters are notoriously fond of flesh, human or otherwise.'

'So that your prospects of recovering any portion of the body are very remote?'

'I'm afraid so, sir. But Superintendent Latham is doing everything he can.'

'And if nothing is found after a reasonable period has elapsed, what then?'

'That's not for us to decide, Professor,' Hanslet replied. 'I suppose the Assistant Commissioner will consult the authorities, and they will advise what steps should be taken. It seems to me, from what Jimmy tells us, there's a perfectly clear case against Gavin Slater. It wouldn't be the first time that a man has been tried for murder, even though the body of his victim is not forthcoming. If a man is clever enough to dispose of the body, it doesn't follow that he should be allowed to get off scot free.'

Dr Priestley made no reply to this remark. His mind seemed to return to some other facet of the problem. 'You have seen both Mr Knott and Mr Gavin Slater, Inspector,' he said. 'Did you notice any personal resemblance between them?'

'Not the slightest, sir,' replied Jimmy promptly. 'They were not in the least alike. For one thing, Mr Knott was fair and broad-featured, while Gavin Slater is dark with a sort of scowling expression.'

Dr Priestley frowned a trifle impatiently. 'Personal resemblance is not necessarily confined to the face,' he said. 'Your reply, Inspector, is an example of the attitude of the majority towards possible resemblance. In comparing any two individuals, we start with their faces. This is perfectly natural. A single glance at the two faces satisfies us. They are not in the least alike. We know that we are never likely to mistake one individual for the other. So we go no further. We do not seek such other similarities between the individuals as may exist. We do not ask ourselves whether they are approximately of the same height, chest measurement and so forth.'

Jimmy wondered if he would ever achieve enough efficiency as an observer to satisfy all Dr Priestley's requirements. He tried to picture the figures of the two men as he had seen them.

'Well, sir,' he replied, after a pause, 'they were much about the same height. I dare say Mr Knott was slightly the taller of the two. And I dare say their girth was about the same.

Slater, I should think, was slightly broader than Knott. But, on the other hand, Knott was probably a trifle fatter.'

'Do you see the possible significance of these personal similarities?' Dr Priestley asked.

Hanslet stepped in before Jimmy could reply. 'I do, Professor,' he said. 'You're thinking about the missing clothes, I can see that. If Jimmy's right, there would be nothing to prevent Gavin Slater wearing Mr Knott's suit and overcoat. He may have kept them because he wished to impersonate him at some time. At a distance and in a bad light, of course. And under circumstances where his limp would not give him away.'

Dr Priestley smiled. 'Why should Gavin Slater wish to impersonate Mr Knott after his death?' he asked.

'I don't know,' Hanslet replied with a slight shrug of the shoulders. 'This isn't my case, you know, Professor. It's Jimmy's. There may be a hint of motive in that theory of impersonation. I'd bear that in mind if I were you, Jimmy.'

'The question of motive certainly requires reconsideration,' said Dr Priestley. 'I do not believe that the theories as at present advanced will eventually prove to be correct. I do not believe that the fates of these two men were disconnected incidents. I cannot suggest what connection may exist between them. To do so, in the light of my present knowledge, would be to indulge in pure conjecture. But I might be able to suggest a possible line of inquiry.'

'I wish you would, Professor,' replied Hanslet promptly.

'I have listened very carefully both to you and to Inspector Waghorn,' replied Dr Priestley judiciously. 'I have noticed that, in the statements of the various witnesses as repeated by you, there are certain inconsistencies. This, of course, invariably happens in any investigation. No two people, however truthful they wish to be, will give the same account of any event or circumstance. But they might be expected to agree upon simple matters of facts familiar to them both. For instance, if I were to ask you in turn which was the nearest bridge across the river to Scotland Yard, you would both, in all probability, reply Westminster Bridge.

'Now, the statements in this case agree with remarkable accuracy. The discrepancies are slight, and deal with details of no apparent importance. But still they exist. I will cite, for example, the matter of the bonus given to Victor Harleston before his death. Will you turn up your notes, Harold, and repeat to us what Mr Slater told the Inspector about the policy of bonuses followed by Messrs. Slater & Knott?'

Harold looked through his notes until he found the required passage. 'This is it, I think, sir,' he said. 'Mr Slater in his statement to the Inspector used the following words: "Our custom has been to grant bonuses only in exceptional cases. For instance, where the recipient has carried out some particularly difficult piece of work, or when his domestic affairs involve a considerable strain upon his income."'

'Thank you,' said Dr Priestley. 'That extract of Mr Slater's statement will be sufficient. Now, the Inspector had previously spoken to Mr Knott about the same subject. Can you find the reference to their conversation on this occasion?'

Once more Harold turned over his notes. 'The Inspector asked Mr Knott whether the granting of bonuses was a matter of routine. Mr Knott replied, "Hardly a matter of routine. It has always been our custom to give a bonus to such of our clerks as has been with us fifteen years and whose service has been in every way satisfactory."'

Dr Priestley nodded to show that no further quotation was

necessary. 'A comparison of those two statements is interesting,' he said. 'The witnesses are two partners of a firm, and their evidence concerns a fact which must have been familiar to both of them. I say it must have been, because apparently the consent of both partners was necessary before a bonus could be granted. Yet their statements are diametrically opposed to one another. Mr Slater says that bonuses were only granted in exceptional cases. Mr Knott says that they were always granted if certain circumstances were fulfilled. How is this discrepancy to be explained?'

The question was addressed to Hanslet. But he merely shook his head and laughed.

'I don't know, Professor,' he replied. 'But it isn't of the slightest importance, for in any case Harleston got his bonus. Both partners are agreed upon that. Whether his family knew that he had got an additional hundred pounds, I can't say. But I should think it more than likely that he said nothing about it.'

'I chose this particular discrepancy merely as an example,' Dr Priestley replied. 'It happened to be a simple one to demonstrate. But I am not fully convinced that it is of no importance. Mr Knott endeavoured to represent the granting of a bonus to Victor Harleston as a perfectly normal event. He did so, no doubt, because he wished to justify his insistence on the grant. But why should the partners have taken such divergent views upon the matter?'

Jimmy ventured to reply to this. 'Mr Slater admitted to me that he disliked Victor Harleston, sir,' he said. 'And though he declared that his personal dislike had nothing to do with his opposition, it probably influenced him in spite of himself.'

'That may be,' said Dr Priestley. 'But were I in charge of this case, I should make inquiries in the offices of Messrs.

Slater & Knott. I should ask how many clerks had received bonuses in the course of the last ten years, say, and I should inquire into the circumstances of each case where such a bonus had been granted.'

'But what on earth would you gain by it, Professor?' Hanslet demanded.

'I might gain nothing. Surely you would be the first to admit that, in any case, the greater part of your investigations proved fruitless. On the other hand, I might ascertain a fact of some considerable importance. I might become in a position to judge between the statements of Mr Slater and Mr Knott. I might learn the respective reliance to be placed on each.'

Dr Priestley seemed disposed to say no more and shortly afterwards Hanslet and Jimmy left the house. But next morning they held a conference in the superintendent's room, in the course of which they exchanged their views more fully than they had yet done.

'You take it from me, Jimmy,' said Hanslet confidentially, 'when the Professor gets an idea into his head, there's always something behind it. If he believes that there's some connection between these two murders, you may take it that a link exists somewhere. And what that link is, we've got to find out.

'Now, I've been thinking this over since last night, as I dare say you have. That point about discrepancies in the statements is a pretty shrewd one. I don't see what possible object Knott can have had in lying to you. It seems to me that the truth is this. Harleston would have got his bonus in the ordinary way, but for Slater's opposition. Slater didn't know that you had already questioned Knott about the bonus. But he did know that Knott was no longer in a position to contradict anything that he might say. So, when you questioned him, he gave you a false impression, to account for Harleston not having received his bonus before.

'You accepted Slater's statement implicitly because you believed that he could have had no interest in either crime. But I'm beginning to wonder whether Slater isn't the link that the Professor hinted at.'

'It's possible, I suppose,' Jimmy replied doubtfully. 'But I don't quite see how.'

'Of course you don't see how. Detection would be an easy enough business if one could always see things like that straight off. We've got to think out the various possibilities and test them in turn until we find the right one. Here's quite a reasonable theory to begin with. The relations between the two partners were not so honest and above-board as appeared. Slater's retirement may not have been due to the reasons he told you. Something may have happened of which nothing has been allowed to transpire. But Knott knew the secret and Harleston shared it with him.

'For some reason, their possession of that secret was inconvenient to Slater. I won't attempt to guess what form that inconvenience may have taken. But Slater determines to put an end to the situation. And the only way to do that was to get rid of both Knott and Harleston.

'Knott presented no particular problem. He was a frequent visitor to Torquay, and could safely be left to the attention of Gavin Slater. There are lots of questions that you didn't ask while you were down there, Jimmy, besides those which the Professor pointed out last night. Was it purely by chance that Mrs Slater was out that night? Or had her father and husband contrived somehow that she should be? However, that's by the way. I think you and Superintendent Latham between you have pretty well got that crime fixed. Gavin Slater was the murderer, no doubt, but was his father the instigator of the murder?

'Harleston was a more difficult customer to tackle. He couldn't be invited to Torquay without arousing his suspicions. He must have known that Slater didn't like him and he would naturally wonder what was behind such an invitation. He didn't go out anywhere and so there was no chance of knocking him on the head in a dark corner. He had to be murdered at home, and Slater must have puzzled his head as to the best way of doing that.

'We agreed long ago that Harleston's murderer must have possessed certain knowledge. And we didn't then see how anybody but a member of his family could have been aware of the necessary details. But Slater might very well have known them. He was still a partner in the firm, and though he had retired from active work, Knott reported to him at frequent intervals. He is certain to have known that Harleston was doing the audit for Novoshave. He was a friend of Harleston's father, and knew all about his family, even to the fact that a share in Hart's Farm had been purchased for Philip. There is no impossibility involved in the theory that he sent Harleston the poisoned shaving cream.

'But that doesn't let out Philip or his sister. I don't for a moment suppose that Slater acted without their co-operation. He probably knew very well that Victor's death would be a relief to them both. So they fixed it up between them. Slater was to supply the means and Philip and Janet between them were to remove the evidence subsequently. All that Philip was asked to do before the event was to hand over one of his tins of nicotine.

'That's the line we've got to work on, Jimmy. I'm not going

to interfere with your case. It seems to me that you've done well enough so far. But, if I were you, I'd get back to Torquay and have another look round. You may find something that will fit in with our theory. And an affair like this is like a jigsaw puzzle. As soon as you get the first few pieces put together, the rest fall into their places quite naturally.'

6

Jimmy's first care upon arriving at Torquay was to call upon Superintendent Latham. The two compared notes.

The superintendent had nothing to report. No traces of the missing body had been found. But he agreed with Jimmy that the time had come to make a detailed search of Mr Slater's house.

They carried this out together without delay. Mr Slater raised no objections. These frequent invasions of the police did not appear to perturb him. But Gavin was furious. He threatened to complain to the chief constable and to the local member of Parliament. Finally he marched out of the house, insisting that his wife should accompany him.

Jimmy, remembering the Professor's remarks, sent for Lizzie. He questioned her as to Mr Knott's arrival at the house. He had come in a taxi from the station. When she had opened the door to him, he had taken off his hat and overcoat and given them to her.

'What did you do with them, Lizzie?' Jimmy asked.

'I hung them up in the cupboard under the stairs, sir,' she replied. 'That's where Mr Slater and Mr Gavin always keep their coats and hats.'

'Let's have a look into that cupboard, Lizzie,' said Jimmy.

'You'd recognise Mr Knott's overcoat again if you saw it, I expect?'

'Oh yes, sir, it was dark blue and rather heavy.'

They looked into the cupboard together. There were several coats of various ages and styles hanging there, but there was not a dark blue one among them. At least, not at first sight. But Jimmy lifted them off their pegs one by one. And beneath a rather dilapidated raincoat he found what he was looking for. 'Why, there it is, sir,' Lizzie exclaimed. 'That's Mr Knott's coat.'

It certainly answered to the description which Lizzie had given. But Jimmy was not satisfied. He looked on the inside and found a strip of linen sewn on to the lining. This strip was marked with the name, 'Edward Knott.'

'Is this the peg that you hung the coat on, Lizzie?' Jimmy asked.

'No, sir,' she replied. 'I hung it on one of those empty ones there. Somebody must have moved it. And I don't know why Mr Gavin hung his own raincoat over it. There are plenty of empty pegs, as you can see for yourself, sir.'

Jimmy had already noticed that. It looked very much as though Mr Knott's coat had been deliberately concealed from view.

'What about Mr Knott's hat?' he asked.

'Mr Knott was wearing a bowler hat, sir, which looked quite new. I hung it on the same peg as his coat, but I don't see it anywhere now, sir.'

But a search failed to reveal any sign of a bowler hat. But there were other places besides the cupboard in which the hat might have been concealed. The superintendent and Jimmy set to work to examine the house from top to bottom. The process took some considerable time. They took one room after another, leaving no corner unexamined. Lizzie, who accompanied them, told them the purpose to which each room was put.

Eventually they reached Gavin Slater's dressing-room. It was plainly furnished with a large wardrobe, a chest of drawers and a few chairs. A single bed stood against one wall and Lizzie, in reply to a question of Jimmy's, stated that it was upon this that she had found Gavin Slater lying on the previous Thursday morning.

They devoted even more attention to this room than they had to the others. They looked under and behind the furniture without finding any trace of the missing hat. Jimmy removed the clothes hanging in the wardrobe, and searched through the pockets. He found nothing to reward his efforts. Then he turned his attention to the chest of drawers. He took the drawers out one by one, looked behind them and then proceeded to examine their contents. The bottom drawer, when he came to it, was full of summer underclothing which had apparently not been disturbed since it had been put away. Jimmy took out the garments one by one and laid them on the floor. But before he had emptied the drawer he felt something hard hidden beneath the underclothing. He withdrew this and found it to be a cylindrical tin. He thought at first that it must be a tin of fifty cigarettes, although, since the wrapping had been torn off it, it was impossible to say so with certainty. He opened the lid and immediately a queer smell greeted him. It was perfectly familiar and he had no difficulty in recognising it at once. The smell was that of a foul pipe, and he knew well enough by now that that was characteristic of nicotine. The tin was about half-full of a thick, colourless, oily liquid. Jimmy glanced at this hastily, then rapidly replaced the lid.

Superintendent Latham glanced at him curiously.

'What have you got there?' he asked.

Jimmy was acutely conscious of Lizzie's presence. 'I'm not quite sure, sir,' he replied. 'But I'd like to take it away for further examination.'

The superintendent made no objection to this. They continued their search, without finding anything else of any significance. Neither the hat nor any suspicious object was to be found in any of the rooms of the house. And then Jimmy suggested that he would like to interview Mr Slater before leaving.

Mr Slater was discovered sitting in front of the drawing-room fire, apparently quite oblivious to the ransacking of his dwelling. He seemed to regard the proceedings of the police much as he regarded spring-cleaning—a necessary evil to be borne with as much fortitude as possible. He answered Jimmy's questions readily enough. His daughter-in-law's absence on the Thursday evening was easily explained and had nothing to do with Mr Knott's visit. She belonged to a bridge circle which met every Thursday evening throughout the winter. It could have been predicted with certainty that Mrs Slater would be out during the whole of that particular evening. She had apologised to Mr Knott for going out and he had accepted her apology with the utmost readiness.

There was nothing more to be done here. Jimmy and the superintendent left the house and paid a second visit to Mrs Puddlecombe. Her previous experience of the police had chastened her considerably, and her answers on this occasion were obviously truthful. Her husband had brought home the suitcase exactly as he had found it, and had opened it in her presence. She was ready to swear that it had contained nothing beyond the articles which she had taken to the pawnbroker's. She agreed that her husband would have kept anything that could have been of any use to him. But since he had found nothing of the sort, he had thought it best to realise what he could on his finds. The cottage was small and was not adapted to the concealment of anything. Jimmy very soon satisfied himself that it contained none of Mr Knott's clothes.

They returned to the police station.

'I'm still curious about that tin you found in Gavin Slater's room,' the superintendent remarked.

Jimmy smiled. 'That's rather a long story, sir,' he replied. 'I'll give you the outline of it, if it won't bore you to listen.' He gave a brief account of the death of Victor Harleston, and of the tin of nicotine which was missing from his half-brother's store. 'And the queer thing about it is, sir,' he concluded, 'that unless I'm very much mistaken this tin contains nicotine.'

'That seems to establish some connection between the death of this man Harleston and that of Mr Knott,' the superintendent remarked shrewdly.

'I fancy it does, sir, but if this is the missing tin, it's rather a puzzle how Gavin Slater can have come by it. Has he got a car?'

'His father owns a car which both Gavin and his wife drive. There's no reason why one of them shouldn't have driven to this place Lassingford, and fetched the tin.'

This seemed reasonable enough, but Jimmy was not altogether satisfied. 'If Gavin Slater used the nicotine to poison Victor Harleston, why didn't he get rid of the stuff when it had served his purpose?' he asked. 'It was incredibly stupid of him to keep it when he might so easily have thrown it into the sea. By Jove, though, I wonder! That's another question we might have asked Lizzie. Do you think one of your men could bring her round here, sir?'

'Certainly,' replied the superintendent. He gave the necessary instructions and then resumed the conversation. 'You ask why Gavin Slater kept the tin of nicotine,' he said. 'Well, it's a matter of experience that even the most accomplished criminal nearly always commits some grave blunder. You'll find the fact laid down in every book on criminal investigation. He proceeds with the utmost ingenuity up to a point and then makes the one fatal mistake. Keeping this tin may have been Gavin Slater's blunder. I'm inclined to think that we ought to get him here and detain him. I expect there are a whole lot of questions you would like to ask him?'

Jimmy agreed that this would be the most satisfactory course. They discussed the question until Lizzie's arrival was announced. She was ushered into their presence looking rather awestruck. The superintendent reassured her in a few words. 'It's all right, Lizzie,' he said. 'We want to ask you one or two questions and we didn't want to disturb Mr Slater's privacy again. Had Mr Gavin Slater returned to the house when you left?'

'No, sir, he hadn't come back then,' she replied.

'Well, never mind. Now, just pay attention to Inspector Waghorn. He wants to talk to you, I think.'

'It's only a small point, Lizzie,' said Jimmy. 'You told us that when you tidied up the studio after Mr Knott's visit you found a glass lying broken on the floor. Where was the other glass?'

'There was no other glass, sir,' Lizzie replied promptly. 'I wondered at the time what could have become of it.'

'You expected to find another glass, then?' Jimmy said quietly.

'Yes, I did that, sir. You see, it was like this. I always put out a tray on the sideboard in the dining-room before dinner. On it I put a siphon of soda and one or two glasses. Usually I only put one, because neither Mr Slater nor Mrs Slater ever touch anything after dinner. But on the night that Mr Knott was staying in the house I put out two glasses.'

'And next morning you found the tray which you had put out in the studio?'

'That's right, sir. The siphon with a little soda was still on it. And there was a decanter of whisky nearly empty which Mr Gavin must have brought in. But there were no glasses and the only one I could find I picked up in pieces from the floor.'

'You are quite sure that there were two glasses on the tray when it was taken into the studio?'

'Quite sure, sir. Mr Gavin took the tray from the dining-room while I was there and I saw then that it had two glasses on it.'

'You haven't found the glass or any bits of it lying about the house anywhere?'

'No, sir. And it isn't in the pantry, for there are two glasses missing from the dozen we used to have. And I know they were all there when I took out the two glasses on Thursday evening.'

Lizzie was dismissed and the superintendent smiled. 'Things seem to disappear from that house in the most amazing way,' he said. 'What's your idea?'

'I'm wondering what became of that second glass, sir,' Jimmy replied. 'Gavin broke one of them to create the impression that he was very drunk that evening. That was probably the one he had used himself. Where is the one used by Mr Knott?'

The superintendent shrugged his shoulders. 'Thrown into the sea with the body, I dare say. I don't see that it's of very great importance, though.'

'It may not be, sir. But I've got this at the back of my mind. Suppose that Gavin Slater kept that tin of nicotine after he had used it to poison Mr Harleston because he meant to try the same trick on Mr Knott?'

'Well, if he did, he seems to have thought better of it. It seems pretty clear that he stabbed Mr Knott with that knife you found.'

'That may have been the last resort, sir. His original plan may have been to have put nicotine in Mr Knott's whisky. But that plan failed, for some reason or another. Mr Knott may have smelt the stuff and refused to drink it. But the glass would remain and would have to be disposed of. Gavin Slater probably threw it into the sea in case anybody should ask questions. What I can't understand is why he didn't throw away the tin as well.'

'Perhaps it might have come in useful on yet another occasion,' the superintendent replied grimly. 'Now I'm going to send word that Gavin Slater is to be brought here as soon as he comes home. You needn't be afraid that he's bolted. My men have been keeping their eyes on him for the last day or two.'

Little more than half an hour later Gavin Slater appeared at the police station, escorted by a police sergeant. During his absence he had apparently been drinking and his manner was even more truculent than usual. He talked about the outrage to his dignity, and threatened the superintendent with all manner of pains and penalties if he were not allowed to go home immediately. The superintendent waited until he had come to an end of his tirade.

'You have only yourself to blame, Mr Slater,' he said coldly. 'It is our duty to inquire into the disappearance of Mr Knott. We have reason to believe that you are wilfully withholding certain information. You have been brought here in order to answer certain questions which Inspector Waghorn will put to you. And I warn you that your replies will be recorded and may be used subsequently as evidence.'

'I don't know any more about Knott than I have already told you,' replied Gavin Slater violently.

'That may or may not be the case. Are you prepared to answer the questions that will be put to you?'

The atmosphere of the police station appeared to have a sobering effect upon Gavin Slater. 'All right, fire away,' he replied sullenly.

The superintendent glanced at Jimmy, who was already thinking rapidly. It was necessary for him to decide what line he should take with the suspected man. It would not do to let him know the full extent to which the facts had been discovered. He might be sharp-witted enough to think out a line of defence to meet the charge. It might be better to keep him in a state of suspense, unaware of how much was known and how much was not.

Jimmy opened with a question which he thought would shake his confidence at the outset. 'At the time of Mr Knott's visit, there was a knife and sheath hanging on the wall of the studio,' he said quietly. 'Who did that knife belong to?'

Gavin Slater eyed his questioner insolently. 'Oh, so that's where it's gone to, is it?' he replied. 'I thought one of you busybodies must have appropriated it. The knife belongs to me, if you want to know.'

'How long have you had it?' Jimmy asked.

'Oh, two or three years, I suppose. I saw it in a curiosity

shop in Exeter and paid ten bob for it. It was just the thing I wanted for a picture I was painting then.'

'And it has hung on the wall of the studio ever since?' Jimmy suggested.

'Until the evening that Knott was with us,' Gavin Slater replied unexpectedly.

Jimmy was aware of the superintendent's significant glance. 'Was it taken down from the wall then?' he asked.

'Why, yes. Knott happened to catch sight of it and asked me what it was. He said he'd never seen a knife like that before. So I took it down and drew the knife from its sheath to show him.'

'How did you withdraw the knife from the sheath?' asked Jimmy quickly.

'Why, the natural way, I suppose. I caught hold of the sheath with my left hand and the hilt of the knife with my right and pulled. Strange though it may seem to the mind of a policeman, the knife came out of its sheath without the slightest difficulty.'

Jimmy picked up an ivory paper knife which happened to be lying on the superintendent's desk. 'Suppose that this represents the knife in its sheath,' he said, 'show me exactly how you held it.'

Gavin Slater took the paper knife. He held the blade of it in his left hand with the little finger nearest the end. His right hand he placed on the handle with the thumb outwards.

'Like that,' he said. 'Anybody who draws a knife does it that way. As soon as it comes out of the sheath, it is in its proper position for action.'

Jimmy nodded. The position of Gavin Slater's hand corresponded exactly to the fingermarks on the knife and sheath.

'You showed the knife to Mr Knott,' he said, 'what did you do with it then?'

'I didn't keep it by me to pick my teeth with, or anything like that. I put it back in its sheath and hung it up on the wall again.'

'Did you do this in Mr Knott's presence?'

'Of course. The thing wasn't in my hands for more than a couple of minutes. As soon as Knott had seen it, his curiosity seemed to be satisfied.'

'At what time did this happen?'

'Oh, I don't know. It was just after Knott and I had gone into the studio after dinner. He walked round for a bit, looking at the pictures and things, and it was then he asked me about the knife.'

'And you had not touched the knife since you put it back on the wall after showing it to Mr Knott?'

'No, I've had no reason to touch it. It wasn't until I noticed yesterday that it had disappeared that I thought about it again. It struck me that perhaps Knott had taken it, since he had shown so much interest in it.'

'Do your guests usually walk off with souvenirs of that description?' Jimmy asked.

Gavin Slater shrugged his shoulders. 'Not as a rule,' he replied. 'But there's an overcoat of mine missing since Knott was with us, and I can't imagine who could have taken it if he didn't.'

'What was this overcoat like?'

'It was a light grey summer overcoat I haven't worn for some time. But I know that on Thursday afternoon it was in the cupboard where the coats are kept, for I happened to catch sight of it. I thought then of having it sent to the cleaners, but when I went to look for it again on Friday morning, it wasn't there.'

Jimmy took a full description of the overcoat. And then abruptly changed the subject. The tin of nicotine had until this moment remained concealed under a pile of papers. He produced it suddenly and placed it in full view of Gavin Slater.

'Where did this come from?' he asked.

'I haven't the slightest idea,' replied Gavin off-handedly. 'What is it? It looks to me like a tin of cigarettes. If so, it isn't mine. I always buy mine in flat tins.'

'You are perfectly certain that you have never seen this tin before?' insisted Jimmy severely.

'How can I be certain?' Gavin Slater retorted. 'All tins of that shape and size are very much alike. And, since you've torn the paper off it, there's nothing to recognise it by. I may have caught sight of it, but I don't remember doing so.'

Jimmy had a feeling that he was not making much headway. So far Gavin Slater had shown no signs of embarrassment at his questions. Either he was amazingly quick-witted, or he had thought out his line of defence well in advance. Jimmy decided to try to fluster him by a rapid change of ground.

'What became of Mr Knott's glass on Thursday night?' he asked quickly.

But Gavin Slater's face maintained its sullen half-contemptuous expression.

'What are you getting at now?' he asked.

Jimmy retained his composure. 'You and Mr Knott had a few drinks together in the studio after dinner, did you not?' he asked.

'Yes, that's right. I don't think he had more than a couple, though, before he went to bed.'

'Did you both drink out of the same glass?'

'Hardly. It is not usual in the circles to which I am accustomed. I carried a tray with the whisky and soda and two tumblers into the studio myself.'

'Then how do you account for the fact that only one tumbler was found in the morning?'

'I don't account for it. It really isn't any business of mine. I shouldn't wonder if the girl broke it and threw away the pieces before any questions were asked.'

Again Jimmy shifted his ground with unexpected rapidity. 'When did you last see Philip Harleston?' he asked.

Gavin Slater's expression acquired a note of surprise. 'I really couldn't tell you, since I have not the honour of his acquaintance,' he replied.

'Oh, come now! You're not going to say that you've never heard of the name of Harleston before?

'I didn't say anything of the kind. I said that I did not know Philip Harleston, which is perfectly true. I know that a man of that name, who was a clerk in the firm, died the other day. Winifred read to my father the letter in which Knott announced the news. But I had an idea that the chap's Christian name was Victor, not Philip.'

'So it was. But you are surely aware that he had a half-brother the name of Philip?'

'I was not aware of it. I never met the fellow, and his family could be of no possible interest to me.'

Jimmy felt a slight awkwardness as he asked his next question. 'You didn't know that he had a half-sister as well?'

Gavin Slater shook his head decidedly. 'I tell you I know nothing about him or his people,' he replied firmly.

'You are in the habit of driving a car, are you not?'

'Yes, I drive and so does Winifred. We take the old man

out for a drive sometimes in summer. And now and then we go for short trips on our own.'

'Then I expect you know your way about fairly well. How would you drive from here to Maidstone, for instance?'

Jimmy had expected the other to hesitate over his reply to this question. But, to his astonishment, Gavin Slater answered at once. 'Maidstone?' he said. 'I should go up the London Road as far as Salisbury, then through Winchester, Guildford and Reigate. It's a good long way, well over two hundred miles.'

'You seem familiar with the road. Have you driven over it lately?'

'Not for eighteen months or so. Winifred and I drove that way to Folkestone the summer before last.'

'Did you pass through a village called Lassingford?'

Gavin Slater shrugged his shoulders. 'We may have done. You can't expect me to remember the names of all the villages on the road.'

'Philip Harleston lives at Lassingford,' said Jimmy sternly. 'And I have every reason to believe that this tin was stolen from his house there, quite recently.'

'Well, if it was, I'm not responsible. I don't go about the country pinching things.'

'Then why did you hide this tin under the under-clothing in your chest of drawers?'

Gavin Slater's face darkened. 'Oh, so you've been rummaging in my room, have you?' he said. 'May I ask by what authority?'

The superintendent stepped in. 'By the authority of a search warrant procured for the purpose,' he said. 'Come now, Mr Slater. We found that tin in your room. And it's up to you to explain how it got there.'

'Somebody must have put it there. I didn't,' replied Slater sullenly.

Jimmy renewed his attack. 'What time did the tide turn last Friday evening?' he asked abruptly.

But the other remained imperturbable. 'I don't know. I'm not a nautical almanack,' he replied. 'You'd better ask one of the local fishermen. They'd be able to tell you, I expect.'

'It's rather an important point,' said Jimmy quietly. 'Suppose, for instance, that anything was thrown into the sea. It would be carried away from shore before the tide turned, and towards it afterwards, wouldn't it?'

'I dare say. I'm not in the habit of throwing things into the sea.'

'But there are occasions when you do, I have no doubt. How many journeys did you make with Mr Knott's suitcase on Friday morning?'

'I never touched his suitcase. He left the house before I was awake, as I told you before.'

'And you still persist that you know nothing about the way in which he left the house?'

'I don't suppose that he jumped out of his bedroom window. I imagine that he opened the front door, walked out and shut it behind him, like any rational being would. And if he hasn't been seen since, it's not my fault. Can't a fellow disappear if he wants to without everybody who knew him being pestered in this way?'

During his examination, Jimmy had written down his questions and Gavin's Slater's answers. He beckoned to him and handed him a pen. 'I must ask you to sign your name to what you have just told me,' he said.

But the other shook his head. 'Not much,' he replied. 'How am I to know what you've been writing down? Let me read

204

all that stuff through at my leisure, and then if I think fit, I'll sign it.'

The superintendent grinned maliciously. 'You'll have plenty of leisure for the purpose,' he said. 'You will remain here until you have had time to think over the matter.'

He glanced at the sergeant, who removed the witness before he had time to protest.

There was silence in the room for a moment or two after his departure. Jimmy felt that the results of his catechism were not altogether encouraging. 'The man seems to be as stubborn as a mule, sir,' he ventured.

'Well, you did your best, anyhow,' replied the superintendent cheerfully. 'I thought you'd be bound to catch him, shifting about from one thing to another like that. He had his story pretty pat, there's no getting away from that. We'll try the same old trick as usual, of course. Tackle him again tomorrow. Ask him the same questions in a different form and a different order and compare his replies. Unless he's a very much cleverer man than I've always taken him for, he's bound to give himself away upon one detail or another. And once we've made a small hole in his defence, there shouldn't be any difficulty in enlarging it.'

Jimmy was somewhat comforted by his superior's optimism. 'I hope we shall get a satisfactory statement out of him, sir,' he replied. 'Meanwhile, I think I'd better take this tin up to London. Superintendent Hanslet will certainly want to see it. And of course, its contents will have to be identified. I'm pretty sure that the stuff's nicotine, but the experts will have to confirm that.'

'Yes, that's about the best thing you can do,' the superintendent agreed. 'I wish to goodness we could find some portion of the body. The tip of a little finger would do. Until then, though we know that Gavin Slater is a murderer, we can't do much with him. It's just one of those cases where we've got to wait until something turns up.'

III

'Stanley Fernside'

I

While Jimmy was carrying out his investigations at Torquay, Hanslet endeavoured to verify the theory which he had formulated. His first move was to send a message to Philip Harleston, asking him to come to Scotland Yard at once. He knew that the atmosphere of the Yard would help to be intimidating, and hoped that by skilful questioning the victim might be driven into a corner.

Philip Harleston answered the summons without delay. He was taken to the superintendent's room, where he was provided with a low chair facing the light. And then Hanslet began a searching cross-examination, covering the familiar ground over and over again. But Philip stuck to the statement which he had already made, and Hanslet entirely failed to entice him into any contradiction.

He then started out on fresh ground, employing much the same tactics as Jimmy had with Gavin Slater. 'Have you any artists among your friends?' he asked.

Philip scratched his head. 'No, I don't think so,' he replied. 'I've never been mixed up with that set.'

'But surely you know a Mr Gavin Slater, who is an artist,' exclaimed Hanslet with stimulated surprise.

Philip looked puzzled. 'I've never met Mr Gavin Slater,' he replied. 'He's Mr Slater's son, isn't he?'

'Yes, he is. But if Mr Slater was an old friend of your father's, you must surely have met his son?'

'I don't remember doing so. In any case, I didn't know he was an artist. And I've only met Mr Slater himself once or twice.'

'You know that your father consulted Mr Slater before he bought you the share in Hart's farm?'

'Yes, I know that. My father always had a great belief in Mr Slater's judgment.'

'No doubt your half-brother knew Mr Gavin Slater?'

'I couldn't say. I never heard him mention him.'

And in spite of all Hanslet's persistence, this was all that he could get out of Philip. He dismissed him with a caution that he might be called upon again at any moment. And then, disappointed of his expected confession, the superintendent started to attack the problem from another direction.

Dr Priestley had recommended the most thorough investigation of Mr Knott's past history. Hanslet decided to follow up this hint. He went to Slater & Knott's offices in Chancery Lane, where he painstakingly interviewed everybody who could tell him anything about the missing principal of the firm. In this way he pieced together quite a lot of information, but only one point seemed to him of any particular significance. This point he elicited from Fred Davies, quite casually. It appeared that Mr Knott had a friend on the staff of St Martha's Hospital. This friend had induced him to enrol himself upon the list of volunteers who offered their blood for transfusion, if necessary. Hanslet made a note of this and continued his inquiries. He learnt that Knott had been a companionable sort of person, with many friends and, so far as was known, no enemies. He liked amusement and spent a good deal of money one way and another. But he never allowed his amusements to interfere with business. He had always been a hard worker and a successful one.

In consultation with Mr Grant, the chief clerk, Hanslet learnt that the business was in a very flourishing condition. 'That is due entirely to Mr Knott,' said Grant confidentially. 'In Mr Slater's time, things were done in rather an old-fashioned way. We had quite a lot of old clients, of course, but no attempt was made to attract new ones. But as soon as Mr Knott took charge, things brightened up a lot. Mr Knott had a way with him. He took the trouble to go out and meet people. He never seemed to have the least difficulty in securing as many new clients as he wanted.'

'Then the profits of the business must have increased since Mr Slater's retirement?' Hanslet suggested.

'I should imagine they had increased very considerably,' was the reply. 'I cannot say by how much, for Mr Knott kept that information strictly to himself.'

The superintendent made no comment and changed the subject. But he put the same question to other clerks of long standing in the firm. They all agreed that the business of Slater & Knott had been on the upgrade since Mr Slater had retired.

This was directly contrary to what Mr Slater had told Jimmy. He had complained that the profits were falling off and had expressed some anxiety as to the future. He would not have done this without some definite motive. Had he wished to afford an explanation of his opposition to the granting of the bonus to Victor Harleston? Rather a clumsy falsehood, if so. Surely he must have some deeper reason. And if so, it was legitimate to link that reason with murders of Harleston and of Knott. Hanslet became still more convinced that Mr Slater's machinations had led to these murders.

Hanslet left Chancery Lane and went to St Martha's Hospital, where he eventually unearthed the friend of Mr Knott. This man, he discovered, had known Mr Knott fairly intimately; they had frequently spent an evening together. In fact, Knott had arranged for them to dine together on the previous Friday evening.

'Did Mr Knott keep the appointment?' Hanslet asked.

'No, he didn't,' the other replied. 'I waited a good half-hour for him, then went off somewhere else. And when I rang up his office next morning to find out what had happened to him, they told me that he had not returned to London.'

'You knew that he had gone down to Torquay the previous day?'

'Oh yes, I knew that. He told me that he was going down to Torquay to see his partner, but that he would be back in time for our meeting. He mentioned that he had an important appointment at his office at three o'clock that afternoon.'

'You persuaded Mr Knott to offer himself for transfusion of blood should emergency arise?'

'Yes, I did. And as it happens he might have been a very useful person to call upon. As I dare say you know, there are four classes of human blood. And if you've got a patient whose blood is class four, for instance, and it becomes necessary to employ transfusion, you've got to be careful that the person whose blood you take is also of class four. If you don't, your trouble's wasted, for the wrong class of blood is no use. Consequently, when anybody offers themselves for transfusion, we take a sample of their blood and test it. We then record the name of the volunteer, under his own particular class. Now, as it happens, we are rather short of volunteers of class one. Consequently, when I tested Knott's blood and found it belonged to that class, I was very pleased.'

Hanslet returned to Scotland Yard with this additional piece of evidence. It was not, of course, conclusive in itself. But it was useful to know that Mr Knott's blood had been of class one. For this was the class of blood that had been found upon the articles brought by Jimmy from Torquay.

In the superintendent's opinion everything was beginning to fit together pretty well. He was annoyed that he had been unable to force a confession from Philip. It seemed to him absolutely certain that Philip must have been in the plot. He no longer believed that Philip had been the actual murderer of his half-brother. But he must certainly have connived at it, if only to the extent of indicating where the nicotine might be procured. But his experience was that criminals frequently broke down when confronted with the first piece of real evidence. Hanslet had every confidence that this piece of evidence would soon be forthcoming.

So when Jimmy entered the superintendent's room upon his return from Torquay he was greeted expectantly.

'Well, have you found anything?' Hanslet asked.

Jimmy produced the tin which he had found in Gavin Slater's room and placed it on the table before the superintendent.

'I found that,' he replied without attempting to disguise the note of triumph in his voice.

Hanslet's eyes sparkled. 'I rather fancy that I've seen tins

211

like that before,' he said slowly. 'Any objection to my opening it?'

'None at all,' Jimmy replied with a satisfied smile. He watched Hanslet open the tin, sniff at the contents and then replace the lid hurriedly. 'The smell seems a bit familiar, doesn't it?' he continued.

'Familiar?' Hanslet exclaimed. 'That's nicotine and you know it. Sit down, my lad, and tell me all about it.'

Jimmy obeyed. He gave a detailed account of his last visit to Torquay, and of the events which had resulted from it. Hanslet listened eagerly. He nodded his head several times as though he had already anticipated the principal points of the story.

'Pretty good!' he exclaimed at last. 'All that confirms my theory, doesn't it? The Slater family, for some reason that we cannot quite fathom yet, decided to murder both Harleston and Knott. They were successful in both cases, but it oughtn't to be very difficult for us to lay them by the heels. This tin of nicotine is just the clue I've been wanting. I'll ring up the Professor and ask if we can go along and see him this evening. He'll be glad to hear that we have solved the problem.'

Dr Priestley's permission having been obtained, Hanslet and Jimmy arrived at Westbourne Terrace shortly after nine. The superintendent was in the highest spirits.

'We've solved that nicotine business between us, Professor,' he said triumphantly. 'I'm very glad to hear it,' Dr Priestley replied. 'As you know, where any problem is concerned, the steps towards the solution are of greater interest to me than the solution itself. I should be very glad to hear how you arrived at the happy result.'

Hanslet, nothing loath, launched into a description of his own and Jimmy's efforts. Dr Priestley listened attentively, but without showing any signs of approval. He waited until Hanslet had finished and then looked at Hanslet inquiringly.

'Well?' he asked.

Hanslet had expected at least a word of approbation.

'Well, the whole thing's pretty plain now,' he said rather lamely.

'To you it may be,' Dr Priestley replied. 'But to my less profound intellect, several obscurities appear to remain. Since the sequence of events appears to you to be so clear, perhaps you will explain it.'

Dr Priestley's manner was not exactly encouraging. Hanslet imagined that the solution of the problem without his intervention had slightly ruffled his *amour-propre*.

'You'd like me to explain what must have happened, Professor?' he asked.

A faint smile appeared on Dr Priestley's face. 'Most certainly, I should,' he replied.

'Well then, here goes,' said Hanslet. 'You remember saying, the last time we were here, that there were certain discrepancies between the statements. As an example, you took the granting of the bonus to Victor Harleston, and pointed out that Slater and Knott had given different accounts of this matter. I have since found an even more serious discrepancy. Slater bewailed to Jimmy that the profits of the firm were decreasing. On making inquiries at the office, however, I found that this was not the case. On the contrary, since Slater's retirement, the position of the firm has greatly improved.

'That shows that, in two instances at least, Slater wished to deceive us. In my opinion, that throws a doubt upon the whole of his evidence. He must be considered at least a possible accomplice. And therefore we cannot rely upon what

213

he has told Jimmy. For instance, we have believed hitherto that Knott's visit to Torquay was at his own suggestion. But since now we cannot trust Slater's account it is quite possible that Knott went to Torquay because his partner sent for him.

'However, I'm getting a bit ahead of myself. I don't know yet what was at the bottom of it all. But it seems to me pretty obvious that Slater for some reason wished to secure the silence of both Knott and Harleston. No doubt we shall discover that reason in due course. I don't think there can be any doubt that it existed. Dead men tell no tales, they say. And Slater decided that the most effectual way of shutting the mouths of his partner and his clerk would be to contrive their exit from this world.'

'You have not yet determined the motive, then?' Dr Priestley remarked blandly.

'I can't tell you why Slater wanted to secure the silence of these two men,' Hanslet replied. 'That he did so, seems to be the only explanation of what follows. Slater, being too old and infirm to take any active steps for himself, enlisted the aid of his son and possibly of his daughter-in-law. It was decided to tackle Harleston first, and the method agreed upon was poisoning by nicotine.

'Now Slater himself admits that he knew that Philip Harleston was established at Hart's Farm. Philip won't at present admit that he had any communication with the Slaters, but that's a detail. No doubt Slater got into touch with him, probably through his son. Philip divulged where the nicotine was kept, and a very elementary theft was staged. I learnt, on one of my visits to Lassingford, that an unknown man in a car had inquired for Philip at a time when he was out. That man was probably Gavin Slater. The same idea occurred to Jimmy when he tried to trap him into an admission. As it happened, he failed at the first attempt, but he may be more successful later.

'Having provided himself with the nicotine. Gavin Slater set out to buy a razor and a tube of shaving cream. We have already been into the details of that dodge. The parcel was no doubt posted to Victor Harleston from Torquay. I think that girl Janet Harleston must have been in the secret. At all events she was very careful to get rid of the paper in which the parcel had been wrapped. The postmark was too valuable a clue to be left lying about.

'Then we come to the man whom Janet says she saw on the doorstep. The trouble about this case is that we can't trust any of our more important witnesses. Did this man exist, or did he not? Janet's statement is entirely unsupported. She may have removed the shaving cream from the bathroom, and poured the nicotine into her half-brother's tea. On the other hand, if the man did exist, who was he? Probably, I think, Gavin Slater. Janet's statement that she cannot give a description of him must not be relied upon. We mustn't forget that she stood to gain by her half-brother's death, and was probably hand-in-glove with his murderer.

'Victor Harleston having been disposed of, the next step was to get rid of Knott. Probably Slater invited him to Torquay on the pretext of talking about some matter of business. One thing is perfectly certain. We have abundant evidence from several different sources that Knott intended to be back in London by three o'clock on Friday afternoon. This would have been possible had he left Torquay at ten-thirty. His sudden decision, as reported by Gavin Slater, to return by the seven-twenty seems incomprehensible.

'The finding of the tin of nicotine in Gavin Slater's bedroom, is to my mind most significant. Jimmy saw that at once.

Nicotine having proved remarkably effective in the case of Victor Harleston, the Slaters had decided to repeat the experiment with Knott. But with Knott, for some reason, nicotine was not employed after all. Jimmy thinks that Gavin Slater tried the dodge of putting nicotine in Knott's whisky. The missing glass seems to bear this out. In that case, Knott may have jibbed at the smell. On the other hand, Gavin Slater may have changed his mind at the last moment and decided to make use of the knife.

'There is no doubt that the knife was used. Gavin Slater admitted handling it, no doubt because he guessed that his fingerprints had been found on it. He waited until Knott was asleep, then stabbed him as he lay in bed. This done, he dismembered the body and carried it in the suitcase to the shore. Then, feeling a bit shaky, no doubt, he polished off the whisky that remained in the decanter and went and lay down in his dressing-room. To my mind the case against him is perfectly clear.'

A silence followed Hanslet's exposition. Then Dr Priestley turned to Jimmy. 'Do you share that opinion, Inspector?' he asked.

'Well, sir, all the evidence seems to point in that direction,' Jimmy replied diplomatically.

Dr Priestley fixed his eyes upon the ceiling. 'Then in that case any comment on my part would be superfluous,' he murmured.

'Not a bit of it, Professor,' Hanslet exclaimed hastily; 'the reason we came here was to hear your suggestions.'

'My suggestions!' said Dr Priestley mildly. 'I can only offer one suggestion, that is, that you should consider and compare the technique of these two crimes.'

Hanslet looked a trifle puzzled. 'I think we've done that pretty thoroughly,' he replied.

'You may have considered them, but you certainly have not compared them,' said Dr Priestley severely.

'I'm afraid I don't quite understand what you're driving at, Professor,' said Hanslet.

'Then I will endeavour to explain. You believe that two murders—that of Victor Harleston and of Mr Knott—were planned and executed by the same person or persons. Is that correct?'

'That's right, Professor. Slater, I fancy, did the thinking and his son did the execution.'

'Very well. Now let us consider these two crimes. First of all the murder of Victor Harleston. Here we have an ingenious plan boldly carried out. Every effort is made to remove incriminating evidence. We must believe that the discovery of the razor employed is due to the victim having thrown it out of the window. Had he not done so, but laid it down on the shelf in the bathroom, it would no doubt have been removed with the shaving cream and the towel. In that case, no clue would have remained which could have implicated anybody.

'Now let us consider the second crime. Here, you will say, the criminal successfully overcame the gravest difficulty with which the murderer is confronted. He was able to dispose of the body in such a way that you have not been able to discover it. But he made no attempt whatever to destroy incriminating clues. On the contrary, he seems to have made a triumphant display of them. Let me enumerate a few of the most striking of these. He omits to wash the knife with which the crime was committed, and hangs it up in its bloodstained condition in a spot where any observant person would be bound to notice it. He disposed of such of the victim's clothes as he thought proper. Why he packed some

217

of these and not others in the suitcase is a problem upon which I will not at present dwell. But he left his victim's overcoat hanging up in the cupboard. Not content with this, he commits an even graver blunder. The pyjamas, perhaps the most damning evidence of all. The rent in them, surrounded by blood, has apparently told its own story. But these pyjamas, instead of being disposed of in the same manner as the body, were hidden at the bottom of an oak chest. Further, as though to implicate himself beyond all possibility of doubt, the murderer hides his alternative weapon, the nicotine, in his own chest of drawers. Then, regardless of any possible risk to himself, he makes his final journey with the suitcase to the shore, at a time when there was not only a possibility but a likelihood of his being observed. Lastly, as a crowning act of folly, he cashes one of the notes which he has stolen from his victim in such a way that it can easily be traced.

'Now, I do not pretend to be a detective. But I claim to have some slight knowledge of human nature. A criminal who displayed such skill in the commission of the first crime would surely never blunder so repeatedly in the case of the second. For this reason alone I cannot believe implicitly in the correctness of your theory, Superintendent.'

'There's something in what you say, Professor,' Hanslet replied. 'But we've learnt a little about Gavin Slater's habits. We know that when he has had too much to drink he becomes hardly responsible for his actions. When the first crime was committed he managed to remain sober. But when the second crime was committed there was a decanter of whisky on the spot, and he couldn't resist the temptation. No doubt, when he had disposed of Knott's body, he got so tight that he didn't know what he was doing.'

'A plausible explanation, certainly. But he cannot have remained consistently drunk until Inspector Waghorn's first visit to Torquay. Even if he were incapable of destroying the clues immediately he had plenty of time to do so subsequently.'

Hanslet shook his head. 'He grew careless, I suppose,' he said. 'It's no use, Professor. If he didn't murder Knott, who did?'

'You may find it easier to answer that question when you discover Mr Knott's body.'

'We shall never do that now, I'm afraid. Those lobsters that Jimmy heard about have grown fat upon it by now. It's a matter of simple logic. Knott was murdered sometime during Thursday night in Slater's house. The only person in that house who was capable of murdering him and of disposing of the body was Gavin Slater. Unless you're going to suggest that somebody from outside broke in and did the job?'

'No, I should certainly not suggest that,' said Dr Priestley.

'Very well, then. You have to admit that Gavin Slater, however clumsily he behaved afterwards, was the murderer. You pointed out yourself the probability that there was a connection between the two murders. That means, I suppose, that the same motive was behind them both and that the same people carried them out?'

'I certainly suggested that connection. But I implied, I think, that it was a connection of motive. Now, as you yourself admit, you have failed to establish the motive in either case. Until the disappearance of Mr Knott, you were convinced that the motive of Victor Harleston's murder was to be found in his half-sister's discontent with her life with him. Now, in order to support your theory of two crimes having been carried out by the same hand, you are forced to imagine a fresh motive. You suppose, without adequate reason for doing so, that Mr Slater had a reason for wishing for the death of Victor Harleston and his partner. It would be just as logical, it seems to me, to imagine that Philip and Janet Harleston had a motive for desiring the death of Mr Knott.'

'I hadn't thought of that,' said Hanslet. And then, suddenly realising the absurdity of the suggestion, he added, 'but of course, that's ridiculous. Those two young people can't have murdered Knott while he was staying at Torquay. That, at least, is certain, for they were under observation at Lassingford at the time.'

'I did not suggest that the Harlestons had murdered Mr Knott,' Dr Priestley replied. 'I merely endeavoured to point out the weakness of your argument. It amounts to this. Appearances, as you say, suggest that Mr Knott was murdered by Gavin Slater. But no motive for this act is apparent. Instead of endeavouring to seek for the true motive behind both these crimes you invent one which will fit in with appearances. And that, as I hardly need point out, is not only illogical, but dangerous.'

Jimmy, a silent listener to this conversation, felt the force of Dr Priestley's criticisms. The lack of apparent motive seemed the only weak point in Hanslet's theory. He had tried to imagine any possible gain to the Slaters for Mr Knott's death, and had failed. The superintendent had told him of his inquiries at the offices of Slater & Knott. Something had certainly been learnt as to Mr Knott's character and habits. But of those who might benefit by his death no hint had been dropped. Mr Grant had believed that his only surviving relative was a married sister, now living in New Zealand. He had no knowledge of Mr Knott having made a will. Since his income would die with him, his heirs, whoever they might be, could only hope to succeed to any capital which he might have saved. And from all accounts, Mr Knott had not been of a particularly saving disposition. Had he really been murdered for the sake of the £750 in notes which he was carrying in his pocket?

But Dr Priestley had resumed his argument. 'I am still convinced that the true motives of these two crimes have not yet been discovered,' he said. 'I am not going to pretend that I have discovered this motive. But, with your permission, Superintendent, I should like to venture a suggestion.'

'I'd be only too glad if you would, Professor,' Hanslet replied readily.

'Very well then. I would recall to your attention the letter alleged to have been written by the general manager of Novoshave to Victor Harleston. With the letter itself I am not at the moment concerned. But you will remember that certain figures had been scribbled on the back of it, presumably by Victor Harleston.

'Now, that the letter is dated January 18th, and there is reason to believe that it reached Harleston on the following day. That is to say, it did not come into his possession until two days before his death. The figures, therefore, cannot have been scribbled upon it before that time. This, I think, suggests that they relate to something in which Victor Harleston was interested immediately before his death. And that something, if it could be discovered, might prove to be of importance.

'Now at the time you showed me the letter, I made a note of those figures. Here they are on this piece of paper. I will read them over to you again in order to refresh your memories.

$$20000 \ - \ 100 \ = \ 19900$$

£100   at £5 2 1   =   £5.104

£20000 at 5.104 × 200 = £1020.8

5.104
_____

£1015.696

'Now, what is the significance of these figures? You will say that they are merely a calculation, probably involving some audit upon which Victor Harleston had been engaged. But, if that had been the case, surely he would have wished to have kept a record of the results. Instead of that, the paper on which the figures were written was torn up and made into spills. This seems to indicate that Victor Harleston made the calculation for his own information alone, and that, once made, he trusted himself to remember it.

'The calculation is an elementary one. The first step in a subtraction of 100 from 20,000. The next two lines show that these figures indicate pounds sterling. One hundred pounds corresponds in some way not indicated to £5 2s. 1d. or 5.104 pounds. This may possibly be a rate of interest to be expected. But the yield is expressed in a somewhat unusual form. If you will consult a table of annuities, as I have done, you will find that £2 2s. 1d. is approximately the income a man of Victor Harleston's age might expect from the purchase of an annuity of £100. The last line explains itself. If £19,900 were to be employed instead of £100, the yield would be approximately £1,015. It seems to me to be within the bounds of possibility that Victor Harleston meant to employ the sum of £19,900 in the purchase of an annuity. He made this simple calculation in order to verify the annual income which an annuity would yield.'

Both Hanslet and Jimmy looked incredulous at this. 'But

he hadn't that sum at his disposal, Professor,' the former exclaimed. 'He only had a life interest in his father's estate. He couldn't dispose of the capital as he liked.'

'Exactly,' Dr Priestley replied. 'That is why I believe those figures to be significant. His apparent means would not have justified such a calculation. But suppose, perhaps as the result of some disreputable transaction, he had acquired, or was about to acquire, the sum of £20,000. Less £100, you will observe, and I would particularly direct your attention to that subtraction. Would not such a sum tempt an unscrupulous person to murder?'

Hanslet smiled. 'There you are, Professor!' he said. 'That merely brings us back to his family. Who else but they could have known about this money?'

'You forget the unidentified individual whom Janet Harleston met on the doorstep. If he indeed existed, he may have seized the opportunity of securing the money while Janet Harleston was out of the house.'

Hanslet looked dubious. 'It all looks to me a bit far-fetched, if you won't mind my saying so, Professor.'

'Hardly far-fetched, I think. I will admit that at present there is no proof of my suggestion. I do not even maintain that it is correct. But where such uncertainty of motive exists, it would surely be good policy to explore all the possibilities.'

'I won't forget this one,' replied Hanslet tolerantly. 'Meanwhile, I wish you'd give me some idea of how I'm to fix the murder of Mr Knott upon Gavin Slater.'

'That, I fear, will prove to be extremely difficult. But again perhaps I might venture a suggestion. Shortly before his visit to Torquay, Mr Knott drew certain notes from his bank. You have secured the numbers of these notes and have circulated them to the banks in Torquay. As a result you have succeeded in tracing one of them. Have any of the others been traced?'

'No, and I don't suppose that they will be now,' Hanslet replied. 'Gavin Slater won't commit the same error twice. From what Jimmy told us, he's pretty wide awake, except when he's had a drink or two. I expect that by now he has destroyed the rest of the notes, or if not, that he's put them in some place where we shan't be likely to find them.'

'That may be,' said Dr Priestley. 'But the more astute the criminal, the greater as a rule is his self-confidence. It might be worth your while to circulate the numbers of the missing notes to the banks in London.'

'Well, it's worth trying, I suppose,' said Hanslet. 'But I'm willing to bet that we shan't hear any more of them. Of course, if Gavin Slater was such a fool as to cash the lot and we could prove it, it would be almost conclusive proof against him.'

'No proof can ever be really conclusive in the absence of Mr Knott's body. The successful disposal of a body is almost certain to secure immunity from punishment for a murder. But it is notoriously a very difficult task to achieve.'

'Well, it's been done in this case, Professor. And what's more, we know how it was done.'

'You cannot prove how it was done,' Dr Priestley objected. 'You have found indications which suggest that Mr Knott's body was dismembered and thrown into the sea. Local conditions enable you to explain why no part of the dismembered body has been found. But you have no definate proof that the body of Mr Knott, either wholly or in part, does not still remain upon terra firma.'

'I wish I thought it did,' Hanslet growled. 'We'd be bound to find it sooner or later, and then the case against Gavin Slater would be absolutely water-tight.'

Dr Priestley glanced at the clock as though to terminate the interview. 'I would recommend you to abandon all preconceived theories,' he said. 'You are confronted, I believe, with a somewhat unusual problem. But this problem is not so complicated as to be incapable of solution. The essential step is to discover the true significance of the events which have caused it.'

2

Hanslet, reviewing matters in his office at Scotland Yard the next morning, felt that he had reached a deadlock. Here were two murders, each elucidated up to a point, but from the superintendent's point of view inconclusive.

The case of Victor Harleston had certain points of ingenuity about it. The method employed might have escaped detection but for the praiseworthy perseverance displayed by Jimmy. The motive was also pretty clear. It ought then to be possible to lay hands upon the criminal. In his heart of hearts Hanslet had no doubt that Philip Harleston had been at the bottom of the affair. It was Philip's obvious duty to confess and so clear the matter up. But, most reprehensibly, he showed no signs of doing so. And, with the evidence at present available, there was no chance of obtaining a conviction against him.

The case of Mr Knott was slightly different. He had been brutally murdered, the object having been to obtain possession of the money he was carrying. No particular ingenuity had been displayed by the criminal except perhaps in the disposal of the body. There could not be the slightest doubt of his identity. But in the absence of the body no charge of murder could very well be maintained.

Following his usual custom when faced with a perplexing problem, Hanslet had had recourse to Dr Priestley. But for once the Professor had failed him. He had shown no practical sympathy with the superintendent's difficulties; he had merely talked a lot of theoretical nonsense, which, though sound enough in its way, did not help matters much. His most recent suggestion had been almost puerile. Hanslet wondered if the Professor's brain could be showing signs of growing old. That fanciful suggestion of Victor Harleston having been possessed of a large sum of money based upon a few figures scrawled on the back of an old letter! It was ridiculous. Almost as ridiculous as the suggestion that the numbers of the notes drawn by Mr Knott should be circulated to the London banks.

Nevertheless, merely as a matter of routine, Hanslet thought he might as well carry out the latter suggestion. He obtained the numbers of the notes from Jimmy and circulated them through the usual channels. Then he turned his attention to the many other matters which were awaiting his consideration.

Late that same afternoon Hanslet received a telephone message. It was from the West End branch of the City and Suburban Bank. If Superintendent Hanslet would call upon the manager he would be put in possession of certain information which might be of service to him. Hanslet lost no time. He went round to the bank at once and was there introduced to the manager. He could hardly believe his ears when the latter informed him that some of the notes of which the numbers had been circulated had passed through his hands.

'I would be very glad if you would tell me the circumstances in full,' he said.

'That is very soon done,' the manager replied. 'On the morning of Saturday, January 26th, we received, by registered post, twenty-five £20 notes. Here are the numbers of those notes, which you will find to correspond with the numbers circulated by you.'

Hanslet compared the numbers given him by the manager with a list which he took from his pocket. There could be no doubt that these twenty-five notes were among those which had been drawn by Mr Knott.

'Yes, that's all right,' he said. 'May I ask who sent you the notes?'

'They were sent to us by one of our customers, Mr Stanley Fernside, together with a note requesting that they should be placed to the credit of his deposit account. I have the note here and you may like to see it.'

Hanslet examined the note with considerable curiosity. It was written on letter paper, bearing the heading of the Midland Hotel, Manchester. Its contents were as follows:

'DEAR SIR,—I should be glad if you would place the enclosed sum of £500 to the credit of my deposit account. I shall be passing through London tomorrow on my way to the continent, where I expect to be detained for some considerable time. As, however, I shall not arrive in London before the bank closes, I am compelled to send the money by post. I should be very grateful if upon receipt of this letter you would send an acknowledgment by hand to my London address.

'Yours faithfully,
STANLEY FERNSIDE.'

The letter was dated Friday, January 25th.

'Will you be good enough to tell me what you know about Mr Stanley Fernside?' Hanslet asked.

'That won't take long,' the manager replied. 'I know very little about him. He has been a customer of ours for the past three years. My first interview with him was when he called at the bank and asked to see me. He said that he wished to open an account with us. I asked him the usual questions and he told me that he was an agent for a firm of American importers. He also told me that he had a flat in London, of which he gave me the address, 12a Banbridge Road, Kilburn. Although this was his permanent address he was very rarely there except at the weekends. His territory covered the whole of Europe and he spent the greater part of his time travelling, both in this country and abroad.

'I was not altogether satisfied with this, since Mr Fernside was a total stranger to me. I suggested that he might give me a reference, and he asked what sort of thing I wanted. I replied that the usual procedure was an introduction from some reputable firm, preferably in London. Mr Fernside replied that he was unaware that this formality was necessary and had not provided himself with an introduction. He would, however, obtain one by next day.

'On the following day he returned. On that occasion he produced an introduction from one of the partners of a well-known firm of accountants, Messrs. Slater & Knott. This introduction stated that the writer had known Mr Fernside for many years and that he had no hesitation in recommending him as a suitable customer to the bank.'

Hanslet concealed his satisfaction at this news.

'Can you tell me the name of the partner who signed the letter?' he asked.

'Certainly. It was Mr Ernest Knott. I am not personally

acquainted with the gentleman, but I took the precaution later of ringing him up and asking him if the introduction was genuine. He replied at once that he had written it that morning and that I need have no hesitation in accepting Mr Fernside as a thoroughly reputable person. I had already agreed to open an account with Mr Fernside, and my conversation with Mr Knott removed any lingering doubt which I might have had.

'Mr Fernside opened his account with notes to the extent of about £200. It was an ordinary current account and it was drawn upon by cheque in the usual way. There was nothing in any way peculiar about it. But some months after the original account had been opened, Mr Fernside came to see me again. He then asked if he could open a deposit account in addition to his current account. I told him that there was no objection to this and he thanked me. Since that time Mr Fernside has paid considerable sums into this deposit account. I may tell you in confidence that the amount now standing to his credit is in excess of £40,000. Curiously enough, Mr Fernside has never entered the bank since his deposit account was opened.'

'Can you give me any sort of description of him?' Hanslet asked.

'No one that would be of very much use, I'm afraid. You see, it's such a long time ago since I last set eyes upon him. But I can recall one or two impressions. He was a middle-aged man, fairly tall but with a pronounced stoop. I remember distinctly that he had a very unhealthy complexion, he was pasty-faced and covered with spots. Another thing I remember is that he seemed rather slovenly in his habits. His clothes were baggy and didn't seem to fit him properly. Oh yes, and each time I saw him he was carrying a very remarkable stick.

It was made of some heavy dark red wood, and had a massive gold knob on the end.'

'You have received money from Mr Fernside from time to time?'

'Yes, but always by post and in the form of notes. And the letters of advice have invariably been dated from various provincial hotels. There was, therefore, nothing extraordinary about the receipt of these notes from Mr Fernside on the 26th.'

'And yet Mr Fernside takes the trouble to explain why he could not bring them here in person,' Hanslet remarked.

The manager shrugged his shoulders. 'People do say a lot of unnecessary things, even in business letters,' he said. 'I suppose Mr Fernside wished to let me know that he was going abroad for some time and the mention of passing through London after the bank was closed followed naturally from that.'

'You have had no communication with Mr Fernside since this letter enclosing the £500?'

'I have not,' the manager replied. 'May I in turn ask why you have thought it necessary to circulate the numbers of these particular notes?'

Hanslet smiled. 'You've been very good in answering my questions, and I'll return the compliment,' he replied. 'The notes paid in to you by Mr Fernside were among a number drawn by Mr Knott from his bank on the 17th. During the course of that night Mr Knott disappeared, and there is every reason to believe that he was murdered. Mr Knott is the gentleman from whom Mr Fernside secured his introduction. I think you will realise why I am anxious to get on the track of Mr Fernside as soon as possible.'

Hanslet left the bank, taking with him the note written by

Fernside from the Midland Hotel at Manchester. He called a taxi and drove to Kilburn Police Station. Here he made inquiries about Mr Fernside and his address. Of the man himself nothing was known. Banbridge Road was a street of quiet shops, each with a small flat above it. The shops were unoccupied at night and the tenants of the flats had access to them by a separate door. The shop No. 12 was occupied by a milliner. 12a was the flat above it. It had been occupied for the past three years and the directory gave the name of the tenant as Stanley Fernside. But nobody at the police station remembered having seen the gentleman.

Hanslet telephoned to Scotland Yard and was shortly joined by an undersized foxy-faced man whom he addressed as Tom. Together they set out for Banbridge Road. Their first call was at the milliner's. The shop was just about to be shut for the night, but they were fortunate in catching the proprietress. She turned out to be an alert, intelligent woman of middle age. Hanslet questioned her about the tenant of the flat above, only to find that she knew very little about him. To the best of her recollection she had only set eyes upon him about half a dozen times. The flat always seemed to be empty, at least she had very rarely heard anybody moving about above her head. She had once or twice seen a gentleman open the door. Her description of him confirmed the bank manager's. He was tall, stooped and walked with a slight limp. And his face was all covered with pimples. She had not seen him for several months past. She was in the habit of locking up her shop at one o'clock on Saturday and not opening it again until nine o'clock on the Monday morning. As she did not live in the neighbourhood, she would not have seen Mr Fernside if he had entered or left his flat during the weekend.

Beside the door of the shop was a second door, number

12a. Hanslet pressed the bell push let into the door-post. He could hear the faint tinkle of the bell upstairs in the flat. But nobody answered it. He rang a second and then a third time. At last his patience was exhausted. 'It's up to you, Tom,' he said.

Meanwhile his companion had been examining the lock of the door. As Hanslet spoke he took a bunch of keys from his pocket. He inserted one of these in the lock and felt it gently. Then he nodded his head as though he had learnt what he had wanted. He looked at the bunch, selected a particular key, and inserted this in the lock. It turned easily and the door opened.

They stepped inside, to find themselves in a narrow hall at the end of which was a carpeted staircase. They climbed this to the first floor where they were confronted by a second door. Tom made as short work of this as he had of the first. They entered the flat, which was in darkness. Hanslet groped round for the electric light switch, found it and turned it on. Then, in the sudden light which flooded the place he saw a spectacle which made him gasp with astonishment.

The door through which they had just passed opened directly into the living-room of the flat. This was of a fair size and contained no more than the bare necessities of cheap furniture. But the whole room was in utter confusion. A painted deal table, which had apparently formed the principal article of furniture, lay on its side with the two upper legs broken off short. Three common wooden chairs lay scattered about the room in various states of disrepair. On a packing-case in one corner stood a small safe. This was wide open and empty. The walls were covered with a sickly green distemper which showed several scratches, apparently of recent date. The window was shut, but the heavy curtain which covered it had been half torn down and hung ungracefully. The floor was covered with linoleum, which showed many impressions of nailed boots.

Tom was the first to speak. 'Looks as if there's been a bit of a scrap in here, sir,' he remarked.

Hanslet made no reply. He walked across the room to a farther door, which he opened. He found himself in a small kitchen, the contents of which were not in disorder. Two doors opened off the kitchen and he looked through these in turn. The first led into a bathroom and lavatory. The second led into a small bedroom, very plainly furnished with an iron bedstead and a wooden chest of drawers. The bedclothes were hastily thrown aside as though somebody had got up in a hurry. The chest of drawers was empty.

The superintendent returned to the living-room which he proceeded to examine minutely. The first thing he noticed was what he took at first to be a damp stain upon one of the walls. It was yellowish-brown in colour and of a peculiar shade. Not for some two or three seconds did Hanslet discover that it was a very rudely executed likeness of a pistol. It had apparently been traced by a finger dipped in some colouring matter.

He turned to the overturned table and moved it slightly in order to examine the broken legs. This exposed to view an object which he recognised at once from the bank manager's description. It was a walking stick of heavy red wood surmounted by a gold knob. The appearance of the knob attracted his attention. On one side of it was covered with a dark incrustation, to which a few hairs adhered.

He laid the stick on one side and continued his investigations. On the wall he found a group of small stains of similar colour to the first. These suggested drops, as though the colouring matter had been sprinkled against the wall. On the linoleum close by the safe was a dark stain of considerable extent.

Hanslet knew well enough that blood stains cannot always be recognised by their colour. But the incrustation on the knob of the stick was unmistakable. It was certainly blood. And that gave the clue to the stains on the wall and the linoleum. These in all probability were also blood. That the room had been the scene of a violent struggle was beyond a doubt.

With Tom's assistance he searched every square inch of it. The edge of the curtain bore a dark stain of the shape of a human hand on which the fingers could be distinguished. From the large stain on the floor by the safe a trail of drops led towards the door. Careful search revealed that these stains extended down the stairs. The last of them was perhaps three inches in diameter and lay just inside the lower door. The safe had clearly not been broken open, but unlocked with its own key, since it bore no signs of violence. It was absolutely empty, and Hanslet refrained from touching it, hoping that expert examination might reveal finger marks. In the bathroom was a wash-basin with a dirty brown line running round inside it a couple of inches below the top.

For the first time Hanslet spoke. 'You're right, Tom. There has been a scrap in here,' he said. 'And I think I begin to see the hang of things already. However, let's be thorough while we're about it. It looks as if there's been a fire in the grate pretty recently, and it might pay us to rake out the ashes.'

Hanslet set to work, and his industry was rewarded by two discoveries. The first was a scrap of paper of which the edges were charred. Its appearance suggested that it was all that remained of a newspaper or periodical, the remainder of which had been consumed in the fireplace. This scrap of paper was about ten inches long. Its width varied from three-quarters of an inch to a quarter. It was blank, but for the printed date which appeared on both sides. This date was Saturday, January 26th. The second discovery was still more amazing. As he passed the ashes through his fingers Hanslet felt some hard body. He blew the ashes away until the nature of this body was revealed. It turned out to be a bullet, slightly flattened at the nose, and on the bullet was an incrustation which strongly resembled that upon the gold knob of the stick.

There was nothing else to be found. Hanslet arranged his finds on the mantelpiece and regarded them with a look of satisfaction. 'Didn't somebody say something about sermons in stones?' he said. 'I don't know anything about that, but there's a complete story in those things there. Now I'm going to make a few inquiries of the neighbours. You'd better stop here, Tom, and see that nobody gets in. I shan't be long.'

The superintendent's inquiries were directed to flats 11 and 13a. He found that the tenants of the former had been away since Christmas and were not expected back for some days. The flat was unoccupied and had been so since their departure. But in 13a he was more fortunate. That flat was occupied by a young couple with a year-old baby. The husband went out to business every day, but the wife very rarely strayed from home. She had known her neighbour by sight, but had never troubled to inquire his name. Her description of him coincided with those which Hanslet had already heard. Tall, stooping, with a palid and pimply face, and invariably carrying a curious-looking stick with a gold knob. She had last seen him on Friday the 18th. She had happened to be looking out of the window about seven o'clock and had seen him enter his flat. He was alone. He was usually a very quiet tenant, and she could never tell whether he was at home or not. Not like the people on the other side of her who had a piano and played it night and day. But for an hour or two on the 18th after seven o'clock she had heard sounds from No. 12a. They had not been very loud and did not last very long. From their nature she had formed the impression that her neighbour was moving his furniture about. Soon after eight o'clock that evening she had heard the door of No. 12a slam. She had looked out of the window and seen the occupant walking away.

This was not very much to the point. Hanslet was more interested in what had happened on Saturday the 26th. Unfortunately, his informant had gone out to see her mother that afternoon, taking the baby with her. She had returned about six o'clock and had noticed a closed car standing outside the door of No. 12a. At that time there was nobody in it, she was sure of that. She had gone up to her own flat and begun to make preparations for putting the baby to bed. Almost immediately afterwards she heard very heavy foot-steps decending the staircase of No. 12a. This was unusual, for the occupant was in the habit of moving about very quietly. She looked out of the window and saw the door open. A man, whose face she could not see, came out. He was carrying on his shoulder a big sack, which appeared to be very heavy. He put this into the car and drove off. She had not given the matter any further thought. But she was quite sure that the man she saw on that occasion was not the occupant of 12a. She had not noticed the car particularly and could only descibe it vaguely as a medium-sized saloon. She had not noticed the number.

This was enough to be going on with, Hanslet thought. He went back to No. 12a and collected his trophies. Then, leaving a man on guard, he took a taxi to the yard.

Here he sat down to consider this new and wholly unexpected development. He made a few notes while his observations were still fresh in his memory, and then sent for Jimmy. To him he unfolded the results of his investigations.

'Now then, Jimmy, my lad, let's hear your explanation,' he said.

Jimmy grinned. 'It's a bit of a puzzle,' he replied. 'But the main facts seem to be fairly clear. Who Stanley Fernside may be or may have been, I'm not going to attempt to guess. The first significant thing about him is that he was an acquaintance of Mr Knott.'

Hanslet nodded. 'Yes, that's the proper starting-point,' he said. 'Well?'

'The next thing about him is that he had a balance of some £40,000 at the bank. I think that's rather important, for a man with all that money doesn't commit a murder for the sake of a few hundreds. Then we come to the most curious thing about it. Fernside somehow came into possession of the notes which Knott had drawn on Thursday the 24th. These notes he posted from Manchester.'

'Hold on a minute!' Hanslet interrupted. 'How do we know he posted them from Manchester? Anybody can walk into a big hotel and pinch a piece of notepaper. He may have posted those notes from Timbuctoo, for all we know. The people at the bank wouldn't have troubled to look at the postmark.'

Jimmy smiled. The superintendent had overlooked one small point. He proceeded to draw his attention to it as diplomatically as possible.

'Oh, I thought you said the letter had been registered,' he exclaimed.

Hanslet stared at him for a moment and then laughed good-humouredly. 'Good for you, Jimmy,' he exclaimed. 'I'd forgotten that for the moment. Of course, if that letter was posted in Manchester, we shall find a record in one of the post offices. They'll have the counterfoil of the certificate of posting. I'll have a message sent to the Manchester police to look for it. That's one to you. Carry on, my lad.'

'The main question is, how did he come by those notes?' Jimmy continued. 'I don't think it's any good trying to answer that until the rest of the facts are explained. Fernside mentioned to the bank manager that he would be passing through London on the 26th. It appears that he did so and went to Banbridge Road. It being Saturday afternoon none of his neighbours happened to see him. And it seems pretty easy to guess what happened to him when he got there.'

'It isn't a matter of guesswork,' Hanslet replied. 'The proof positively stares one in the face. He had a safe in his flat, and some gang or other decided that it might be worth their while to crack it. They hit upon a Saturday afternoon for the job, knowing that all the shops would be empty and shut. They worked the usual dodge. Having provided themselves with keys to fit the doors, they drove up in a car. The chap who was to do the job went into the flat, the other chap or chaps kept a lookout. Fernside must have turned up almost immediately afterwards, I think. He let himself into his flat and found the cracksman already in occupation. He went for the fellow with that stick of his and gave him a pretty nasty knock by the look of it. But the other chap whipped out a gun and shot him. But Fernside wasn't killed outright. He managed to get to the window and tore the curtain aside,

I suppose with the idea of calling for help. Then the cracksman closed with him and overpowered him. They made a pretty mess of the furniture between them, I can tell you. Fernside once overpowered and I expect trussed up, the rest was easy. There was no further need to break open the safe. All that was necessary was to take Fernside's bunch of keys and find the right one. And that's just about what's happened. With any luck, we may find some fingermarks on the safe, and if we do, that'll put us on the track.

'While the safe was being opened, Fernside died of his wounds, I fancy. The cracksman then had to dispose of the body—a difficulty which he had not foreseen. He hadn't got the sea at his back door, so to speak, like your friend, Gavin Slater. But he didn't like to leave the body where it was. Anybody might have come upon it and there would have been a hue and cry at once. So he put it in a sack which he had with him. There must have been a good deal of blood on his hands by the time he had finished and he washed them in the basin in the bathroom. Then he carried the sack downstairs with blood dripping from it and put it in the car. And where the body may be now goodness only knows.'

'What about that diagram drawn on the wall which you say looks like a pistol?' Jimmy asked.

'Ah,' exclaimed Hanslet sapiently. 'That's a very interesting point. There are some crooks who seem to take a positive delight in leaving their trademarks behind them. It's not at all uncommon for a criminal to leave a definite mark of identification. You're too young to remember the chap who gave us such a lot of trouble and who's never been found to this day. He was a specialist in opening unoccupied houses, and for some reason he had an extraordinary trick of soaking himself in scent. This scent persisted for months, and as soon as a theft was reported, we got in the habit of sniffing for it. Every policeman in London knew it as the thieves' smell. You would have thought it would have been a very valuable clue, but we never found the fellow in spite of it.

'This chap gives us another example of the same kind of thing. Apparently he's a bit of an artist and has a fancy for drawing pictures on the wall. We'll have to search the records and see if in any previous cases a similar picture has been found. Now I've had a busy day and I'm going home. It will be good practice for you to set your thinking box to work and tell me in the morning what conclusions you've come to.'

Jimmy was ready enough to exercise his brains on the problem. He regarded the murder of Mr Knott as in a sense his own case, and the extraordinary affair at Banbridge Road was obviously not unconnected with it. The first thing to discover was what connection had existed between Fernside and Mr Knott. That Jimmy thought would be easy enough to discover. Somebody in the offices of Slater & Knott would surely be able to throw some light upon it. The two must have been old acquaintances. Mr Knott, on being applied to for an introduction, had stated that he had known Fernside for many years.

But as Jimmy had already realised, the most important factor was Fernside's possession of the notes drawn by Mr Knott. Jimmy could think of several theories to account for this, but they all seemed to him, for one reason or another, highly improbable. The first was that Fernside had murdered Mr Knott. He could only have murdered him while he was staying with the Slaters at Torquay. Could he have followed him there and broken into the house during the night? The idea sounded utterly fantastic. Would a man with a bank balance of such dimensions murder another for the possession of £750? If he had murdered him for some other reason not yet apparent would he have taken the notes?

A variation upon this theory was that Stanley Fernside and Gavin Slater were one and the same. But the description of Fernside differed entirely from that of Gavin Slater. There was only one point of resemblance between them, and that was a very slight one. One of the witnesses had said that Fernside limped slightly. This question of identity could easily be put to the test. Fernside was known to have been in London between six and seven o'clock on the 18th. If Gavin Slater could have been proved to have been in Torquay during that period, the identity was disproved.

Had Fernside obtained the notes from Gavin Slater? That opened up an almost unlimited field of speculation. Fernside might have been in the conspiracy against Mr Knott. He had met Gavin Slater in Torquay after the murder. In that case the Slater family must already have known of his existence. Discreet inquiries upon this point might prove fruitful.

Finally, there was a theory which vindicated Fernside from all complicity in the murder of Mr Knott. According to this Mr Knott had drawn the notes for the purpose of giving them to Fernside, and had actually done so before his arrival at Mr Slater's house. Mr Knott might have mentioned in the course of conversation that evening that he had drawn £750 from the bank. But he omitted to mention that he had paid them away. The Slaters had understood him to mean that they were still in his possession and had therefore mentioned the notes to divert suspicion from themselves in case inquiries were made. This seemed fairly plausible. Fernside had sent to his bank notes to the value of £500 only. Perhaps that was the sum which he had received from Mr Knott, who had retained the balance. The note which Gavin Slater had changed had been part of this.

Fernside's innocence would explain his letter to the bank and his return to London. But in spite of Hanslet's explanation the events which followed that return seemed to Jimmy deeply mysterious. The evidence of a struggle having taken place in the flat appeared overwhelming. As a result of it, according to the superintendent, Fernside had been killed and his body taken away. But why should a gang of crooks encumber themselves with a body of which they would eventually have to dispose? Surely they would have left it where it was, to be discovered in due course? The body itself would give no clue to the murderer. And that design upon the wall? Why a pistol of all things in the world? Was it merely a piece of bravado? An intimation that the murderer carried a gun and would not hesitate to use it? It might be so. But Jimmy couldn't help wondering. It seemed to him that clues so deliberately fabricated were more likely to be misleading than boastful. The design of the pistol naturally suggested a search for an armed murderer. Could this be an attempt to lay a false scent at the start?

The date of the occurrence in the flat was at least definitely established. The car had been seen standing at the door on the afternoon of the 26th. The scrap of paper found by Hanslet, so obviously the remains of a newspaper or periodical, bore the same date. It did not follow from the paper alone that the murder had been committed on that date. But one cannot buy a newspaper before the date of publication. The murder then must have been committed on or after that date.

Hanslet had shown Jimmy the scrap of paper. There could be no doubt whatever about the date. At one extremity of the paper was printed January 26th. As the other was printed Saturday. And, as though to make perfectly certain of the date, the same words were printed on either side of the paper.

This seemed as conclusive to Jimmy as it had to Hanslet. And in addition, Jimmy felt that the type and its arrangement was somehow familar to him. Where had he seen it before? He racked his brains over this for some few moments. Then suddenly he remembered. And, as he did so, he laughed aloud. The scrap of paper so carefully cherished by the superintendent was valueless as evidence of date.

Jimmy recognised it now clearly enough. It was part of the heading of a page of the *Radio Times*. Now the *Radio Times* is on sale on Friday. It contains the programmes for the ensuing week from Sunday to Saturday. If this particular copy had contained the programme for the 26th, as the heading seemed to show, it could have been purchased as early as the 18th. Was this another false clue? Had this scrap of paper been left behind in order to indicate a false date? And there was some slight significance to be attached to the 18th. This was the day upon which Fernside had been heard in his flat apparently moving the furniture about. But had those sounds been really those of the struggle?

For the moment Jimmy was tempted to consider this as a possible solution, until the manifest impossibility which it involved appealed to him. If Fernside had been murdered on the 18th, how could he have come into possession of the notes drawn by Mr Knott on the 24th? Fernside must have been alive on the 24th, so much at least was certain.

The maddening thing was that Fernside, alive or dead, had disappeared. His evidence might have solved the mystery of Mr Knott's murder. Now, that murder seemed to be involved in greater mystery than ever. Jimmy felt himself confronted by a series of trails which faded out before they reached their conclusions.

The whole chain of circumstances, as he reviewed them, was completely baffling. It began with the death of Victor Harleston. That at first had seemed difficult to explain. But Jimmy himself by dint of perseverance had found the clue. The discarded safety razor had revealed the manner of Victor Harleston's death. But it had not led to identification of his murderer. Whatever Hanslet might think, Jimmy was convinced that neither Philip nor Janet had had anything to do with it. His conviction was based upon psychological rather than logical grounds. He would not commit himself so far as to deny that they might be potential murderers, though his mind revolted at the idea so far as it concerned Janet. But neither of them possessed sufficient ingenuity of mind to plan and carry out a murder of such skill and subtlety.

Then came the disappearance of Mr Knott, following so shortly upon the death of his clerk. Jimmy agreed with Dr Priestley that there must be some connection between the incidents. Mr Knott had so obviously been murdered during his visit to Torquay. The only person who could have murdered him was Gavin Slater. That is, unless a whole series of improbabilities were to be admitted. Everything pointed to Gavin Slater's guilt, whatever Dr Priestley might say. He had certainly committed some amazing blunders. But then he was notoriously addicted to drink, and, when under its influence, he would be incapable of clear thought. Unfortunately, he had succeeded in the most difficult portion of his task. He had disposed of the body so effectually that no trace of it could be found. For that reason, although his guilt was practically certain, there were grave difficulties in the way of bringing him to justice. Finally, this last exasperating development. Dr Priestley, with an almost uncanny prescience, had suggested a search for the missing notes. Quite unexpectedly this search had been successful. But it had led not to the elucidation of Mr Knott's murder, but to the discovery of yet a third crime. The existence of Stanley Fernside had been revealed. But the man himself had vanished, leaving only his wrecked and bloodstained flat behind him.

Puzzle his brain as he might, Jimmy could find no rational explanation of the sequence of these events. The only theory that he could form was utterly fantastic. Harleston, Knott and Fernside had been associated in some mysterious affair. This had been known to a gang of crooks who had exterminated them one after another in quick succession. A melodramatic theory, certainly, but to Jimmy wholly improbable. For what had the murderers gained by their wholesale slaughter? Certainly not Fernside's fortune, which was still safely deposited at his bank. And, more puzzling still, that deposit had existed before the first murder, that of Victor Harleston. Was there anything to be gained from a consideration of the hints which Dr Priestley had let drop? The suggestion about the notes had certainly proved profitable, up to a point. The other suggestion, that Harleston might have been about to invest a sum of £20,000, seemed fanciful. And yet Dr Priestley's explanation of those scrawled figures had been certainly plausible. £20,000, of which £100 had been subtracted. Dr Priestley had particularly stressed that transaction. Was there any hidden significance in the sum of £100? Victor Harleston had received that sum shortly before his death. That had been the amount of the much disputed bonus which he had received from his firm. But he could not have expected that bonus to be increased to £20,000 in the near future. That would have been purely ridiculous. Jimmy went home to bed at last almost convinced that the problem which confronted him was insoluble.

As it happened, he did not see Hanslet again until the following afternoon. And then the Superintendent sent for him. 'I've just rung up the Professor,' he said curtly. 'You and I are to go round and have a chat with him this evening.'

Hanslet's tone was not encouraging but Jimmy ventured a question. 'Have there been any fresh developments?' he asked.

The Superintendent scowled. 'Developments!' he exclaimed. 'I haven't time to talk to you now. You'll hear all I've got to say this evening. But if you find me sticking straws in my hair before we're through with this case you mustn't be surprised.'

3

When Hanslet and Jimmy reached Westbourne Terace that evening, they found that Dr Oldland had been invited to join the party. After a few preliminary remarks Dr Priestley turned the conversation to the subject at issue.

'You wish to consult me, I understand, Superintendent?' he said.

'I do, Professor,' replied Hanslet fervently. 'Perhaps you can make some sense out of what I'm going to tell you. I can't. To begin with I took your tip about the numbers of these notes. I circulated them and found that £500 worth had been paid into his deposit account at the West-End Branch of the City and Suburban Bank by a man called Stanley Fernside.'

Dr Priestley nodded. 'That does not altogether surprise me,' he said quietly.

'Possibly not, but the sequel will. I got hold of this man

Fernside's address, and went round to his flat. And, if you've the patience to listen, I'll tell you exactly what I found there.'

Hanslet gave an exact description of what he had found in Banbridge Road. Dr Priestley listened to the details with a faint smile, but asked no questions. 'The condition of the flat suggested a certain theory to you,' he remarked when Hanslet had finished.

'It did, Professor. The evidence seemed as plain as though a written description had been left behind. But, of course, I didn't leave it at that. I put in the experts, and their report came in this afternoon. And what to make of them I'm blest if I know.

'First of all the safe. I had hoped that they would find fingerprints on that. But they didn't. They report that there are no traces of fingerprints anywhere about the room, even on the stick. It seems as though everybody concerned in the affair must have worn gloves. The sale of gloves ought to be forbidden in the interests of justice.

'The absence of fingerprints is bad enough, but there's worse to follow. I asked the experts to examine and report upon the various stains about the place. These included the marks on the wall, on the floor, on the curtain, and in the wash-basin in the bathroom. All these were identified as bloodstains. Each set of stains was examined and tested in turn. But, if you'll believe it, those confounded experts declare that the marks on the walls, the floor and the curtain were not made by human blood. They were made by the blood of some animal of the cat tribe.'

Oldland laughed. 'That seems to admit all sorts of possibilities,' he said. 'An animal of the cat tribe would include anything from a tiger to a newborn kitten.'

'So the experts have explained to me,' Hanslet replied tartly.

'But I've no reason to suppose that Fernside kept a menagerie in his flat. The fourth stain, that on the inside of the wash-basin, was undoubtedly human blood. The basin had undoubtedly been used by somebody to wash his or her hands. Although the water had been run off, the soap and blood had left an incrustation which made identification possible.

'Now we come to the stick. I've already described it to you. I was careful not to handle it overmuch when I found it. But the experts have examined it very carefully. They found first of all that it was badly cracked, as though a heavy blow had been dealt with it. The knob at the end, which isn't gold by the way, but some form of pinchbeck, was badly dented. The incrustation I found is human blood, and the hairs sticking in it human hair. The experts point out that those hairs were apparently torn out by the roots.'

'Suggesting of course that somebody had been knocked on the head by the stick,' Oldland remarked.

'Exactly. That's the only common-sense point about the whole affair. Finally we come to the bullet. I told you that it was flattened at the end and had something that looked like blood upon it. It was blood, and human blood at that. You'll say, doctor, that this suggests that it had been fired at somebody and wounded him. But it doesn't.'

'Why doesn't it?' Oldland asked.

'Because the experts swear that the bullet had never been fired at all. Oh, I know. It doesn't make sense, but I can't help that. At least, if it has been fired, it wasn't from the weapon for which it was intended. I'll explain.

'The bullet has been identified. It was intended to fit an old-fashioned type of revolver of .45 calibre. The bullet itself shows signs of having been manufactured many years ago.

Now the rifling of the pistol for which this bullet was intended is very deeply cut. A bullet fired from such a pistol shows unmistakable signs of grooving. But this particular bullet shows none and its diameter has nowhere been diminished. Therefore, it was not fired from the revolver. If it was fired at all, it must have been some smooth-bore weapon of the same or slightly larger calibre than the bullet.

'Now I can make no sense whatever of all this. If the animal blood had been on the stick and on the bullet one could have formed some sort of idea, however fantastic, of what had happened. One might have supposed that Fernside, on returning to London, had found that a tiger had somehow strayed into his flat. First of all he attacked it with his stick, and then he produced a duelling pistol, or something of the kind, from his pocket and shot it. But even that nightmare won't account for the facts. It must have been Fernside who was hit on the head. And I absolutely refuse to believe in a tiger which uses sticks and pistols with which to defend itself.'

Dr Priestley glanced benevolently at the exasperated superintendent.

'I find the facts not altogether inexplicable,' he said. 'I imagine that you have made inquiries concerning this man Stanley Fernside?'

'I've spent the whole day doing nothing else. I can't hit upon any trace of him. I've sent men round to make inquiries of all the American importers that I can hear of and none of them have any knowledge of any such person. You remember that he told the bank manager that he was going abroad. It struck me that I might get on his track that way. If he were going abroad, he would have to have a passport. So I went to the passport office and made inquiries there. They have no record of any passport existing in the name of Stanley Fernside. Jimmy has also been making inquiries following out an idea of his own.'

'I started with the fact that Mr Knott had introduced Fernside to the bank,' said Jimmy. 'I went round to the offices of Slater & Knott and made inquiries there. Nobody had ever heard of Stanley Fernside. And Grant, the chief clerk, is convinced that if Mr Knott had known him for many years he would at least have been acquainted with the name. I even made inquiries of Novoshave, just on the off-chance, but I've had no luck there either.'

'At my request the Manchester police have made inquiries,' Hanslet resumed. 'They have found the certificate of posting of a registered letter in one of the smaller post offices. It is dated January 25th and the letter is addressed to the Manager, the City & Suburban Bank, West-End Branch. As it happens the clerk remembers the posting of the letter. On the afternoon of the 25th, about six o'clock, a man came into the post office and bought a registered envelope. The clerk noticed that he had a pale face covered with spots and was carrying a dark red stick with a gold knob. He took the envelope to a desk, inserted something in it, sealed it up, and handed it in for posting.

'That proves, I think, that Fernside was in Manchester on the afternoon following the murder of Mr Knott. There is no record of his having stayed at the Midland Hotel, but that is not altogether surprising. He could have secured the notepaper without staying there. And that's the only trace of him I can find so far. There's only one hope left so far as I can see. His pimply face and that stick he carried seems to have made him rather conspicuous. I shall circulate a description on these lines.'

'I fear that if you do so your trouble will be wasted,' Dr Priestley remarked dryly.

'Well, if he's dead, it will be,' Hanslet replied. 'Is that what you mean, Professor?'

'No I think that the man who calls himself Fernside is still alive. But it would be useless to seek for him under that description. Does the appearance of the flat, coupled with the expert's report, suggest nothing to you?'

'Nothing that makes any sense, Professor,' Hanslet replied moodily.

'Because you allowed yourself to be misled by the appearance of a struggle. Suppose that a struggle had never taken place, and that the bloodstains and the other phenomena were capable of a simple explanation?'

'Then all I can say is that I should very much like to hear that explanation.'

'Then I will attempt to formulate a theory which might account for the facts. Fernside, for some reason of his own, wished to create the impression that he was no longer alive. Now there are obvious difficulties in the way of creating such an impression. The most convincing evidence of all, that of the dead body, cannot be produced. It is very unlikely that Fernside was acquainted with anybody sufficiently like him to serve this purpose. He was therefore driven to make appearances as convincing as he could in the absence of the body.

'Unfortunately for him, he under-estimated the ability of the experts. He did not realise that they could distinguish between human and animal blood, for instance. And he overlooked the fact that it is easy to tell whether a bullet has been fired or not. And his dispositions were made, I think, not on the 26th, but on some previous date.'

'But everything goes to prove that the events in the flat happened on the 26th,' Hanslet objected.

Dr Priestley glanced at Jimmy. 'Do you agree with that, Inspector?' he asked.

'Well, sir,' replied Jimmy with an apologetic glance in Hanslet's direction. 'It occurred to me that that scrap of paper might have been part of the *Radio Times*. And if so it might have been put in the fireplace as early as the 18th.'

Dr Priestley nodded approvingly. 'That is a very good point,' he said. 'Then we have the evidence of the sounds heard in the flat on the 18th. This, I think, is when the furniture was disarranged and broken. And I have very little doubt that the bloodstains were produced at the same time. If that is the case then Fernside himself created these appearances since he was seen to leave the flat on that date.'

'But why should he want to create a false impression as to the date, Professor?' Hanslet asked.

'Because it was essential to his scheme that he should be thought to have been alive on the 25th. But we can return to that point later. For the moment let us consider how he could have created the appearances which have so greatly puzzled you. He had provided himself with the necessary instruments. Among these were included an ordinary domestic cat, an old revolver bullet extracted from its cartridge case, and the current copy of the *Radio Times*. His first action, I expect, was to kill the cat and pour its blood into the wash basin. With this source of supply in hand, he made stains on the floor and the trail of drops leading to the door. He dipped his hand in it and then touched the curtain. He sprinkled some of it on the wall and with his finger traced the pistol design of which you speak. What did you make of that curious decoration on the wall, Superintendent?'

'I put it down to the work of some gang or other,' Hanslet

replied. 'That sort of thing is not altogether uncommon, as I dare say you know.'

'Fernside may also have known this, and drawn the likeness of the pistol to mislead you. But I am inclined to think not. I believe the design had a definite purpose. You were, I feel sure, intended to find the bullet. But Fernside realised that it would not do to leave it in too obvious a place. Your suspicions would have been aroused if you had found it, for instance, standing in the middle of the mantelshelf. Therefore it had to be hidden, and the fireplace was a very suitable place for the purpose. But you might not have raked out those ashes, and so the bullet might have escaped you. Fernside's problem was to indicate to you the existence of a hidden bullet. He did this by drawing the pistol on the wall. This would have suggested to you that the blood in the room came from a wound caused by a firearm. You would then naturally have searched for the bullet, and sooner or later you would have found it.

'Fernside, like most criminals, could not resist the attempt to gild the lily. He had already done enough to suggest a violent encounter, in which he had been severely wounded. But he must needs improve upon his work. By this time he had, I think, exhausted the blood of the cat, and washed out the basin. For his final touch of realism, he required a further supply of blood, and this he secured by cutting or pricking his own finger. Having cracked his walking stick, possibly by bending it across his knee, he smeared the knob with this blood. He then smeared the bullet in a similar way. Finally he washed his hands, of which one of the fingers was still possibly bleeding, in the basin. This would account for the traces of human blood found in it.

'The last act in the comedy took place on the afternoon

of the 26th. Fernside drove up in a car and entered his flat, carrying an empty sack under his coat. Here he waited a favourable opportunity. No doubt he was watching through the window, and saw his neighbour return home. Then he filled the sack with something in order to bulk it out and stamped heavily down the stairs. He put the sack in the car and drove off. You already believed in the existence of a dead or wounded man. So that when you heard about the sack you assumed that it had contained the body. Fernside had shown tolerable skill in the achievement of his object. It was merely his ignorance of the powers of science that induced him to employ a cat. And he should have used a bullet which had actually been fired instead of one extracted from its case. By the way, with regard to the human blood found, did the experts' report contain any further details?'

'Merely that the blood on the stick, the bullet and the wash-basin appeared to have come from the same person,' Hanslet replied. 'In each case it was of the same class, number one. But look here, Professor, what was Fernside's motive in all this? You say that he wanted to create the impression that he was dead? Why? Had he committed some crime? You might say that his possession of the notes suggested that he had murdered Knott. Or at least that he was in league with Gavin Slater. Is that the idea?'

Dr Priestley smiled. 'Stanley Fernside has undoubtedly committed a very grave crime,' he replied. 'But that crime was not the murder of Mr Knott. Although I have no doubt that he knew more about the disappearance of Mr Knott than any of us.'

'You mean that he put Gavin Slater up to the job?' Hanslet suggested.

'No, I think that Gavin Slater was an unconscious tool in his hands. But let us examine Stanley Fernside a little more closely. I think we shall find that he exhibits rather striking peculiarities. He is in the possession of a considerable balance at the bank, which he apparently acquired within the course of the last three years. How did he accumulate this large sum? It could surely not have been the profits of his alleged occupation.

'Then, in spite of his comparative wealth, he rents a flat in an obscure quarter of London. I do not imagine that the inhabitants of Banbridge Road are in receipt of large incomes. Nor, as I judge by your description, did he surround himself with any attempt at luxury. The flat is, I think you said, very plainly furnished.'

'It contains only the barest necessities,' Hanslet replied. 'And even these are of the cheapest quality.'

Dr Priestley nodded. 'Just so. Now let us turn to another of Fernside's peculiarities. He is rarely seen at his flat, and never during the week. Having opened his account, he never again appears at his bank. In fact, he only appears when it suits his purpose to do so, as, for instance, in Manchester on the 25th. He alleges that he spends the greater part of his time travelling at home and abroad. But you have been unable to trace his possession of a passport. And apparently he is unknown to people with whom he might be expected to be familiar. It would almost seem that he possesed the power of rendering himself invisible. Does all this suggest nothing to you?'

'Only that he was up to no good and kept himself out of the way as much as possible,' Hanslet replied.

'He was up to no good, of that I have no doubt. But how did he contrive to keep himself out of sight? There is, I think, only one rational answer to that question. Stanley Fernside only existed when it suited his purpose to do so.'

Hanslet looked puzzled. 'I don't quite follow you, Professor,' he said.

'And yet my meaning was sufficiently clearly expressed. Stanley Fernside was a second personality, a disguise if you like, assumed at his convenience by some other person.'

'Well, that's possible,' Hanslet admitted. 'But it doesn't carry us much further. He may really have been John Smith and not Stanley Fernside. We know precious little about Stanley Fernside, and nothing whatever about John Smith.'

'We know this at least about John Smith,' Dr Priestley replied quietly. 'He was sufficiently well acquainted with Mr Knott to induce him to give him an introduction as Stanley Fernside.'

'That would be splendid, if Mr Knott were still alive,' said Hanslet rather tartly. 'But, since he isn't, I don't see that it carries us much further.'

As some glimmering of the truth occurred to Jimmy he made a sudden movement in his chair. This attracted Dr Priestley's attention. 'Well, Inspector,' he said, 'have you any comment to make?'

But Jimmy was far too diplomatic to step in where his superior knew not how to tread. 'I was wondering what crime Stanley Fernside could have committed, sir,' he said.

'There is, I think, very little doubt that he is guilty of murder,' said Dr Priestley in a matter-of-fact tone.

'But dash it all, Professor, you've just said that you didn't believe he murdered Mr Knott,' Hanslet exclaimed.

'Mr Knott is not the only victim whose death remains unexplained. I believe that Stanley Fernside, as we will continue to call him for the present, is guilty of the murder of Victor Harleston.'

Hanslet opened his eyes wide at this. And then he laughed heartily. 'Oh come now, Professor!' he exclaimed. 'You're always rubbing it in to me that conjecture unsupported by fact is a worse crime than murder. And if that isn't pure guesswork I don't know what is. Why, there's nothing on earth to connect Stanley Fernside with the murder of Victor Harleston!'

'Exactly,' replied Dr Priestley tranquilly. 'And that is the whole strength of his position.'

Hanslet shrugged his shoulders. 'I suppose you've some grounds for what you say. But to begin with, what possible motive could Fernside have had for murdering Harleston?'

Dr Priestley glanced at him sternly. 'You have from the first misunderstood the motive underlying the whole chain of events,' he said. 'You found an apparent motive for the murder of Victor Harleston, and this contented you. You were disinclined to seek for some deeper motive, not visible upon the surface. And yet, that such a motive existed can be deduced from the facts in your possession. It is possible to formulate the nature of that motive, and, upon further investigation, to prove its existence.'

Hanslet considered this for a few moments and then shook his head. 'I'm afraid I haven't got there, Professor,' be said.

'Perhaps because you have neglected to consider certain indications. A few days ago I drew your attention to certain discrepancies in the statements of the various witnesses. First of all, with regard to the custom of Messrs. Slater & Knott in granting bonuses to their employees. In this respect the statement of either Mr Slater or Mr Knott was incorrect. Then, as to the prosperity of the business since the retirement of Mr Slater. It appears from your investigations that the business has flourished from that time. On the other hand,

Mr Slater complained to the inspector that the profits were falling off.

'Now it seems to me that it would be very instructive to have this point cleared up. This could be done without much difficulty. It would be necessary to ascertain the nature of the agreement between Mr Slater and Mr Knott, as to their respective shares of the profit. Mr Knott was, of course, aware of the amount of the profits, but he is said to have kept this knowledge strictly to himself. You will probably find that all record of this has disappeared, with Mr Knott. But it should not be impossible to obtain a fairly close estimate. This having been done, it would be a simple matter to find out whether Mr Slater had obtained his correct proportion of these profits. If he has not, then Mr Knott has been guilty of consistent fraud.

'I believe that this was actually the case. Mr Knott represents to his partner that the profits were decreasing. Mr Slater's blindness would prevent him from checking the actual figures. He seems to have had implicit faith in Mr Knott, and probably accepted his statement without question. Mr Knott was thus enabled to appropriate large sums of money which should by rights have been divided with his partner

'Now let us turn to the murder of Victor Harleston. You deduced quite correctly that the murdered man must have possessed certain special knowledge. Such, for instance, that he had been engaged upon the audit of Novoshave Ltd., that his half-brother Philip possessed a store of nicotine, that Novoshave Ltd., were about to issue a new type of razor, to be known as model K. You thought at first that this special knowledge could only be available to some member of the Harleston family. Later, as your investigations proceeded, you learnt that Mr Slater might have acquired it. But you have overlooked the fact that one person must certainly have possessed it. That person was Mr Knott. As the head of their firm of auditors, he would be fully conversant with the policy of Messrs. Novoshave. His knowledge of Philip he no doubt acquired from his partner, who had been concerned in the purchase of the share of Hart's Farm. It is a matter of common knowledge that fruit farmers employ nicotine in quantities.'

'Do you mean that Knott put Stanley Fernside up to murder Harleston?' Hanslet exclaimed. But why, in Heaven's name?'

'Victor Harleston was murdered because he had become aware of Mr Knott's frauds. Of that I think there is not the slightest doubt. Harleston was blackmailing his employer. He began by demanding that he should be granted a bonus—that would account for the different statements which you have heard on that subject. Knott was compelled to use considerable persuasion to induce Mr Slater to agree to this. But naturally he represented to you that the granting of the bonus was a very ordinary matter. He did not wish the subject to be pursued too closely.

'But Harleston was not content with a mere £100. Knott was completely in his power. Harleston could at any moment go to Slater and tell him the state of affairs. Proceedings would have been taken and investigations made. In that case Knott would have been completely ruined.

'So Harleston made a further suggestion. His silence could be bought. And he fixed the price of his silence at £20,000, less the £100 which he had already received on account. Knott would be forced to agree to this proposition. But he had no intention of completing the bargain. He pointed out to Harleston that he could not lay his hands upon £20,000 at once. The money was invested and securities would have to be realised. He promised to pay the money on a certain date, and that date, I expect, coincided very closely with Harleston's death. I have already told you my interpretation of the figures found on the back of the letter. This theory would explain the source of the money that Harleston expected to receive.'

'Well, Professor, we can find out about the profits and the share of them received by Mr Slater,' said Hanslet. 'If it turns out to be as you say, I'll believe that Knott had a motive for murdering Harleston. But why was he murdered himself two days later?'

Dr Priestley smiled. 'Was he murdered?' he asked conversationally.

'Of that at least, the proofs are convincing,' replied Hanslet confidently. 'If he had committed suicide, his body would not have been disposed of so neatly.'

'From the first, the facts struck me as a trifle too convincing,' said Dr Priestley. 'Every possible clue came to light and each at its appropriate time. The bloodstained sheet, the knife with which the crime was committed, the fingermarks of the murderer, the victim's suitcase, stained with blood and containing some but not all of the victim's belongings. Only the body was missing, and of that an adequate explanation was forthcoming.

'And yet I am convinced that no murder was committed. Knott staged his disappearance to escape the consequences of his crime. He did it with the utmost efficiency, but I venture to think with rather too much emphasis. He had first of all to create the impression that his disappearance was involuntary. He did this by making it appear in advance that he had every intention of returning to London by three o'clock on Friday afternoon. You obtained evidence of that intention from every side. From his office, where he had made an important appointment. From his friend, with whom he was to dine that night. From the owner of the garage where he kept his car. It was all most convincing.

'From the first, I think, he meant to fix the guilt upon Gavin Slater. He had to provide a motive, so he drew a sum of money which he carried on his person, exhibiting it both to Mr Slater and his son. Not a very convincing motive, perhaps, but he knew Gavin Slater's reputation. It would be assumed that he had got drunk and was therefore in a state when he was hardly responsible for his actions. The sight of the notes might then have been a sufficient motive.

'As to what happened that night at Torquay, one can only conjecture. But I think it is possible to reconstruct the events with a fair degree of accuracy. The statements of both Mr Slater and his son can be accepted as substantially correct. Knott and Gavin Slater were left together in the studio after dinner. Knott asked the other to show him the knife. He said that he would have to leave by the early train, knowing that Gavin Slater's repetition of this statement later would sound very suspicious. He asked Gavin Slater to change a five pound note for him. He encouraged him to drink whisky until he saw that he was well on the way to a state of insensibility. And then he went to bed.

'Mrs Slater came home about midnight, and no doubt Knott heard her enter her room. Then, after allowing a sufficient time to elapse, he took action. He had taken upstairs with him a tumbler, which is said to have disappeared. In this he collected a supply of his own blood, probably secured by the opening of a small vein. With this, he smeared the sheet and the interior of the suitcase. He removed the pillow-case and subsequently took it away with him. That, in my opinion, was rather a clever touch. It would be assumed that the pillowcase had been soaked in blood and that the murderer had destroyed it. He then dressed in his underclothes and lounge suit and put the remainder of his belongings in the suitcase.

'His next scene of operation was Gavin Slater's dressing-room. Here he found a pair of shoes, which he wetted liberally with salt and water. And at the same time he hid the tin of nicotine in the chest of drawers.

'That tin of nicotine is to me very significant. I have no doubt that it was the one stolen from Philip Harleston. But why had Knott kept it so long? I think he wished to have a supply of poison available. If his guilt were to be discovered, it would secure him a rapid death. But now he felt that even though his guilt were suspected, no search would be made for him. The nicotine might now be disposed of. How better than by employing it to cast a further suspicion upon his supposed murderer?

'Knott then went downstairs, carrying his suitcase, his pyjamas, and the glass with the blood in it. The suitcase, I suppose, he left in the hall. The other things he took into the studio where Gavin Slater was lying fast asleep. Or he may have waited until he heard Gavin Slater stumble up to bed. That I cannot say. In any case, having reached the studio, he took down the knife, being very careful not to obliterate Gavin Slater's fingermarks. He unsheathed it, dipped the blade in the blood, and sheathed it again. Then he put it back on the wall, feeling sure that it could not escape an observant eye. He made a suitable slit in his pyjamas to correspond with the width of the blade of the knife, poured some blood round this and put the pyjamas in the chest. His work was now accomplished, and it only remained for him to leave the house.

'This, he did, I think, at about six o'clock. He took with him his suitcase, his own hat, and Gavin Slater's overcoat. He also had about him the pillowcase and the glass which had held the blood. He simulated Gavin Slater's limp, so that in the uncertain light he might be mistaken for him. I have no doubt that the man seen by the gas-worker was actually Knott.

'Whether or not he had studied the set of the tide, I cannot say. Probably he had, for he seems to be a man who leaves nothing to chance. At all events he threw the suitcase into the sea, trusting to its being discovered and washed up. The object of the suitcase, of course, was to suggest the means of disposal of the body. The tumbler he threw into the sea separately, careless of whether it were found or not.

'His only care now was to leave Torquay unobserved. He did not care to risk the possibility of recognition at the station. He probably walked for some distance out of the town and then picked up an omnibus. At all events he reached the railway at some point and thence took a train to Manchester.'

'Where I suppose he had a rendezvous with Stanley Fernside,' Hanslet remarked.

Dr Priestley smiled. 'Stanley Fernside suddenly stepped into the picture at this point,' he replied. 'But is not that gentleman's identity yet apparent to you? As a criminal, Knott is a very interesting study. He had decided to commit one crime, and a second was thrust upon him. His endeavours to escape the consequences of these crimes have at least the merit of ingenuity.

'I have no doubt that the idea of defrauding his partner had been present in his mind for many years. As soon as Mr Slater retired he began to put his plan into action. He meant

263

to accumulate a sum of money which would enable him to live in comfort for the rest of his days without the tiresome necessity of attending to business. Being of an extravagant disposition, he found himself unable to save that sum by honest means. Hence the system of fraud which I have supposed. But there was always the danger that the fraud would be discovered. He decided that at a certain time Knott should disappear, leaving in his place a different person to enjoy the proceeds of his industry. That is why he created the fictitious Stanley Fernside.'

Hanslet looked incredulous but said nothing. After a short pause, Dr Priestley continued. 'The only object of Fernside's existence was to accumulate a bank balance. For that purpose he must produce proof of his existence and possess a genuine address. Knott provided these for him. His disguise was so simple that it can hardly be called such. The difficulty of disguise varies with circumstances. For instance, it would be very difficult for Oldland to disguise himself in such a way that I should not recognise him if I remained long enough in his company. On the other hand, if I met a stranger in the street, the first time disguised and the second time not disguised, I would probably not suspect that I had seen the same individual in both cases.

'Knott had considered this fact and applied it very cleverly. The artificial production of a pallid and spotty complexion is a matter of no great difficulty. It is equally easy to simulate a stoop or a limp. But where he showed a stroke of genius was in carrying an unusual stick. This was bound to attract the eye, and at the same time avert attention from, say, his features, or the colour of his eyes. You will observe that all the descriptions you have obtained of Fernside mention the stick and the spotty complexion. These, in fact, are the only peculiarities which seem to have been noticed. Knott counted on this being the case. Further, he was very careful not to appear as Fernside to anybody who knew Knott. And he only appeared as Fernside when it was strictly necessary for him to do so.

'His original intention, I think, had been to retire when he had accumulated sufficient funds. The personality of Knott would then have been obliterated. Stanley Fernside would have taken his place and drawn money from the bank as he required it. But Victor Harleston's discovery interfered with his plans and he was forced to revise them.

'He planned and carried out the murder of Victor Harleston with considerable skill. But later he was obsessed by the guilty conscience which is the curse of all criminals. It is very unlikely that the police would ever have discovered his guilt. But he was taking no risks. It was time for Knott to disappear in such a way that his disappearance would be accepted as final. And, lest the connection between Knott and Fernside should somehow be discovered, it was necessary that Fernside should disappear as well. Fernside's disappearance would, of course, have been only temporary. When the murder of Victor Harleston and the disappearance of Edward Knott had been forgotten, Fernside would reappear and claim his money from the bank. He would no doubt then be furnished with some plausible story to account for the condition of the flat in Banbridge Road.

'But let us return to Knott's behaviour on reaching Manchester after his disappearance from Torquay. Here he perpetrated the one fatal error which the most astute criminals are said to commit. He sent some of the notes which he had himself drawn to the Fernside account. Probably he did not wish to carry so large a sum about with him now that it had served its purpose. He cannot have overlooked the possibility that the police would ascertain the numbers of those notes and the consequent danger that they would be traced. It was one of those inexplicable actions with which we are all familiar.

'It wouldn't have been any good to us but for your hint, Professor,' said Hanslet. 'What made you think that those notes might be found in London?'

'By a logical process of reasoning,' Dr Priestley replied. 'I was never convinced that Knott had been murdered, mainly, I think, because the evidences of that murder were a shade too convincing. If no murder had taken place, then Knott must have disappeared voluntarily. He would then be compelled to seek some hiding place while he was, so to speak, manufacturing a new personality. I did not then know that this personality was in readiness. And the most secure and easily accessible hiding-place is undoubtedly London. I did not anticipate that Knott had committed the folly of paying the notes into a bank. But I thought that possibly he might be compelled to change one or more of them and that in this way he might be traced.'

'When did you first suspect Knott of having murdered Victor Harleston?'

'Not until I learnt of his disappearance. And then I asked myself the reason of this. Could it have had any connection with the death of Victor Harleston? You and the inspector had already formulated a condition with which Harleston's murderer must comply. And I saw that Knott was one of the few persons who could fulfil that condition.'

'The lack of apparent motive didn't worry you then, Professor?' Hanslet suggested slyly.

'The motive was not difficult to deduce. You yourself

suggested it, although you did not see the correct application of your suggestion. You guessed the existence of some secret shared by Knott and Harleston alone. But you were convinced that both had been murdered in consequence of this secret. It did not occur to you, therefore, to reflect whether or not Knott might have murdered Harleston.'

'Well, I'd like to lay my hands on the chap,' exclaimed Hanslet viciously. 'He's given me a lot of trouble and made me look a bit of a fool into the bargain. But he's had time to get clean away, and it'll be a hopeless job to find him. Never mind, I'll set every man on the force on his track.'

'That, if I may say so, would be an extremely foolish proceeding,' said Dr Priestley. 'Knott has shown himself to be a very clever man. He is probably watching the course of events with the closest attention. He has no doubt completely changed his appearance for the third time, and is probably living somewhere quietly under conditions which give rise to no slightest suspicion. If you institute a search for him, he will know that he is suspected, and he will make no further sign. If, on the other hand, you appear to let the matter drop, you will inspire him with confidence. Let it be understood that you accept the fact of Edward Knott's death, and that you are not concerned with the disappearance of Stanley Fernside. Then, sooner or later, an attempt will be made to draw from the funds lying to the credit of Fernside, and thus you will obtain the necessary clue to his whereabouts.'

Hanslet perceived that Dr Priestley had nothing more to say. He rose and prepared to take his leave.

'Well,' he said with heavy jocularity, 'it's been a knotty problem, anyhow.'

Oldland sighed wearily. 'I've been waiting for you to say that all the evening, Superintendent,' he murmured.

4

Hanslet, after consultation with the Assistant Commissioner, decided to take Dr Priestley's advice. Investigation into the murder of Victor Harleston was apparently abandoned. Jimmy was allowed to assure Janet and Philip Harleston that no further suspicion rested upon them. Superintendent Latham of Torquay was taken into the secret and Gavin Slater was released from detention. But behind the scenes Hanslet did not relax his activities.

His first action was to investigate the affairs of Messrs. Slater & Knott. No record of the actual profits of the firm could be discovered, and it seemed probable that Knott had made away with this before his disappearance. However, an independent accountant was employed, and after a long and careful inquiry, he arrived at an approximate idea of what the profits since Mr Slater's retirement should have been.

The deed of partnership, of which Mr Slater had a copy, provided that after the latter's retirement Knott should be awarded a fixed annual sum in recognition of his activities. After the deduction of this sum, the profits were to be divided between them equally. Comparing the sums which Mr Slater had received with the estimated profits, it was found that Knott must have defrauded him to the extent of some £40,000. This agreed very closely with the sum which had accumulated to Stanley Fernside's credit.

Dr Priestley's theory was so far justified. And in the course of his investigation Hanslet discovered several other small points concerning it. He paid a visit to Lassingford and questioned Janet Harleston very closely as to the man she had seen upon the doorstep upon the morning of her half-brother's death. He learnt that she had never been to the offices of Slater & Knott and had never to her knowledge seen Mr Knott. But upon being shown the photograph which Jimmy had secured, she agreed that so far as she could remember it bore a considerable likeness to the man. This, though not very satisfactory in itself, was a step in the right direction.

Hanslet's next step was to examine Knott's car, which he removed to Scotland Yard for the purpose. In the tool box he found a grease-gun. This had been newly filled with ordinary motor-car grease. The proprietor of the garage where the car was kept said that he had not filled it. In fact, he had never used the grease gun, because he had an apparatus of his own with which he greased Mr Knott's car periodically. Hanslet handed over the grease gun to the analysts, telling them of his suspicions. They found that the grease was slightly contaminated with nicotine.

The superintendent was overjoyed at this, since it confirmed the guess he had made very early in the inquiry. Knott had undoubtedly used the grease-gun to force the poisoned shaving cream into its tube. He had then cleaned it thoroughly, as he supposed, and repacked it with grease.

Mr Topliss, the general manager of Novoshave Ltd. stated that he had had a conversation with Mr Knott shortly before the audit took place. In the course of this conversation he had mentioned the new model razor which was about to be placed on the market. Mr Knott had asked whether the new model was yet obtainable and had been told that it was not. During the same interview, Mr Knott had taken a packet of sheets of the firm's notepaper and had made notes upon the top sheet. Mr Topliss believed that he had taken this and the remaining sheets away with him.

This gave Hanslet a new idea. He had learnt that in Mr

Knott's room at his offices was a safe of which he had been told that nobody but Mr Knott himself possessed a key. He had this safe opened by the makers. It was empty but for a few unimportant documents, mainly of a private nature. These documents he handed over to the fingerprint department at Scotland Yard. The department found several fingerprints upon them, all of which appeared to belong to the same individual. It was, therefore, a legitimate assumption that these fingerprints were Mr Knott's. He then submitted the sheets of Novoshave letter paper, which he had found in Mr Harleston's desk at No. 8 Matfield Street. These also bore fingermarks identical with those found upon the documents. Knott then must have put these sheets of letter paper in the desk. This was another example of his thoroughness. He had foreseen that the bogus letter to Harleston might be found. The discovery of the blank sheets in the desk would suggest that somebody in the house had compiled the letter. Janet declared that Mr Knott had never visited the house in Matfield Street. If he had placed the sheets in the desk, it could only have been during her absence. Yet another indication that he had been the man whom she had seen on the doorstep.

Hanslet next turned his attention to establishing the identity between Edward Knott and Stanley Fernside. It was significant that the blood found in the flat in Banbridge Road and that found in Mr Slater's house at Torquay was of the same class. But, unfortunately, the experts could go no further than this. Science was not sufficiently advanced for them to declare that the blood came from the same individual. However, the superintendent was enabled to obtain one or two valuable hints. He submitted the letter written by Stanley Fernside from Manchester and several specimens of Mr

Knott's writing to the handwriting experts for examination and comparison. They found certain characteristics common to both. The writing of Stanley Fernside was unnatural and strained, as though deliberately disguised. But certain of the strokes, and above all the proportions of the letters, showed a close affinity to the writing of Mr Knott.

Jimmy, who was associated with Hanslet in the inquiry, had a stroke of luck. He had been given the task of making a thorough and minute examination of Mr Knott's rooms in Crozier Court. He found, entangled in the carpet of Mr Knott's bedroom, several loose hairs. These were subjected to microscopic examination, together with the hairs found on the knob of Stanley Fernside's famous stick. Both of these samples of hair were found to have the same rather unusual peculiarity of structure. They were of identical colour and showed that their owners were at least of the same age. It was impossible to say definitely that they came from the same head, but the probabilities in favour of this were very strong. Another fact ascertained by Jimmy was this. A large tabby cat had for a long time been in the habit of prowling about Crozier Court. It had vanished some time within the past few weeks. By diligent inquiry, Jimmy established that it had not been seen since Friday, January 18th.

Meanwhile the manager of the West-End Branch of the City & Suburban Bank had been requested to communicate at once with the police should any attempt be made to draw upon the account of Stanley Fernside. As the weeks went by and nothing was heard of that elusive gentlemen, Hanslet began to grow restive. More than once he had almost made up his mind to publish a description of Knott, together with his photograph, but Jimmy, who had greater faith in Dr Priestley's wisdom, managed to dissuade him. And at last patience was justified. Towards the end of April a message came from the bank manager. A cheque bearing the signature Stanley Fernside had been presented.

Hanslet went at once to the bank, where he was shown the cheque. It was payable to James Parkington, and had been presented through a bank at Felixstowe. Hanslet and Jimmy took the next train for that town and went straight to the bank on their arrival. Having presented their credentials, they were given all available information. Mr James Parkington was the proprietor of a private hotel and when paying in the cheque had mentioned that it had been given to him by one of his customers.

They secured the address of the hotel, which was only a short distance away. It was quite small and unpretentious.

'Just the sort of place our man would choose,' exclaimed Hanslet triumphantly. 'Now, if he's at home, this affair will be ended at last.'

As they approached the door, an elderly man, walking with the aid of a stick, came out. In their eagerness to apprehend Knott they paid no attention to him. He glanced at them and seemed to hesitate for a moment. Then, with more agility than he appeared to possess, he set off down the street at a smart walk.

Had it not been for this display of nervousness, he might even have then escaped. But already something in his bearing had attracted Jimmy's attention, and his sudden haste seemed suspicious.

'Hold on a minute,' Jimmy exclaimed. 'I'd like to have a closer look at that chap.'

He went off in pursuit. Jimmy was normally a fast walker, but the elderly man seemed more than a match for him. They covered nearly the whole length of the street, the distance between them increasing rather than diminishing. Then Jimmy broke into a run. Hearing his footsteps behind him, the elderly man threw off all pretence of infirmity. He, too, broke into a smart run, heading away from the centre of the town towards the open country. But when it came to running, Jimmy proved the better man of the two. He had been a rugger blue at Cambridge, and was now even fitter than he had been then. After a few paces, he began gradually to overhaul his man, and it was evident that sooner or later he must overtake him.

But, after all, the glory of the capture was not to be his. Hanslet was less impetuous, both of foot and head. He stopped a passing car, jumped on the running board and told the driver to pursue the fugitive. He overtook and passed Jimmy. Then, as the car drew alongside his quarry, he jumped off the running board and laid his hand upon his shoulder.

'I want a word with you,' he said.

It was obvious that the man's nerves had deserted him. He had at last believed himself safe, and the sudden appearance of Hanslet and Jimmy, whom of course he had recognised, had completely demoralised him. He stood there, breathless and shivering, until Jimmy came up.

'Well Jimmy, here's the man you wanted to see,' said Hanslet grimly.

Jimmy looked at him searchingly. The man had changed his appearance as far as possible but had made no attempt at disguise. He had evidently realised that a permanent disguise is the most difficult thing to maintain. Beneath the beard and heavy moustache, Jimmy discerned the features he recognised.

'You are Edward Knott,' he said positively.

The man's lips quivered weakly. 'I don't know what you mean,' he replied. 'My name is Stanley Fernside.'

'Then you can tell us what happened in your flat in Banbridge Road last January,' said Hanslet. 'I'm sorry to interrupt your seaside holiday, but I shall have to ask you to come back to London with us.'

In the cold atmosphere of Scotland Yard he gave up all further attempt at pretence. He admitted that he was Edward Knott and, confronted by the proof of the frauds upon his partner, he admitted his guilt. He seemed relieved when his statement had been taken down and he signed it.

Hanslet paused. He seemed on the point of ordering his removal from the room. Knott watched him, as an animal at bay might watch the hounds confronting it. Then, after a tense silence which seemed to last an age, Hanslet spoke.

'How did Victor Harleston find out what you were up to?' he asked almost casually.

Knott went livid and his fingers clutched the arms of his chair convulsively. 'Harleston!' he exclaimed. 'What has he got to do with it?'

'With the fraud, very little, I imagine,' Hanslet replied. 'But I shall charge you with murdering him through the agency of poisoned shaving cream. You may as well save yourself the trouble of denying the crime. We know exactly how you carried it out. All right, that will do for the present.'

Knott was led away, seemingly in a kind of stupor. But next day he expressed the desire to make a statement. He was allowed to do so, and dictated a full and detailed confession.

He had planned and carried out the murder exactly as Dr Priestley had deduced. Harleston had requested a private interview with him just before Christmas. At that interview he had said that he had spent a considerable time calculating the profits of the firm. He had by chance seen the last two quarters' cheques paid to Mr Slater. The amount of these cheques seemed unaccountably small and he proposed to suggest to Mr Slater that he should make investigations. But of course, if Mr Knott could satisfy his misgivings he would say no more about the matter.

The interview had lasted for some considerable time. In the end Knott had undertaken to secure for Harleston a bonus of £100 at once, and to pay him the sum of £20,000 less the £100 on January 21st. Knott confessed to Hanslet that he had never had the slightest intention of paying Harleston the money. The delay would enable him to consider how he could best be got rid of.

That evening, as it chanced, he saw a reference to the case of Count Bocarmé. Nicotine, administered with greater dexterity, seemed to him the very thing for his purpose. He bought a work upon toxicology and read up what he could about nicotine. And in the course of his reading he learnt that it was used for spraying fruit trees.

This piece of information seemed heaven-sent. Mr Slater had told him that Philip Harleston was the manager of a fruit farm. Next day he went to Lassingford and made very careful inquiries. He got into conversation with one of the men employed on Hart's farm and learnt that nicotine was used and where it was kept. He also learnt that Philip was out all day. He then explored Philip's cottage, and saw that the padlock of the store would be easy enough to open.

A couple of days later he returned to Lassingford. He had provided himself with a number of keys and with one of these he managed to open the padlock. He abstracted the tin of nicotine and drove back to London with it.

For the rest, his methods had been exactly as deduced by Dr Priestley. He had arranged that the parcel containing the razor and the shaving cream should reach Harleston on Saturday the 19th. He guessed that Harleston would try the experiment, if not on the following day at least very shortly. He had spent the greater part of Sunday morning hanging about Matfield Street, but nothing unusual appeared to happen in No. 8. On Monday morning he took up his post again. Very shortly after his arrival Janet had rushed hatless from the house. He had spoken to her and entered the house as she had left it.

There he had acted as swiftly as possible. His object had been to remove the damaging clues and substitute others. He had been unable to find the razor and dared not spend time looking for it. He did the best he could, left the house before Janet returned and went to his office.

But the crime once committed he had misgivings as to his own safety. The fact that he had not been able to recover the razor disturbed him. He feared that it might be found and somehow traced to him. He had already made his arrangements for the disappearance of Edward Knott, but he had not intended to put these arrangements in force so soon. Under the circumstances he now decided that Edward Knott should be murdered by Gavin Slater. Choice of Gavin Slater was based not only upon a profound personal dislike. During one of his previous visits to Torquay, Gavin Slater had tackled him upon the subject of his father's income from the business. How was it that the profits were progressively decreasing? It occurred to Knott that Gavin Slater had his suspicions, and that if he could be hanged for murder these suspicions would go no further.

The curious point in his confession was that he declared

that he had given no thought to the numbers of the notes which he had drawn. That the police would secure these numbers, and use them in their investigations, had not occurred to him. His reason for asking Gavin Slater to change one of them had not been that he wished him to be found in possession of the notes. He wished to establish beyond question that he had that large sum of money about him, since this would supply the motive for his murder. He had already impressed the fact upon Mr Slater. But Mr Slater was an old man and might well have forgotten the incident. He thought it better to impress the notes upon the mind of his son as well. And that had been his sole reason for producing the notes in the studio and asking Gavin to change one for him.

This explained his gigantic blunder, which had led to the identification of Stanley Fernside with Edward Knott. Not having considered that the numbers of the notes which he had drawn would have been known to the police, he had no hesitation in sending the greater part of them to the City & Suburban Bank. The letter to the manager had been merely to establish the fact that Stanley Fernside must have been attacked in his flat on the 26th. Actually the appearances had been produced on the 18th.

He was tried for the murder of Victor Harleston, sentenced and executed. Both Hanslet and Jimmy were congratulated upon the successful outcome of the difficult case. The latter, his faith in Janet being thus triumphantly justified, became a frequent visitor to Lassingford in his spare time.

Dr Priestley, discussing the arrest with Oldland, was inclined to be censorious. 'A most disappointing criminal,' he remarked. 'He committed his crime with a skill and audacity worthy of a better cause. And then he allowed himself to become too clever. The staging of his own murder, was, as I thought at the time, far too melodramatic. It was too full of clues to be convincing. And the ridiculous affair at Fernside's flat was a mistake. If Knott had been less anxious to secure his own safety, he would probably be at liberty at this moment. He sealed his own fate by attempting too much.'

'You might add to that that he under-estimated the powers of logical deduction,' replied Oldland slyly.

THE END